The Mote in
Andrea's Eye

TiTANic

Other Five Star Titles
by David Niall Wilson:

Deep Blue

The Mote in Andrea's Eye

David Niall Wilson

Five Star • Waterville, Maine

First Edition
First Printing: June 2006

Published in 2006 in conjunction with Tekno Books and Ed Gorman.

Set in 11 pt. Plantin by Christina S. Huff.

Printed in the United States on permanent paper.

Library of Congress Cataloging-in-Publication Data

Wilson, David Niall.
    The mote in Andrea's eye / by David Niall Wilson.—1st ed.
        p. cm.
      ISBN 1-59414-453-2 (hc : alk. paper)
      1. Hurricanes—Fiction.   2. Missing persons—Fiction.
    3. Bermuda Triangle—Fiction.   I. Title.
    PS3573.I456885M68 2006
      813'.6—dc22   2006002671

I want to thank Win Wenger of Project Renaissance for the design of the pumps that might, or might not be able to stop hurricanes. Win consulted with me throughout the writing of the novel and was incredibly helpful. You can find more about Win and his work at www.winwenger.com.

I'd also like to thank Mr. Jack Williams, Weather Editor at *USA Today,* for his work and for consultation on Operation Stormfury, and hurricane fighting in general.

I'd like to thank my agent, Robert Fleck, and Janet Berliner for a good thorough going-over of the manuscript that revealed some flaws and fixed some holes. Normally, I'd say this was my agent's job, but he didn't rep this one, so thanks!

I would also like to thank the love of my life, Patricia Lee Macomber, for the off-the-cuff remark, "I wonder why no hurricane ever got lost in the Bermuda Triangle?" and for her undying support of my life, and my work. Without her, this wouldn't be happening.

Included in the mix of those who contributed are my daughter Stephanie, who kept a diary through our own ordeal when Hurricane Isabel hit and for the image of "U-Boats." Her brother, Billy, is our resident storm expert and wants to study hurricanes and tornadoes. I hope he brings none of his work home! I'd also like to thank my sons, Zach and Zane, for letting me bore them during our long truck drives with the story of this book—and for still wanting to read it when I was done.

Last, but certainly not least, I'd like to thank the cast of characters whose names have been used to create this work. Most of them work with me every day, and they were good sports to let me make off with their names when I got home. Thanks to: Kathy O'Pezio, Matt Scharf, Jeff Gray, Randy Sherman, Lisa George, Pam Jones, Dan Satalino, Mike Pooler, Keith Foster, Linita Thompson, Jake Marriner, John Carlson, Seth Andre, John & Alicia Kotz, Vance Richards, Jamie Bradshaw, Arvis Purvis, Jack Howe, Terri Hill, Charles Lynch, Rick Johndrow, Susie Stoots, Michael Penn, Leslie Clayton, Al Menard, and Jay Greenwood.

PART ONE

Outer Banks of North
Carolina—1942

Chapter One

The sunrise was a deep, blood red that faded to orange, as its light grew more intense. Andrea sat on the top step of her back porch and watched, her morning orange juice forgotten and her eyes wide. She always watched the sun rise over the beach, its rays coloring the white-capped surf and drawing the long shadows back from rocks on the beach and the pier in the distance. This sunrise was different; she'd never seen the sky so red, and it bothered her. It was as if someone had drawn Mickey Mouse and made him green.

With a quick glance over her shoulder and up the wooden steps that led to the kitchen door, she rose and stepped down onto the wooden walk. It stretched toward the beach and she stared at it longingly. She wanted to feel the wet sand between her toes and to gather seashells from the shore, but she knew better than to wander off without permission.

The squawk of the radio broke the early morning silence as her father turned up the volume and twisted the tuning knob. The sound slipped past her in odd, disjointed bits of conversation and paused once to let a short snippet of music escape into the morning. Andrea closed her eyes and let the notes drift around her, soft saxophone and very faintly a woman's voice, then there was the familiar squeal, and she heard a man's voice. The volume was set too low for her to make out any words, but she knew that he would speak on into the morning, until her father left the kitchen and her mother took control. Then it would be *Kate Smith Speaks*, and more news.

Andrea knew there was a war. She didn't really know what a war was, but she knew that it was more important than just about everything. Names like Churchill and Hitler rolled out of the radio's speaker in a steady stream, but none of it made much sense to her. She remembered happier mornings when the radio had found the music and stayed there. On those mornings her mother would already have been out on the porch, sipping her coffee and smiling as Andrea wandered down to the beach to play in the damp sand.

A couple of years before, her daddy had retired from his job in the Navy. He'd been home ever since, working on the house, sitting late into the night with Andrea's mother, the radio on low, the soft roar of the surf in the background. Before the war, the two best times in Andrea's day were those just before sleep, and the hour after breakfast, when her parents smiled and held one another close, aware of her and loving her, but caught up in their own little world. She liked to wander in and out of their smiles, lost in her own thoughts.

Now there was tension in the air that had not been there before, and the radio, which had brought the soothing music and ushered in the best parts of the day, was a constant, droning backdrop. The crackle and pop of static through the speaker charged the air with something, making everyone nervous. Her father spent a lot of time staring into the ocean, sometimes alone, and sometimes with a few of their neighbors.

There weren't many homes near theirs, but her father spoke often about growth and property values. There was talk of a ferry boat—Andrea had heard it as fairy boat, and had brought more laughter and smiles to her parents' faces with questions about elves and Tinker Bell—that would take visitors out to Ocracoke Island. The war had stopped that, as well, but the war would pass.

That was what her parents said, and the radio said, but Andrea had grown so accustomed to the war's presence that she doubted the truth. It was the pop and crackle static in the back of her life, and it didn't seem like the kind of thing that, once it had come, would ever really go away.

She hoped the music would come back, but she feared that the radio had learned a new language, and it made her sad. She couldn't understand half of what was said, but she knew from the expressions on her parents' faces that it wasn't good.

The sun had lifted from the waves by the time the door at the top of the stairs finally opened and her mother stepped through. Andrea saw the morning breeze catch her mother's hair and lift it gently, as if trying to blow it back into the kitchen. In contrast, the open door sucked the voice from the radio into the world of the beach and the sunlight, and softened it. As the door closed once again, Andrea caught the word U-boat and wondered. Her mind conjured images of boats in the vague shape of a horseshoe, and then she quickly dismissed them.

Her mother took her usual seat in one of the white chairs flanking the small wicker table on the porch. She had a porcelain cup and her pink Thermos carafe with the glass handle on the lid. The morning sun winked off that handle, and Andrea smiled. Her mother caught the expression, and just for a moment, the war and the voices crackling away behind the kitchen door disappeared. The two smiled, and the morning sun's warmth took on a reality that had been lacking only moments before.

Then Andrea turned and ran off down the walkway to the beach. The wood slats were buried in drifting sand, and had become a soaked amalgam of creosote and salt water.

Andrea's feet made dull slaps on the wood, and then she hit the beach, and slowed. The soft, drifting sand was hard to run through. Her ankles sank in and there was a soft crunch, like she was grinding something to dust every time she planted her foot. Ahead were the damp sand near the water, and the soft ripples of sunlight dancing across the waves.

She carried her mother's smile with her down to the water's edge and wiped away the red morning sky and the crackling radio voice with the wonder of sun and seashells. There were several rocky outcroppings on the small stretch of sand, and when the tide retreated she found tiny kingdoms in the pools of water they left behind, small caves and cuts in the rock that didn't release all of the ocean's life when the water swept back, but held them and kept them safe, sparkling in the brightening sun.

This was her time, and her world, and she entered it happily, safely guarded by her mother's soft watchful presence.

On the porch, her father left the kitchen as well, bringing the radio with him. He set it on the wicker table and fussed with the cords that lay along the deck, looking for the end of the extension that would bring the news back to life.

Thomas Jamieson was a tall man, holding his almost fifty years with grace. Thirty years in the U.S. Navy had hardened his frame and chiseled salt-sharp lines into the features of his face, but his eyes were dark and expressive, and he still moved with the confidence and energy of a teenager.

His wife, Lilian, watched him with detached concentration. Her gaze drifted back to the beach, caught Andrea's form in the sunlight and lingered protectively. Thomas could handle the recalcitrant electrical cords without her help; her eyes and her thoughts were never far from the safety of her daughter.

The times had beaten it into her. Every time she heard a report of the war, she cringed inside. It had seemed such a distant, meaningless part of her life. Thomas fought the wars, and he did so thousands of miles away. Then, when he was done and their world was safe, he returned.

She'd spent her mornings and evenings writing letters and gathered with huddles of other lonely wives, fighting their own battles against time and boredom. Some had fallen by the wayside, or failed under the pressure, but Lilian Jamieson had waited. This time together at the end of that wait was to have been their reward. This home on the beach, far enough from the military gray of the ships and the neon brilliance of the bars that had lured so many of Thomas' friends away from their families, even when their days of fighting had ended. So many pitfalls and traps avoided to get to where she was, sitting in the sunlight, sipping coffee and watching the daughter that had come to her, heaven sent, in the later years of her life.

Now the voices that came to them through the radio warped it. The wars that had been so far away a year before had actually reached within sight of the U.S. shoreline, not many miles from where her daughter stared out over the waves. German submarines had torpedoed merchant ships, sending them flaming to the bottom of the sea, and when they did this those Nazi sailors were within miles—not thousands, or hundreds of miles—but tens. Ten was far too small a number for safety, and though the radio spoke of patriotic unity and the strength of Allied forces, the ships still sank, and the stability she clung to had grown uncertain.

The radio crackled to life, and Thomas grunted with satisfaction. He slid into the chair across from her and cupped his coffee mug between his hands. Lilian watched him for a moment as he furrowed his brow and cocked an ear to the newscaster's nasal voice. Thomas' expression was so serious and concentrated that she had to stifle a smile. He had spent so many years in the thick of it all, so many years in command, making things happen and setting things right, that it pained him to be removed from it. His retirement had limited his involvement to hunkering over this radio, or the neighbor's radio, or the radio down at the barbershop in town. He was a spectator, part of the world he'd sworn to protect, and she saw by the way the veins rose on top of his hands that he ached to do more.

"Did you see that sunrise?" she asked him, trying to divert his attention.

He glanced up and paused as his thoughts rearranged, then he smiled quizzically. "No. That's odd, I always used to watch it—like a ritual. Now it seems . . ."

His words trailed away and she nodded her understanding.

"It was red," she said, turning to stare down at the beach. Andrea kicked up sand just shy of the water's edge, and Lilian smiled. "It looked, just for a while, like the clouds were bleeding into the ocean."

Thomas' smile dipped to a frown. He shook his head, caught himself, and turned to follow his wife's gaze.

"What is it?" she asked.

"Probably nothing," he said, his voice, and his mind, suddenly very far away. "Just remembering something. On the ship we never wanted to see that red sky in the morning. You've heard the old rhyme, 'sailor take warning.' It's hard to get things like that out of your system."

Sensing some deep-rooted thing gripping a part of her husband that she couldn't reach, Lilian rose and walked around the table. Without hesitation, she slipped into his lap, surprising him only for an instant. His strong arms wrapped her tightly, and they stared out across the water together.

"It will never really be gone," she whispered into his ear. "It's all part of you, and I—we," she turned and tilted her chin toward Andrea, "love every bit of it."

He hugged her tightly and leaned back, letting her head fall against his shoulder. She had always liked this—sitting in his lap and held close, and safe. The times it had been possible had been too few, and now that he was here, every day, she basked in it.

The radio crackled, and she listened; only half-interested.

"More reports of the hurricane that rocked the Bahamas are just in. There have been twelve deaths reported and untold damage to property and homes. There are reports of flooding, homes blown from their foundations, and at one point a tidal wave washed miles inland, crushing everything in its path. This storm is headed east-northeast. Initial reports indicate it might strike the eastern coast of Florida as early as this evening. Residents are being warned to evacuate the area, and tropical storm warnings have been issued up and down the coast."

Thomas didn't stop rocking her, but she felt him grow tense.

"They said it would hit Florida," she said. "We should be fine."

Thomas nodded, but he didn't say anything. He stared out over the waves as if he could draw the storm's intention from them and ease his mind.

"We'd better get Andrea in," he said, lowering Lilian from his lap and standing slowly. "I'm going to run into town for some supplies. It never hurts to be ready, and it *is* storm season."

Lilian sighed, but she nodded. "I'll get her. I know she'll want to go with you."

The radio announcer rattled on to the close of his report,

and then announced that *Kate Smith Speaks* would be up next.

Thomas entered the house and let the door slam behind him. Lilian started down the steps to the sand below, and her daughter. The wind, which had made her hair dance so gently when she first came outside, had picked up slightly, and the waves looked choppier, though it might have been her imagination.

Thomas was right. It never hurt to be prepared.

The truck wound its way back down the long road toward their home, passing the sparse neighboring houses and leaving the town lights behind. It was late afternoon, and the sun, which had come up so bright and red, dropped toward the horizon slowly in hues of magenta and lavender. It was beautiful, but the wind that whipped against the windows and buffeted them on the road, combined with the clouds of dust and sand devils dancing through the gloom gave that beauty a dark edge.

The radio in the truck crackled and faded in and out of tune. The announcer's words seemed to stretch as he ran through the news. The Germans were still advancing, but that meant little to Andrea. She tuned him out, much as the jouncing of the truck tried to do, and waited for the bright, cheerful jingles and snatches of music that rose between news stories.

There were more reports on the storm. It had not struck Florida, and people there were returning to their homes. There was talk that it might hit somewhere further up the coast, even in North Carolina, but no one seemed to believe it. All day long Andrea had followed her father around in the grocery store, the hardware store, and on a quick stop at the diner, where she'd had an ice cream sundae, and her father had sipped black coffee and talked about the war with two men sitting at the counter. The storm had come up, but the answer was always the same.

"We haven't had a storm here in a long time," one young man had said. He didn't seem old enough for the statement, to Andrea, but she kept her silence and ate her ice cream, letting the smooth chocolate slide down her throat, cooled by rich vanilla.

"We've been hit a few times," another man said, "but we always ride it out. Best thing to do is just batten down the windows and take your yard furniture inside."

"What about that storm back in '33?" Andrea's father asked. "I heard that out on the island they were up on their roofs."

"That's the island," the first young man replied, grinning. "It's always worse out there. Besides, this one may not hit here at all."

It had gone back and forth like that all day long, but in the end, Andrea's father loaded up their truck with plywood, planks, nails, groceries, candles, and a lot of other things—so many she'd lost track and begun to wish for home, and her beach.

Now the light on their porch was visible in the distance and drawing closer, and Andrea was exhausted. She leaned on her father's shoulder and smelled the comforting odors of flannel and tobacco. He glanced down at her, then back to the road, and she knew he was smiling. It was a good moment, and the pleasant sensation only lessened slightly when they finally pulled up beside the house and saw that two other vehicles were there ahead of them.

The neighbors had gathered, and she knew that the only thing that remained was to find out if they were here to discuss the war, or to worry over the coming storm. It wouldn't matter to Andrea. She would take her book and her crayons and slip off into a corner. Sometimes they called out to her and asked her questions, but when the grownups talked she got lost quickly, and she didn't know anything about the war. The storm worried her more, but the supplies in the truck had calmed her. Her father was taking it seriously, and he would take care of her.

The wind whipped sand around their legs and the sky grew dark and black as they climbed the stairs and slipped into the warmth of the big kitchen.

On the beach, the waves crashed against the rocks. It was high tide, and the waterline was higher than usual, but no one noticed.

Chapter Two

The kitchen was brightly lit, and the aroma of coffee wafted out the door the moment her father opened it. Andrea slipped inside and ducked past her mother, who smiled down at her as she passed. There were three neighbors gathered around the table, Muriel O'Pezio, who was the nearest neighbor, sat on one side of the table, and across from her were Keith Foster and Jeff Thompson.

Muriel was older than Andrea's parents. She was tall and slender with wispy gray hair that she kept feathered back from her face and very bright, blue eyes. Her dog, Jake, was curled in a big ball of lazy muscle at her feet. Jake was a bulldog, but not the kind you saw in the cartoons. He was white with a patch over one eye like the dog on the *Little Rascals*. He lifted his head off the floor when Andrea and her father entered, and he cocked his head, causing one ear to rise comically and his tongue to loll as he watched her skirt the edge of the table on her way to the next room.

Muriel's home was the only one you could see from the porch out front, or from the beach, and it was built along the same lines as Andrea's home. The structure was raised from the ground on heavy creosote-soaked supports in case of flooding, giving it the impression of a building built on stilts. Andrea waved at the woman often when she saw her on the beach, and liked to play with Jake down by the surf, though Andrea's mother did not trust the dog.

Keith Foster and Jeff Thompson had driven out from nearer to town. They were friends of her father's, and Andrea knew them pretty well. Mr. Foster had been in the Coast Guard, and Jeff Thompson was an army man. They stopped by once or twice a week to listen to the radio reports of the war, and discuss things with her daddy over beer, or coffee, or—if the evening dragged on long enough—both.

They all three liked to tell stories, late into the night, and sometimes Andrea would sit just apart from them and pretend to play with something, or to read her book while she listened. It was hard to imagine her daddy, or either of the other two men, with guns, fighting wars and sailing across the ocean on huge gray ships, but it was fun to think about it, filling in the details from her own active imagination.

Mr. Thompson reached down and ruffled her hair as she passed, and Andrea blushed, pulling away slightly. Mr. Thompson chuckled, and Andrea put on a short burst of speed, darted through the door into the next room and stopped there to catch her breath. Mr. Thompson was always messing up her hair, or calling her kiddo. He smiled a lot, and usually had a piece of chocolate or a dime ready if the hair ruffle didn't bring a smile. Andrea liked him, but she didn't want to be caught up in the adult conversation.

When that happened, her part was invariably to stand in the middle of the room, shuffling uncomfortably from one foot to the other while they all exclaimed over how tall she was, and how long her hair was getting, or asked her if she'd met any boys this summer. It was always the same, and they would forget any answers she gave almost as soon as the words were out of her mouth. She knew this because the next time she saw them they asked the same questions again. They never told her what they were talking about, or asked her opinion.

Her crayons were right where she'd left them, and she grabbed them and searched the floor until she found her notepad. With these in hand, she crawled up onto the couch, where she could look out the window toward the beach below, and settled in. There was something about sitting on the couch that made it possible to hear the radio clearly, even though it was in the next room. Her parents' voices were muted, but she heard the broadcaster loud and clear.

It was hard to tell, but the announcer seemed to be a young man. He spoke quickly, giving things emphasis with raised tones and slowing his speech at the important points. He talked about someone named Rommel, and the name sounded vaguely familiar, but Andrea tuned it out. She stared out across the ocean and frowned.

She had sat in that same position more times than she could remember. Something was different. She flipped the pages of her notebook to the last picture she'd drawn. In the colorful image she saw the beach, the rocky outcropping halfway to the water line, and beyond that the white-capped waves. The picture had been drawn in the evening, and the sky was colored with the hues of sunset, a very pretty palette of lavender and orange with white fluffy strips of cloud overlaying it all. In her picture she'd made one of the clouds look a little like Jake, the dog.

Andrea glanced back at the beach. The water swirled around the base of the rocks, much closer than she'd ever seen it before. There was no moonlight. All she had to illuminate the beach were the two large electric lights her father had installed on the porch. In that dim, focused break in the shadows, the water was ominous, creeping up and over the rock and rolling around behind it in surges. The frothy white of the waves was thicker than usual, as if agitated.

Curling her legs up under her, she leaned over the back of

the couch to watch more closely. She didn't want to let it out of her sight, though she couldn't have told anyone why. The water should not be up around the rocks; she knew that. She was about to turn away, to go to the kitchen door and find a way to get her mother's attention so she could show her what was happening, but at that moment the sky lit with a brilliant light. It looked like a giant firefly blinking on out over the water, and Andrea watched, mesmerized.

Then the crash came, like thunder only louder. The windows in front of Andrea's face shook with the impact of the sound and rattled in their frames like a line of skeletons. Andrea turned, leaped from the couch and ran toward the kitchen, but the adults already blocked the door, and then were through it. They rushed to the couch and stared out over the water. A flame burned where she'd seen the light, a candle floating in the inky darkness. It seemed very small and far away, but the strobed image of the huge flash still hovered before Andrea's eyes.

At first, no one said a word. They lined up on the couch. Andrea's mother scooped the girl into her arms and stood just behind the men, staring out the window toward the beach. Muriel came up beside them, but no one looked to her, or acknowledged her late arrival. Then, as suddenly as the silence preceding the huge crash of sound had begun, it ended. They all talked at once and pointed toward the window. The springs of the couch squeaked and complained.

"What the hell was it?" Mr. Thompson asked incredulously. "What *is* it?"

"Torpedo," Thomas Jamieson said through gritted teeth. "A damn German torpedo. They must have gotten one of the ships trying to make it in ahead of the storm."

There was another moment of silence, then Lilian spoke, very softly.

"So close," she said. Her voice was little more than a whisper, but they all heard her. "Oh my God, they are so close."

The men whirled and headed for the door, grabbing for hats and jackets as they went. Andrea's mother spun slowly and watched them rush out into the darkness, but she said nothing. She, Muriel, and Andrea watched until the last of the men had exited and the door was closed tightly behind them, and then they spun back to the window and the flickering, dancing fire that burned—impossibly—on top of the water.

In the background, Andrea heard the radio. It was the same young man, but now he was talking about the storm. She heard the words "North Carolina," and "evacuation," but they meant little or nothing to her. She was worried about the light out on the water. She wondered where her father had gone, and for how long. She remembered the early years of her life, all spent alone with her mother for company—and her toys. She felt how tense her mother was now, how tightly she was being held—almost painfully.

Andrea pushed the announcer's voice aside and stared out at the beach. She saw that her daddy and his friends had made their way onto the sand and were headed toward the water, where they might see better, or hear something else, if the attack hadn't ended. Andrea burrowed her face into her mother's neck and shivered.

She remembered the way the water licked and teased at the base of the rocks on the beach, and now, watching her daddy hurry onto the sand, she saw that the waves had drawn nearer still. The rocks had become a small island, their tip dripping with foam, and their base awash in a swirl of dark water. She watched that water creep up the stone, and she clutched her mother tightly.

None of the adults took any particular notice of the water.

They gazed steadily out over the water at the fire, burning in the distance. Andrea understood that the fire had been an explosion, and that whatever they were, and however strange the names sounded ringing in her ear, the Nazis and the U-boats were responsible. She knew that this frightened her mother, and that, in some ways, it excited her father. He knew that the men were out on the beach, glaring at the fire as if they could put it out by blowing on it, or stamping whatever caused it under their feet. She knew, also, that they almost wished there would be Nazis on that beach, whoever the Nazis were, so that they could rush them and attack with their bare hands.

What seemed a very long time later, her mother dropped her gently back onto the couch, and the women returned to the kitchen. The scent of fresh coffee filled the air, and the bustle of pans and wash of sink water told Andrea her mother had retreated into things she was comfortable with and left the men to the fire on the beach—and Andrea herself to the rising, licking waves.

Muriel had turned the radio down low, not quite willing to give up the steady stream of voices and announcements, but not wanting—just for a short time—to be buried in the dire predictions and wild pronouncements of that young man so far away, flinging his words through the air.

Wind whipped against the windows, and the first spatter of rain rattled across the glass. The streaked view this gave of the beach distorted everything, and moments later, when the rain grew steadier, even the light from the fire disappeared from sight. Andrea still watched, though there was nothing to see, as if her silent vigil could fend off the encroaching waves and the strange threat of U-boats and Germans. She wanted to go to bed, close her eyes, and wake up to another morning on the beach.

The door crashed open and the men stamped inside, wet

and scowling, dripping water onto the linoleum kitchen floor in large puddles. They gathered at the table, where Lilian had poured fresh, hot coffee. There was a bottle on the table, as well, Scotch, Andrea knew. She thought it was odd that the drink her daddy liked best had the same name as the tape she used to wrap Christmas presents—that was why she remembered what it was called. Now she wondered why every time something was wrong, that bottle became the centerpiece of the table.

Her mother never touched it to drink, but she would pour. There were special glasses, a little bit bigger than the ones Andrea used for orange juice, but glass, and very heavy. When someone dropped ice into them, they gave off a ringing *clink!* That was the sound that made the final separation between Andrea and the adults. She had come to learn that once the Scotch bottle was on the table, voices grew louder. The ruffling of her hair would be harder, sometimes even painful, and things that the grownups said to her became even more incomprehensible than usual.

She picked up her almost forgotten crayons and notebook and headed to her room to draw, and to sleep. The windows shook, buffeted by a powerful gust of wind, and she was grateful that her room was near the center of the house. She had no windows.

Behind her, she heard Mr. Thompson's voice rise over the others, just for a moment.

"Well," he said, "I don't know about the rest of you, but I'm headed back to the place to pack. I'm going to get the family on the road before morning and head inland. I've got relatives in the mountains, and I guess maybe it's about time I gave them a visit."

Andrea paused in the hallway outside her door and listened.

"We're going to ride it out," her father's voice boomed in response. "I'll start battening things down tonight. I picked up everything we should need when I was in town."

"I guess I should have had someone out from the city to help at my place," Muriel said. Her voice was higher in pitch, and sounded somewhat frightened. "I haven't done a thing to prepare, but I don't have anywhere else to go. Nowhere that would take Jake . . ."

There were some mumbled responses. Andrea thought it was likely that her mother had invited the older woman to stay and sleep on the couch, but a few moments later she heard Muriel's shaky goodbye, and the door closed. The others left one by one, Andrea knew by the sound of their car doors and engines, roaring off into the night. The rain fell in steady sheets, and she hoped that Muriel and Jake had made it home okay. The memory of that creeping, swirling water came back with chilling clarity.

When her mother finally came through the door to announce that it was bedtime, Andrea was coloring furiously. She'd placed the earlier picture of the beach on her bed beside her notebook, and now she was working on another. This picture was a warped version of the first. The sky, instead of the muted lavenders and purples of the other sunrise, was a wash of deep red, dripping down from dark clouds. The beach was half as wide as it had been in the earlier picture, and water surrounded the stones, wrapped around their base like great white-tipped fingers in a death grip.

Her mother glanced at the pictures, and when Andrea looked up, it was just in time to see a quick wash of something dark flashing behind the familiar brown eyes and swirling, shiny hair.

"Why is Mr. Thompson leaving?" Andrea asked, choosing her words carefully. She didn't want a quick pat on the cheek, she wanted a real answer, but if her mother got upset, there would be no chance again until the following morning.

After a moment, her mother sat down on the bed and turned to her. Andrea was shocked at how tired her mother looked, how fragile.

"A lot has happened tonight," she said at last. "Mr. Thompson thinks that the storm that's coming in will be very bad. He's taking his family away to a place that will be safer."

"Why aren't we going?" Andrea asked.

"Your daddy thinks we'll be fine here, honey. There hasn't been a big storm here since 1933, and this is a good, strong house. We'll be fine."

Andrea dropped her eyes to the picture she was working on, idly sliding the red crayon back and forth across the sky. Before she could form another question, her mother rose again, leaned close, and kissed her on her cheek.

"Get some sleep, baby," she said. "It'll all seem better tomorrow. I promise."

Outside, the wind howled promises of its own, and Andrea heard the pounding of her father's hammer as he placed the sheets of wood he'd bought over the windows of their home.

Andrea drifted off to sleep, still clutching the red crayon. As the world fell away to darkness, she dreamed of churning, rushing water, eating away at the sand beneath their home and washing like gripping talons around the foundation poles. The sky was a deep red, like the color of your eyelids if you closed them and stared into a bright light, veined with clouds and dancing with lightning.

In the distance, her father's steady hammering became the firing of huge guns, and the wind faded to the whistle of shells through the air. Andrea slept fitfully as the wind rose in force and volume, and her father retreated inside to wait it out.

In her dream, she watched a boat shaped like the letter

"U" swirling down and down into the black depths of the ocean, caught in the clutching, gripping fingers of the waves and drawn far, far away. As dawn approached, her features finally eased their tense, twitching battle with the unseen, and the dreams fell away to black.

Chapter Three

When Andrea woke, it was very dark. She knew that her door was open a crack, and there should have been some light leaking in from the hallway. Her mother always left a small lamp on in the bathroom so they could find their way in the dark.

Andrea rolled carefully out of her bed and stepped to her door. There was no light anywhere, and she heard a roaring sound, like she was standing too close to the railroad tracks. Wind slammed into the wall and windows in a violent gust. The walls hummed with the effort of holding it back and the floor shifted just slightly beneath Andrea's feet. She cried out, stumbled into the hall, and crashed painfully against the wall.

Hurried footsteps sounded from the direction of the kitchen, and she heard her mother's voice. It was soft, almost a whisper. Andrea stared into the shadows and tried to make out her mother's form. As her eyes grew accustomed to the lack of light, she saw that it wasn't absolutely dark. There were shades of gray, and she saw the door at the far end of the hall leading into the living room.

Andrea stood and was suddenly scooped up into her mother's arms. She was getting too big for this, but in that shivering, shaking darkness with the voice of the wind crashing against their walls like a nightmare version of the Big Bad Wolf, Andrea clung to her mother's shoulders, wrapping her arms and legs so tightly and suddenly that Lilian staggered slightly under the onslaught.

They hurried down the hall toward the living room. It was dark in that room as well, but as they slipped out of the hallway, Andrea caught the flicker of candlelight from the kitchen. Long shadows flickered and rippled across the wall where the windows should be. That space was dark. How could it be so black? How could it be so dark?

As her mother turned toward the kitchen and carried her through and out of the room, Andrea kept her gaze locked on that wall, and on the windows. In a flash, images of the night before—the waves creeping and gurgling up the beach to drown the outcropping of stone—the brilliant, almost blinding flash of fire over the water and then the smaller flame, burning in the distance—the crash that had not really been thunder—filled her mind. All of it was gone, as if the rocks, the beach, and the ocean itself had been erased, swept away and left as blank space.

Andrea slid to the floor in the doorway of the kitchen and turned. Her daddy sat, his hands wrapped around a coffee cup, staring into the flame of a single candle on the table. The windows in the kitchen were dark too, but with the dim light Andrea could make out more detail. She saw a hint of wood grain through the glass, and again memories shifted into place. She was wide awake now, and she remembered the pounding, the hammering that had ushered her into her dreams. Wood covered every inch of glass. Wind pounded at the plywood and pressed it inward, shaking the walls again and again.

Andrea glanced up at her mother and saw the fear etched deep and hard into that familiar face. She saw it, and the darkness encroached on her own heart. She felt a chill, as if the wind had penetrated the window and the walls, bringing its icy breath to blow down the back of her neck and whisper to her that the water was out there, gurgling and growing, clawing at the base of her home, and it was hungry. She stepped to the table and laid her hand on her father's knee.

When he looked up, he smiled. Andrea weighed that smile and all that it meant against the fear in her mother's eyes.

"Morning, princess," he said. "I was wondering if you were ever going to wake up."

Andrea looked around at the shadows. How could it be morning? How could there be a day without a sunrise she could watch from the beach? She had seen rain, even been through some bad, windy storms, but this was different. Everything had shifted. The house shook again; she clutched her father tightly and buried her head in his chest, working her way up into his lap and staying there. It was even darker with her face pressed into his shirt, but the warmth and the familiar scents softened the edges.

Her mother slid into the seat across the table. The radio, for once, was silent. There was no power, no way for electricity to reach them. No way to know how bad the storm was going to be, how long before things would go back to normal, or how their neighbors were doing. Closed in the box prison that had been their home, the three of them huddled together quietly.

When she couldn't stand the silence any longer, Andrea asked, "When will it stop?"

She didn't direct the question at either parent in particular. If the radio had answered her, she would have been happy to hear it. She would have been happy to hear about Nazis and U-boats, or to hear Benny Goodman playing on his clarinet. Anything would be better than the horrible silence in the room and the awful roaring and crashing from outside.

"I don't know, princess," her father said, placing his hand protectively on her head. "I just don't know."

Then, very suddenly, the entire house was gripped and shaken. Andrea screamed, her mother cried out and fell to the side. Her chair toppled loudly, and everything tilted away from the beach. The candle slid toward the edge of the table and somehow, thinking calmly even in the midst of sudden tumult, Thomas Jamieson reached out and caught it, preventing it from falling.

There was a horrible groaning sound, and Andrea heard the rush of water, the crash of surf, and behind it, always there, the screaming of the wind, blended now with her mother's screams.

The house thrummed like a violin string that had been plucked hard and left to resonate, waiting for the next time the finger would draw it back and release. With a sudden wrench, one of the boards across the living room window facing the beach lurched outward, and then ripped away in the wind. Gray light streamed in. Andrea was nearly blinded by it, even though it was not bright, and she couldn't focus.

Her mother had risen from where she'd fallen. Blood streamed down her cheek from a cut beside her eye, but she paid no attention to it. She stared out through the doorway into the living room, and beyond. Andrea watched her as she stepped away from the table and closer to the doorway. Her eyes were dull and glazed.

"Lilian," Andrea's father called out. "Get away from there."

Andrea's mother didn't hear him, or if she did, she ignored him. She stepped full into the door's frame and stood like a statue, gazing out through the water-streaked glass.

With a curse, Thomas Jamieson moved. He stood quickly, reached out and pinched the candle's flame dead between his thumb and forefinger. He grabbed the candle then and tucked it between himself and Andrea, whom he held tightly and easily with one arm.

Something tore loose on the roof. Andrea heard it, like the sound of a saw when you bend it back and forth, and then something whipped into the gloom. Some part of what had been the roof was not there any more, and the wind clawed the hole, worrying at the shingles and board around that spot. The sound of running water beneath their feet was joined by a steady pouring splatter from the corner. Andrea turned and saw that water had found its way in from above, somehow. There was no light—no hole to the sky—but there was enough of an opening to let the water in and it was dripping down the wall toward the floor, making a dark stripe against the bright, cheerful white paint.

Her mother turned at this new sound, this new invasion of her home. She saw the water, and moved without a word to her cabinets. Andrea's father stepped forward, as if to stop her, and then held back. It didn't matter, and if this small act of defense helped her to cope with the moment, he wasn't going to take that from her. At least she wasn't standing un-protected in the doorway.

Lilian Jamieson dropped to one knee and placed a large saucepan beneath the dripping water. Some of it slipped down the wall behind the pan and reached the linoleum anyway, but the simple act of fighting back energized her. She bustled about the room and gathered all the pans she could find, pulled towels out of drawers and placed them near the leak to cut off the water from the rest of the room.

Andrea and her father watched in silence for a moment and then resumed their seat. The chair they were in was turned with its back to the short section of wall beside the doorway to the living room. Andrea's mother was behind that door on the other side, reaching into one of the upper cabinets. Something sucked the air from the room, and Andrea brought her hands up to cover her ears. The floor gave another shiver and then, with incredible force, the window in the living room burst inward. The wind screamed and howled and followed the glittering shards of glass. It crashed through the kitchen doorway and slammed into the wall beyond with incredible force.

Andrea's father wrapped her tightly in his arms and leaned toward the wall, shielding her with his back. They were all screaming, and the house groaned again, leaning one way, then shivering back the other as the foundation held, and new waves of water and air sliced over and around them. Everything moved at once. Curtains ripped from their rods and whipped through the doorway like giant bats. Lamps and dishes, anything not attached solidly to a wall or a floor, tumbled and spun, lifted into the air and smashed into the far wall of the kitchen.

Andrea tried to turn her head to see her mother, but her father gripped her too tightly. In the periphery of her vision she saw the edge of the door. It had swung inward and tight back against the counter where her mother had stood moments before, but there was no way to know how hard it had hit, or where her mother was now.

The shrieking of the wind didn't let up. Andrea screamed and screamed into her father's chest, but the words were caught in the grip of rushing air and torn away before they could reach her ears. She didn't know if her father screamed. She'd heard him, just once, then nothing but the wind, and the bits and pieces of their home, and their lives, flashing through the doorway into the kitchen and hammering against the wall, leaving chinks and cuts, battering the plaster into dust.

Then her father moved. At first Andrea was afraid the wind was ripping him away from her, and she clung more tightly, but he gripped her firmly and pressed her into the corner. That space was like a dead spot in the air, and this was more frightening still. It felt like the pressure was building to the point where it would blend with the howling wind and suck them into the maelstrom of water, debris, and destruction.

Her father placed her on the floor and leaned in very close. He put his lips to her ear and screamed so she could hear him.

"I'm going to get mommy," he said.

Andrea's eyes were very wide, and she wanted to reach out and clutch his arm, his legs, anything that would keep him from letting go of her and leaving her in that quiet pocket in the corner—anything that would keep him from placing himself in that doorway, or beyond it. Numbly, she nodded, and he was up. She saw his back as he pulled his way to the edge of the doorway, then he dove across the gap toward the cabinets and the sink beyond.

Andrea watched him, her eyes wide and her arms wrapped so tightly around her legs that her joints felt as if they might stretch, or snap from the effort. For a second Thomas Jamieson was caught in the wind, and he staggered. Midway in the span of the doorway, he took the full brunt of the wind; a wind they would later learn was just over a hundred miles per hour with gusts up to nearly a hundred and ten miles per hour. He slipped, slid a foot toward the back wall, and then another, fighting to press through to the relative safety on the far side of the door. Andrea screamed again.

She clamped her eyes closed tightly and rocked back and forth. She pressed the small of her back into the wall and felt the vibration throb through her. She didn't want to think about her father, caught in that wind and slammed against the wall, or walking through a sudden spray of glass and debris. She didn't want to think about his body slumped just out of reach of anyone who might help him. She didn't want to think about her own position, pressed against a wall that shook and vibrated like it was about to be ripped from the ground without his strong arms wrapped around her.

Tears streamed from the corners of her eyes and dried instantly on her skin. She shook so hard that the strength left her arms and her legs, but she still held tight to her knees, and she did not look. Not until something touched her leg, and she screamed and tried to scoot across the floor. She had nowhere to go; she was trapped in the corner.

Then she saw it was her father. He had her mother beside him, her arm over his shoulder, and he pressed them through the whipping air in the doorway and down to the floor. Andrea's mother slid down the wall to sit numbly by her daughter, and the two of them hugged tightly.

Thomas Jamieson was not done. He grabbed the kitchen table by one corner and dragged it closer, then dropped to the floor beside his wife and daughter. He used the table's legs to drag it closer still. They ducked down and he pulled it to the wall in the corner, using the tabletop as a shield in case anything ricocheted off the ceiling, or the wall.

The back wall had taken a horrible beating. As the three watched in stupefied amazement, it gave way. The plaster peeled from the boards and crumbled, spraying outward and busting through the wood and shingle surface of the outer wall. They could see the deck, and the stairs out back clearly, and Andrea saw the world beyond their home again. The screams she'd finally gotten control of burst free again.

Trees lined the road, tall trees, but now these were bent nearly double. She saw them rock down, slip back up, then rock down again as the winds pounded and buffeted the upper branches. Some of the trees were already gone, and others fell as they watched. One moment they were there, and the next would follow a huge, violent crack, and the tree was simply gone.

But that wasn't the scary thing. The scary thing was—when the trees fell, they never hit the ground. There was no ground. Where their driveway and the road should have been, there was nothing but water. Their car was either gone, or submerged. The trees that soared above the road were not so tall anymore, and the porch, which looked down its fifteen long stairs to the ground, was only slightly above the level of that water.

Dark shapes moved in the water, floating things, bobbing things, trees from their yard and from places Andrea could only imagine, danced madly among white-capped waves, beaten to a wild froth by the wind.

Without the back wall to build the pressure, the wind roared through their home, each gust taking away another bit of wood, or plaster, peeling back more shingles and plywood from the roof. The kitchen table, which had seemed an almost silly precaution, helped to block the worst of the rain.

It went on and on. Andrea needed something to drink, and she was hungry. She needed to use the bathroom, but she didn't move. She curled into her mother's arms, her legs across her daddy's lap, and the three of them clung to one another as if that contact could prevent the wind from tearing any of them away, or dropping them into the surf that slapped over and over again at the foundations of their house. As if their closeness could be stronger than the trunk of a two-hundred-year-old oak tree and prevent them from cracking, falling, and bobbing away in the waves.

Hours later, maybe only a few, maybe more, Andrea slipped into blackness. She was cold, wet, shivering with exhaustion and hunger, and she simply let it slide away and drew a more familiar darkness over her mind, like blinds across a window where the sun beating in was too bright.

When she woke, the sun shone right in through the roof, and she was alone, lying on the floor of the kitchen with that bright light blocked by the yellow Formica topped table. She was wrapped in a warm blanket, and her head lay on a soft pillow.

She lifted her head and heard the sound of softly lapping water. Her head pounded, and she suddenly understood what her mother meant when she said she had a headache. She felt drained, and she ached from needing to use the bathroom, and from thirst. She couldn't decide which thing was worse—which thing she needed to do more.

And she wanted her parents. Rising slowly and carefully, Andrea slipped out from under the kitchen table and stood in the wreckage that had been the kitchen. She heard voices from the direction of the living room, and she followed them, moving slowly and holding the wall tightly with one hand.

The voices came from the living room, and she moved toward them. As she stepped into the doorway and saw the devastation, the water stretching out in all directions and her mother leaning on her father's shoulder, seated on what was left of their couch, crying softly, it all hit her. All of it, the wind, the noise, the images of her father being swept away in the wind. Andrea took a step toward her parents, opened her mouth to speak, and found that her lips and tongue were too dry to form the words.

Her mother lifted her head and reached out a hand, but things whirled, and Andrea slumped to the floor and back to the darkness. From a great distance, she heard someone calling her name; it faded into whirling emptiness, and was gone.

Chapter Four

This time Andrea was only unconscious for a few moments. She woke in her mother's arms, seated between her parents on the old couch. Lilian had covered it with towels, which had soaked up much of the moisture in the cushions. The sun streamed in through the shattered window and the brilliant rays had dried it further. Andrea shook her head from side to side slowly and blinked, trying to bring the room into focus.

She knew she was in her living room, but so much was broken, stained, and damaged that it was hard to believe it was the same room she'd sat in the night before with her notebook and her crayons, watching the water lick its way slowly up the side of the rock on the beach. It was hard to imagine the faraway explosion and the way it had shaken the windows and the walls, but only enough that you knew it was there—enough to drag your eyes to the window and the ocean beyond. That explosion had been on the outside. This destruction, this *invasion* of her home was inside as well.

The walls were streaked and stained from the rain. Jagged holes had been torn in the plaster, the siding, and the roof. Furniture was overturned, broken, or just missing. And there was the silence.

It wasn't that there was nothing to hear. Andrea heard birds. She heard the lapping of water, a sound she'd heard countless times among the rocks on the beach, but never so close to her home, and never beneath her feet as they rested on the floor of her living room.

The silence, she realized, was the lack of voices. Her parents were not talking. They watched her and waited to make sure she was okay. Her father's face was etched with deep lines of concern, and staring into his eyes she saw that he was very tired. She wondered if he'd slept at all, and thought it was not likely. He was protecting them, and there had been no way to do that and to sleep, so he'd chosen to stay awake beyond the bounds of what was normal, or even safe.

Andrea saw that her mother had fared about the same as the living room, and the house. Her hair shot out in all directions at once, and the carefully applied makeup Andrea was so used to had feathered out and melted. It made her mother's eyes look like large bruises. There were real bruises too, ugly blue-black lines that crossed over her mother's lips and another on her chin. There was also the small cut by her eye. Somewhere a Band-Aid had been found and applied.

Memory surfaced with sudden clarity, and Andrea remembered the window bursting inward, the awful howl of the wind as it invaded their kitchen, and the edge of the kitchen door she'd been able to make out from her father's arms. That door must have hit hard to leave the bruises she now saw, and a small twinge of pain caught in Andrea's heart. She leaned in close and gave her mother a gentle hug.

The silence, however, was still more than this. It was the lack of the radio. The war was gone. The burning hulk of a ship attacked by the U-boats was gone. Even reports of the storm would not reach them now. The sounds she heard were those of this particular place on the earth, and those who were there. There was nothing more, or less, than that.

Andrea stood and turned toward the hall that led to where her bedroom and the bathroom had been. It was funny to think of it that way, but she didn't really know, did she? The rooms might be there, or they might not. There were walls missing, windows shattered, and great patches of roofing had been yanked out by the nails and cast into the storm as it passed. Beyond the room they sat in there might be nothing left at all.

"It's okay, honey," her mother spoke. They were the first clear words Andrea had heard since the storm, and they sounded odd, too loud and somehow detached from reality.

Her father said, "The hallway and your room are fine. They're in the middle of the house. The bathroom is there too. It doesn't flush—there's no water."

Thomas Jamieson fell silent at this. They all held that silence for a long moment, and then, without warning, her mother burst into laughter. It rang out loud and tinny and wrong, just for a second. Then her father was laughing too, and as she realized why, Andrea joined in, leaning on the battered wall for support. Here they were, stranded in the middle of more water than they ever hoped to see again, with it lapping at the supports of their home and rolling over and around the shattered trunks of trees that had been tall and beautiful only a few hours earlier, and they couldn't flush the toilet.

"It will be fine," her father told her. "I'll lower a bucket and fill it with sea water. The pipe isn't backed up, so I guess it washed away in the storm, or broke. If we pour water down the pipe fast enough, it will clear."

Andrea didn't care at that moment. Her body was screaming at her in a hundred different voices, demanding a hundred neglected things be taken care of, and she knew she was going to have to start answering soon. She stepped carefully around the corner and disappeared into the hall beyond.

She heard her parents' voices behind her, still laughing, and a weight lifted from her heart.

It was going to be okay, she thought. The storm had battered their home, but it still stood. The storm had battered them, as well, but they were alive and able to laugh. The water would eventually slide back into the ocean. It had crawled out at first, hungry and seeking, and then it had rushed out, overflowing the beach and roaring to pound at the foundations and tear away trees that were already gripped in the impossible strength of the wind, but it would have to go back to the ocean. Floods receded. Andrea had never seen a flood before, but she'd read about them, and she remembered that word clearly. What floodwaters did was recede, and these would have to do that eventually.

She closed the bathroom door behind herself and pressed the round wall switch that controlled the light. Nothing happened. She stood for a moment, looking at the switch, then burst out laughing again. She turned away from the door and the house groaned. Nothing moved, but that sound sliced through her like a hot knife. What was it? Was the house going to collapse?

Suddenly, being alone in the unlighted room was too much for her. Andrea quietly opened the door, just a crack, and finished as quickly as she could.

Before returning to the living room, she turned left and made the short walk to her own room in the center of the house. Her door was still open. She slipped in, fumbled around in the shadows for a moment, and came up with her notebook, her crayons, and a pen. With these treasures clutched tightly in her hands she hurried back to the living room. She sat on the floor beside the couch, leaned against the cushions at her mother's knee, and spread her notebook out on the floor.

She wanted to draw. She didn't know *what* exactly. The picture she'd been working on when the storm hit stared up at her from the page. The colors were stark and vivid. The blood red sky, the angry waves, all of these brought memories to the surface of her mind and she pushed them away. She did not want to draw those things again. She didn't even want to think about them, though it was hard not to when she was sitting in the middle of her living room in a patch of sunshine that wouldn't be there if the storm hadn't ripped a hole in the roof.

She flipped to the next blank page and stared down at it. She grabbed the pen and placed the tip on the paper, but she couldn't decide what to do with it. She could write something, or she could draw. The problem was that all of the things filling her head, the images she could most easily transfer to the paper, were bad ones. She wanted something else.

Then her mother cried out. "Oh, Thomas, look!"

Andrea's father turned to stare out through the shattered window where his wife pointed, and then he stood very suddenly. Andrea stood as well, forgetting the paper and crayons for the moment, to see what had caught her parents' attention.

It was a boat. It wasn't a big boat, and there was no motor. It was the short, flat kind, wooden and half-full of water. One of the oars still hung over the edge, like a long broken insect's leg. The waterlogged craft rolled with the up-and-down motion of the waves, not more than a yard or two away from the wall of their house.

With her knees on the couch, Andrea was able to get a better look at their situation, as well. The water came about nine steps up the fifteen on their stairs. It had not reached the floor of the house, though waves had crashed up and around them. It was possible, she thought, that it had already dropped some, though it showed no sign of it at that moment.

"I'm going after it," Thomas Jamieson said quickly. He was moving then, taking off his shoes and socks and pulling his shirt over his head. "Lilian, see if you can find me some dry clothes, and bring me the nylon rope from the cupboard, if it's still there—you know, the one we bought for the clothesline?"

"Tom," Andrea's mother started to speak, but she bit the words off mid-sentence. She knew he wasn't going to listen to her, if she asked him not to go, and he was probably right. They needed the boat. They needed something.

Lilian rose and headed to the kitchen. Andrea stared at her father, then leaned out the window to watch the boat. It had floated off to the left of the house and out toward the ocean, moving more quickly than she thought it should, and suddenly she thought about current. She knew that rivers had them, and she knew that the ocean did too. What if the water wasn't done with them? What if it was just using that old boat as a lure, like catching a fish? What if it just wanted her daddy to dive in so it could grab him, yank him down, and drag him away?

Her mother stepped back into the room with a long coil of thin nylon rope in her hand. Andrea's father took the rope, hugged his wife quickly and snapped a comical salute at Andrea before heading back to the kitchen and the door.

He was excited, and his exhaustion of a few moments before seemed to have dropped away completely. Andrea could tell he wanted to do this almost as much as she didn't want him to. Thomas Jamieson was a man of action. He'd picked that up in the Navy and he'd never let it go. He rose early, went to bed late, drank too much coffee, and he got things done.

Andrea walked into the kitchen behind him and stood to the side as he opened the door. The porch outside was still there. He reached out with one foot and pressed down on the wood flooring. There was no give. He stood there in the sunlight, wearing only his pants for a moment, then he turned, took the rope from Andrea's mother and started around the corner of the house, keeping up against the wall as he followed the winding porch that skirted most of their home. Four steps and he'd rounded the corner.

Andrea and her mother hurried back to the living room. They wouldn't be able to see him until he neared the boat. To Andrea's dismay, it was even further away than before and it showed no sign of slowing its progress. It was probably fifteen yards off.

They heard a splash, and in a few moments her father's head bobbed into view. He was a good swimmer, and the current was in his favor. He had the rope tied around his arm and trailing off behind him, and Andrea saw that he must have tied it off to one of the rail supports on the porch. She hoped it would hold if he needed it.

He reached the boat pretty quickly and threw a hand over the side of it, gripping tightly. Andrea could see he was straining against the pull of the current. He fumbled in the water, splashing and thrashing as he tried to find a way to wrap and tie the line to the boat with one hand. It wasn't working. Though he had a firm hold on the line, and on the boat, he was losing ground. The nylon rope slid slowly through his grip, and the boat floated steadily out to sea.

The rope was still looped around his shoulder, but he was running out of line too quickly, and the current threatened to drag him free of the safety of the line completely. Andrea gripped the back of the couch and watched with her eyes wide, biting her bottom lip. Her mother stood beside her, not moving. Andrea did not look up to see her mother's expression. She wanted her mother to be brave, to be certain her father was going to be back with them, dripping wet and laughing in a few more minutes, but she was afraid that was not the face she would find. Her mother was too still, her arms and her back too stiff, for bravery.

Then, with a sudden lurch, her father swung one leg up and over the side of the old wooden boat. It dipped a little lower in the water, canted to the side and shuddered. In the next instant, her father was inside the boat. It rode lower, filled almost to its top with water, but he had a hand free. Andrea couldn't see what he was doing for sure, but in a moment, both his hands were loose from the rope, and it grew taut as the weight of the boat and its one-man crew squared off in a bizarre tug-of-war with the porch rail.

Thomas grabbed the one limp oar and tried to turn the boat so its nose pointed at the house, but it was too heavy. The water weighed it down and made it sluggish and clumsy. Andrea saw the strain, saw her father's frustration as he yanked the oar from the water and tucked it back into the boat.

Then, to her amazement, her father grabbed one side of the boat, turned, and placed his feet against the other side. With a heave he threw himself backward, and the boat rose, slowly at first and then gaining speed. Water sluiced off over the sides and out the ends. The hull lifted, held, balanced for just a second, and then it flopped over, upside down in the water, and her father disappeared into the waves.

Lilian leaned out the window then, with a gasp, and Andrea wrapped her arms around her mother's legs.

"Thomas," Lilian cried. "Oh Thomas, no . . ." The word trailed off, and Andrea felt the tension drain from her mother's body, felt the strength ebb. The two of them teetered, off balance like the boat had been, but Andrea planted her feet and held her mother upright.

In the next moment they saw him. First a hand, then the other, followed by an arm, appeared over the side of the old boat. Her father clung there for a moment, rested, and then, with a tremendous effort, he flipped the boat again, righting it, and clambered back over the side.

Without the load of water it had been carrying the boat bobbed like a cork in the sunlight. After only a moment of rest, Thomas took the line in his hand and pulled it back to the house, hand over hand. The boat moved slowly at first, but once he had a rhythm, it went more quickly. The current still tugged him in the opposite direction, but with the resistance cut back to normal, the water had lost its hold, and the distance between boat and house dwindled rapidly.

Andrea and her mother left the window and went to the kitchen. Lilian sat at the table and placed her hand on the radio, as if she could give it life by the laying on of her hands and get a promise from the young man so far away that her husband was okay and that this nightmare would end. She wanted to be told they would be safe again, somewhere far from this ocean, and this beach.

Andrea slipped out the door. Her mother called after her, but she paid no attention. The porch had held her father. It had held up against the drag of the boat, and it would hold her. She made her way carefully around the corner of the house, sticking close to the wall as she'd seen her father do, and in moments she'd reached the stairs.

Her father was just stepping from the boat onto the bottom stair. He saw her, smiled, dripping wet and obviously very tired.

"Hey, princess," he said, "I got it."

Thomas told Andrea to step back, and he dragged the old

boat up the few remaining steps above the waterline and onto the bare floor of the porch. He wanted to tie it into place and to go over it, inch by inch, looking for holes and making repairs.

"I don't know if we'll need this to get out of here," he said. "The water could drop away as fast as it came in, or they might send rescue squads out from town, or from the Coast Guard. It's good to have it here, just in case."

Andrea nodded, but secretly she thought it was much more important that he was back with them. She wanted to explain to him what she knew of floodwaters, and how they recede, but she just hugged him, dripping and wet, and followed him back toward the kitchen.

Before they rounded the corner, a sound caught her attention. It wasn't loud, but it was familiar somehow. She put her hand to her forehead and scanned the waves.

In a moment she saw them. Muriel and Jake stood on the porch of their house. Muriel waved her arms frantically. It was Jake's bark Andrea had heard. They were too far away to make out details, but it looked like the back half of Muriel's home had collapsed.

"Daddy?" Andrea said, tugging at his arm.

"What is it?" he asked, turning.

She pointed, and he followed the line of her finger to the porch far out across the water. As he looked up, a large chunk of wall gave way, and the far end of Muriel's porch dropped into the water.

This time when Jake barked, they both heard him. And they heard Muriel scream.

Chapter Five

Andrea's mother joined them on the porch when she heard her daughter cry out in fear. She wasn't a particularly brave woman, but she wasn't letting one more bad thing happen, particularly not to her daughter. Not if she could be there to prevent it. She stepped out of the kitchen and followed Thomas' gaze across the water, over and through the broken, twisted remnants of treetops, to what remained of Muriel's house.

It was difficult to make out details over such a distance, but it was clear that a large portion of the woman's home was simply not there any longer. Muriel waved her arms and screamed to them, but only the faintest sound reached across the distance. Lilian, Thomas, and Andrea heard Jake barking clearly, his voice was deeper, and louder. Lilian's heart fluttered.

Just for a moment she imagined herself in the other woman's place, alone on that porch with the walls falling down around her, no one there to hold her, or to set things right. There was a loud screech of metal as the end of what they all knew was Muriel's living room collapsed into the waves and tried to draw the rolled aluminum roof down with it. The torn metal dangled precariously and sent a huge shiver through the entire structure.

It wasn't holding. Something was different about the way Muriel's home had been built. Something in the foundation was weaker, or the materials that had been used. Maybe the ground beneath the support timbers wasn't as solid. It didn't matter. What did matter was that if something wasn't done — and soon—Muriel would be gone. She would go the way of the trees and the road, drop into the water and be sucked out to sea, taking Jake along with her.

Thomas scanned the sky, hoping against hope to spot a helicopter, or that off on the skyline they'd see some sort of rescue boat chopping its way through the waves. There was nothing but the birds, and the sunshine. It was around noon, and the latter was bright and warm—mocking the cold terror of the moment.

"I have to try and help her," Thomas said, turning toward Lilian. "You know we can't just leave her there."

"It's too far," Lilian said. Her voice started out weak, but as she spun toward Thomas her eyes flashed, and it grew stronger. "You barely got that boat back here to the house with a rope tied on," she said. "How do you propose to make it all the way to her house with one paddle? We only have one rope, Thomas, and it isn't long enough."

"I have to try," Thomas repeated. "There has to be a way."

Andrea heard the soft crack in the back of her father's voice. He was tired; maybe too tired to do whatever it was he was thinking about doing. Maybe he was too tired too think it through clearly. She stepped closer and hugged him again, and felt his still-wet pants leg against her cheek.

He stared out over the water, thinking. Every moment that they stood there, Muriel grew more frantic. Her voice must have grown hoarse, because though they could see her calling out to them, only Jake's booming bark echoed across to them now, and even that seemed to have faded.

Then her father pulled away gently and stepped around

his wife and into the kitchen beyond. He went through into the living room, turned into the hall, and disappeared. When he came back out, he had changed his clothing, this time donning shorts that would free up his legs and a T-shirt. He also had another rope, a shorter one, and his hunting bow.

Andrea stepped aside, but her mother stood firm in the doorway and blocked his way back to the porch.

"It's too far, Thomas," she said again. "Someone will come. They will come and rescue us. You can't get to her and we need you here."

He stepped up to her, leaned his bow on the wall, dropped the shorter rope to the floor, and took her in his arms. There was no hesitation in the motion. He pulled her tight against him, so tight that Andrea was afraid her mother might crack in two. She watched them; saw how well they fit together, like two parts of a puzzle. Her father's legs were very white against the dark blue of his shorts. Trails of blue veins ran under his skin, mapping the years of hard living and work he'd required of his body.

"I could never live with myself if something happened to Muriel while we stood here and watched," he said at last. "I wouldn't sleep another night of my life, and I'd hear that damned dog in my nightmares.

"I can get there. I'll tie off to what's left of that big oak halfway across, and then I'll tie off to her place and get her down. It's going to take time, and I'm going to need help. When I get to the tree you'll have to cast the line off here, and when I get back to the tree I'll shoot the line back. I'm going to need you to be strong, and to tie me off again so I can pull us across. It's going to be heavier with Muriel and the dog in the boat."

Lilian shook her head from side to side as if she could erase his words, or make them retreat, but there was no talking him out of it. Andrea knew it as well as her mother did. Once Thomas Jamieson had decided to act, for good or for ill, it was best to get out of his way and let him get to it so he didn't have to stop to move you before he did it anyway. Andrea stepped in close, and for a moment—just a single, slow moment in time—they stood wrapped in one another's arms and shared the warmth of their bodies and the silence.

Then Jake barked again, and her father pulled away, moving quickly to the boat. The nylon rope was still tied to it, and he unfastened it, working quickly. He attached the shorter, thinner line he'd brought from his closet to one of his arrows. The other end of this he tied to the nylon rope then pulled on it as hard as he could to test the strength of his knot. Andrea had watched her father tie all sorts of knots, bows, and hitches, arcane names he had tried to explain to her as he worked with a length of rope sitting in the old wicker porch chair late at night, his glass of Scotch at his side.

She had watched him for hours as she sat reading, or drawing, looking over out of the corner of her eye to see what he was doing. He wound the rope in and over itself, whipped loops around and around, and pulled, and each time he did so a knot of a different shape would appear. Then, after studying his handiwork for a moment, he'd untie it and start over, tying something new.

Andrea had forgotten the names of the knots, but she knew that each had a special purpose. Some were for splicing two ropes together; some were for holding things tightly together. This one, she decided, was the one that tied her to her father, and she paid careful attention.

"Daddy," she said.

He turned to her and glanced up. "What is it, princess?"

"What kind of knot is that?"

He glanced down at the two ropes. They were bound to one another with a knot that looked something like a pretzel.

"They call this one a sailor's knot," he said, tugging it again. "It's a special knot that is very strong, and it doesn't slip easily, even if it gets wet." To emphasize what he was saying, or to reassure her, he strained his arms. The knot didn't slip.

Andrea nodded slowly and committed the name to memory. She would learn to tie it, she decided. Tears had formed at the corners of her eyes, and she didn't know why. She glanced out over the water toward Muriel's house. The woman had quit waving her arms, but she still stood there, watching—staring at Andrea's porch and waiting to be saved.

Thomas tugged the boat back to the edge of the stairs and carefully lowered it down. He tied it off with a third piece of rope, one that had been dangling from the boat's prow, broken free of whatever berth had once held it, and went back into the kitchen. When he returned he held one of Lilian's handled pots.

"In case I need to bail," he explained. "I don't think there's any leaks, but there was a lot of water in it when we found it. No sense getting halfway there and sinking the boat."

He ruffled Andrea's hair, but he was already staring off over the water. The sun had advanced across the sky, leaving its noontime seat, and falling slowly toward the darkness a few hours distant. He would have to be back before that happened. There was no way to do what he planned to try in the dark—no way at all. Maybe he couldn't do it in the light either, but he was going to try.

Working quickly and methodically, he tied off one end of the rope to the thick, four by four support of the porch rail. He showed Andrea, and her mother, how to untie it, going over the process more than once to be sure they'd be able to pull it off once it had been pulled tight. The rope was long enough to get him to the tree—midway to Muriel's porch, but no farther than that. Once he reached the tree, he'd have to tie off there, reel in the line, and try to get the end of it to Muriel to be tied off again.

Andrea looked out at the tree, watched branches and debris bobbing by on the waves, and noted that a light wind had risen. It sent little ripples across the surface of the water, and reminded her of the howling, uncontrollable wind that had ripped through their home not so many hours before. There were no clouds, but weather could change quickly.

Her father picked up one of the arrows and attached it to the shorter, thinner length of rope. Once again he tied the knot carefully, and tugged to be certain it would hold. Then he picked up the bow, nocked the arrow, and sighted on the tree. It wasn't an easy shot. The bow was powerful, but to cross all of that water with the rope dangling behind it was a different story than just flying straight and hard. He aimed very high, and for a point well beyond the tree. Though it had broken off cleanly, there was a nest of branches left poking up out of the water, and Thomas knew if he got the line across there he'd able to draw it back and catch it on something.

He let the arrow fly. It shot up at a sharp angle, and for a moment it looked as if it might fall short of the tree, but it didn't. It arched over the top branches and dropped into the water just beyond. Thomas laid his bow aside quickly and pulled the rope in with a quick, hand-over-hand motion. The arrow caught several times, then slid free, but at last he gave a hard tug, and it held. Keeping tension on the line, he walked it down to the post where the near end was tied off, and loosened the knot. He drew the slack through and then tightened it again. The rope hung just above the water, dangling between the house and the tree.

Andrea's mother stood just outside the kitchen door, watching. Her eyes were dull, and she moved very slowly. She hadn't said a word since he'd pushed her gently aside to get to the porch. Andrea stepped to her mother's side and wrapped her arm around her mother's legs, but she got no reaction. Lilian's eyes were fixed on her husband, or on some point far beyond him. Although the three of them were all on the porch together, there was a line of tension you could sense stretched out between them, and Lilian was afraid to cross over it.

Thomas was not. He turned to his wife and daughter, wrapped them a final time in his arms, and whispered. There was no reason to whisper. No one was near enough to hear, and what he told them was no secret, but his tone, and the way he made them lean close to hear him, gave the moment power it would have had otherwise.

"I'll be back."

Then he turned, and he was gone. It took only a moment for him to slip back into the boat and maneuver it around the side of the porch to the line stretching out into the flood. The craft was clumsy with just the one oar, but Thomas pulled it from the oarlock and used it like a paddle, and in moments he had the line between his hands. He turned to face the tree and placed his feet firmly to either side, braced against the boat for balance.

With the same quick, sure movements he'd used to pull the rope taut in the tree, he made his way slowly out into the current, and across to the far side. He had the bow and several more arrows at his feet.

Andrea moved to the rail and watched. Her heart pounded, and she pressed her lips together tightly. She prayed silently for the rope to hold, for his arms to be strong enough, for the current not to move too fast, for the storm not to return, and most of all—for her daddy back. She couldn't see his face, but she held that last image of it close, his lips barely moving as he promised to come back.

Her mother did not move to the rail. She watched, but she still hadn't spoken, and Andrea was worried about that too. She didn't know whether she could count on her mother's help when the time came to cut the line loose. She couldn't even tell—through the dull expression and vacant stare—if her mother was really watching the progress of the boat across the way, or if she had retreated to some dark, private place inside where Andrea could never follow.

So Andrea watched and gave a little cheer when her father reached the near side of the tree. He turned then, waved at her and shook his fist in the air—a sort of victory dance. Then he was moving again, working his way around to the far side of the tree where the arrow had caught tightly between two branches.

Andrea grabbed her mother by the leg and tugged her toward the rail.

"Come on, Mommy," she said. "We have to untie the rope like Daddy said. He's halfway there."

Lilian shook her head and glanced around in confusion. She didn't really seem aware of her surroundings, and it took several long, deep breaths for clarity to return to her tired eyes. When it did, she moved all in a rush. Thomas was seated in the boat on Muriel's side of the tree. He held his hand aloft, waving. Lilian began frantically tearing at the knot.

"No, Mommy," Andrea said, kneeling beside the post. "You have to pull on this one—it loosens the knot."

At first her mother didn't seem to hear. She tugged and shook the rope, her hands wrapped around the knot as if it were a puzzle she couldn't fathom. Then her eyes cleared another notch, and she reached for the loop that Andrea had pointed to. Clutching this she worked it free and pulled. The knot unraveled quickly; the tension from the damp line stretched over such a long distance dragged it round and round the post, then free. It splashed into the water and immediately Thomas pulled it in again. He was tied off to the tree and rocking gently in the waves, but he seemed in no particular danger or stress.

Andrea watched the rope slide off into the water like a snake, and she wanted to reach for it. She wanted to grip that line, either to follow it out to the boat, or to use it to drag her daddy back. It was too late. All she could do was wait, and watch. It seemed to take a very long time, but at last the rope had disappeared completely and she saw her daddy turn toward Muriel's house.

The first shot didn't reach the porch. She saw him stand, saw him pull back and release the arrow, but a moment later he was pulling again, pulling it back to himself.

"What if he can't reach her?" she asked her mother. She turned, just for a moment, saw that her mother was paying no attention, her own eyes locked on the small boat and the big man in middle of all that water.

"What if he can't get back?" She whispered this last, and only the wash of the water against the bottom of the stairs answered.

The second shot was better. This time the arrow angled up to the right of where Muriel stood, cowering against her house in fear.

Andrea's mother spoke softly, not really to Andrea, but out loud, at least. "She probably thinks he might hit her with the arrow," she said. "She's about to fall in the ocean and drown, but she's afraid he's going to shoot her."

Muriel overcame her fear. Andrea saw that her father was

shouting across the water to her, giving her instructions. Maybe he was telling her it would be all right, that he was going to get her out of there. Whatever it was that he said, it was enough to get her started, and a few minutes later, the boat was moving again, launching from the far side of the tree and into the deep, wet expanse once more.

The closer her father got to Muriel's porch, the smaller he became, until all Andrea and her mother could make out was a tiny speck bobbing up and down on the waves, and Thomas' head. He made good time across the water, and the sun was still high in the sky. Maybe there would be time. Maybe it would be okay.

The steps leading down from Muriel's porch to the beach were still there. She had been backed as far away from them as possible, but it was to these steps that Thomas pulled the boat. He reached up, took Jake by the collar, and coaxed the big dog down the stairs and into the boat. He turned back, but Muriel had backed away from the top of the stairs and turned toward the remnant of her home.

Andrea wanted to scream at her to come back out, to get into the boat and get moving. Muriel would not have heard her. Andrea saw her daddy climb out of the boat and onto the stairs. He moved slowly, as if he was uncertain of every step. Then he walked to the door of Muriel's house and he disappeared as well.

"What are they doing, Mommy?" Andrea asked. When she got no answer, she gripped her mother's arm and yanked. "What are they doing?" she cried.

"I don't know, honey," her mother said. "I just don't know."

Then her father reappeared in the doorway. He stood facing away from Andrea and the water, staring back into Muriel's house. He waved his arm to Muriel, who showed up in the door moments later. She had something in her hands, and in a moment, it glinted in the sunlight, and Andrea knew what it was.

Her birdcage.

Andrea had been to Muriel's house a few times, and in the living room there was a cage where the woman kept a large, grumpy green parrot. The bird was so old its feathers were ragged. Andrea's mother had said once that it looked as if it were always molting. It was that cage that Muriel held in her hand as she returned to the doorway.

It was that glint of light that Andrea would always remember. Something groaned. The sound was loud, like a passing locomotive, or a huge plank of wood bending and starting to give way, snapping like the mast of a ship, or one of the trees in the storm. The sound started low and ominous, and rose quickly in volume to a tearing shriek of tortured metal and wood.

As Andrea and her mother watched in horrified silence, the floor on the far side of Muriel's house collapsed. It fell away from the porch, crumbling down and back. The extra weight of Thomas' body had proved too much for the weakened structure, and somewhere in the frame of the building, the last of its strength evaporated in the late afternoon sunlight and was sucked out and down.

Muriel screamed, and Andrea heard her father's surprised, outraged bellow. She saw the two of them, suspended in the air about a foot above the level of the porch, caught on the trailing edge of the house's floor as it tipped up and back. Their arms pinwheeled crazily. Muriel clutched at the cage and toppled forward. Thomas tried to grip her around the waist and leap, but their combined weight was too much. His foot caught on the lip of the doorframe and they fell between the porch and the house.

Andrea screamed. She brought her hands up to the sides of her face, grabbed her hair and pulled so hard that it nearly ripped out of her head, but she didn't feel it. Her gaze was riveted on the scene across the water. Her ears rang with the echoes of the screams, punctuated by Jake's suddenly loud and violent barking. The dog leapt from the boat and back to the stairs, climbing to the porch, but there was nothing he could do but stare over the edge into the frothy water below and bark crazily.

Andrea clutched the rail. She rose up on the tips of her toes and stared, trying to see if her father would surface in the water below, if he would swim to the boat, holding the bird cage high. She pictured him that way, with Muriel's thin arms wrapped around his neck from behind. She saw them, in her mind, dragging themselves up over the side of the boat and dragging Jake back in after them, shooting the arrow and starting the long trip back.

She closed her eyes and prayed and willed it to be true.

"When I open my eyes," she said fiercely, biting her lip painfully, "I'll see them. They will be coming home."

When she opened her eyes, all she saw was the small boat, bouncing up and down on its tether. The house beyond was gone, all but a small bit of the frame that poked up at an angle. There were no swimmers, no birdcage or Muriel. Her father's arm did not appear over the side of the boat, or at the foot of the stairs, and on the ruined porch, staring down into the water and wreckage below, Jake had begun to howl.

When the Coast Guard boats came through, early the next morning, they picked up Andrea, her mother, and after a long, exhaustive search for Thomas Jamieson and Muriel, they took the dog Jake on board, as well. The animal came immediately to Andrea and lay down, shivering, at her feet.

She wrapped him in a tight hug, buried her tear-streaked face in his fur, and did not look back as the boat turned out to sea and started down the coast. Lilian Jamieson, still in shock, lay on a cot in one of the cabins, covered in several thick, green wool blankets.

Slowly, leaving nothing untouched, the floodwaters receded.

PART TWO

Weeksville Naval Air Station, NC—1963

Chapter Six

The airfield buzzed with activity as aircraft were towed from the hangars by bright yellow service vehicles. Pilots and their crews circled each plane, inspecting wings, fuselage, landing gear, and other equipment carefully. They matched the readings from fuel and hydraulic gauges with the proper readings on their clipboards and noted any discrepancies. It was nine o'clock in the morning, and the sun shone bright and hot on the tarmac, sucking streams of hot air from the runway.

Phillip Wicks stared down the length of it and off into the fields beyond. He saw a line of trees, but the images were warped and patchy, distorted by the waves of heat. It was a beautiful day for flying, but the weather over the airstrip wasn't his concern. Not this time, anyway. It was the weather over the ocean he had on his mind.

The pre-flight checks had gone smoothly, and he was confident that his co-pilot, a stocky young aviator by the name of Matt Schmidt, could handle the rest on his own. Phil had another stop to make before he was ready to climb into the cockpit, and he had just about enough time left to make it happen.

The control tower loomed on the left, and behind that were hangars, service bays, and a number of squat, nondescript brick buildings. They were left over from World War II. Some were still in service, housing various branches of the service in small detachments. Others housed the odd government agency, or special projects that didn't rate new accommodations or top priority.

The last of these, a two-story office complex, was surrounded by a bustle of activity and a small fleet of vehicles. Out in front a single panel truck was parked with the call letters of the local news station on it. This truck had a number of wires and cables running out of its rear, and there was a smaller center of activity near the rear doors. Phil made a note to enter the building at the far end and avoid the news truck completely.

Phil was a tall man with wavy brown hair and deep-set blue eyes that glittered if the light caught them just right. He had made a long study on the art of catching that light. You play what you're dealt, he liked to say, and his smile was an asset that had gotten him both into and out of more jams than he could recall.

Skirting the truck, its crew, and the streams of technicians and laborers filing in and out the main door, Phil turned left, walked the fifty feet to the corner of the building and pushed through a set of glass doors. There was no sign to tell him what building he had entered. Inside was a wide set of stairs, standard military style with high-gloss tiles and polished metal, non-skid, reinforced edges. The walls were a uniform "champagne."

His footsteps echoed as he climbed, and the doors closed slowly behind him, shutting off the sounds of trucks and traffic and the distant whine of aircraft engines.

Down the hall from the stairway, double doors opened onto a long hallway that ran the length of the building. Office doors opened to either side of that hall, most of them locked and dusty. About halfway down, one set hung open, and light spilled out into the corridor. Above this door a simple wooden plaque had been hung. It read, "Operation Stormfury."

Inside were desks, file cabinets, electronic equipment, an old quartermaster's chart table, and several radarscopes. All of these latter were manned by sailors in dungarees, their eyes pressed to the rubber hoods that blocked light from the screens. Their fingers danced over various intensity and focus controls. There were several officers and at least one pilot gathered around the chart table with maps spread out over its surface, and at the largest of the desks, buried behind piles of manuals and computer readouts, Andrea Jamieson scribbled furiously on a legal pad. Every few moments she shook her head in disgust, tore loose the page she'd been working on, and crumpled it angrily.

One of the radar operators called out a set of coordinates to the men at the chart table, and annotations were made. There was a long, sectioned arm that stretched across the drawing surface. It could retract to one side, or be drawn across the surface of the map. The mechanical arm made more exact course plotting possible. It was a compact team, and every member was focused on his or her particular task.

Phil stuck his head in the door quietly and looked around. He recognized the pilot at the table, another of the men assigned to his mission. He took in the radarscopes, and the desks. From where he stood, all he could see of Andrea was the top of her head, rising and falling as she wrote, crumpled, tossed, and started over on whatever it was she was working on.

Phil stepped into the room and walked to the chart table. The men looked up as he approached. Earl, the other pilot, nodded to him, but the others barely acknowledged his presence. They were intent on the lines they traced on the chart. Phil stepped closer and looked down.

They were charting a course past Bermuda and on a line

with the coast of Florida. The airfield was inland, but still on the track they were carefully marking out.

"Is it going to hit here at all, do you think?" he asked no one in particular.

When none of the others offered an answer, Earl glanced up again. "Looks like there will be some wind, and some rain, but it shouldn't be too bad. It's been a long time since a storm got a direct hit this far inland. We should be okay."

The sound of another sheet being torn from the legal pad drew Phil's attention. When he turned, he saw that Andrea had stood. She had her hands flat on the desk, and her eyes blazed with—something.

"Don't you ever think that," she said, "and even if you do think it, don't say it here. If you get used to storms not hitting, then you get lazy. If you convince yourself it won't ever happen, that every one of them will pass right on by because the last two, or three, or twenty of them passed on by, you'll become a statistic. We deal in those statistics here."

She grabbed a handful of the computer printouts, huge folding sheets with lines and lines of numbers, text, and characters, and shook it at them.

Phil stood very still. He hadn't seen the outburst coming, and from the look on his face, neither had Earl.

"I'm sorry," the pilot said. "I didn't mean to make light of it." He turned back to the table, grabbed his goggles and flight gear from the corner, and clapped one of the officers on the shoulder. "Keep an eye on it for us, Lieutenant."

Andrea still held the printout in her hand. She watched as Earl wound his way around the radarscopes on the far side of the chart table and headed for the door without a backward glance. Phil watched her. After a moment, he repeated his question, this time addressing her.

"Ma'am," he said. "Do you think the storm is going to hit

here? I'm not just curious for the sake of it. I'll be flying out over your storm in a little while here, and I'll be taking a lot of men and aircraft with me. We've got a mission to complete, and when we're done, we have to come back. If we're going to have a hurricane on our tails, or even close, then I need to have an idea of it before we go."

She stared at him, and her hand lowered slowly until the papers rested on the cluttered desktop. Her lips moved, but she didn't speak immediately, not so that he could hear. She was obviously having trouble calming herself after the outburst, and he wondered what had sparked it. Earl's comment was no different than a thousand others he'd heard—possibly not the brightest way to look at hurricanes, but certainly not worthy of an attack.

"I'm sorry, Captain . . ." she hesitated.

"Wicks," he said, stepping closer to her desk and holding out his hand. "Phil Wicks. I'll be flying point today."

She released her hold on the papers and took his hand. Her lips curled into an embarrassed smile. "I'm sorry about a moment ago," she said. "I take storms very seriously. We all do."

She realized that she'd held his hand too long and pulled hers back quickly. To hide the blush that rose to her cheeks, she stepped around her desk and walked past Phil to the chart table. The lieutenant moved aside as she approached, and Phil followed her, watching as she pointed to the line of the approaching storm.

"This isn't a hurricane yet, Captain," she said. "It's a tropical depression. The winds are only about sixty miles per hour. It's moving quickly though, nearly twenty miles per hour, and we believe it will slow down here," she pressed her finger onto the chart on a line with where they had plotted the course. "It may strengthen here, perhaps to a Category One storm—meaning about seventy-five-mile-per-hour winds. We are counting on it to strengthen, but not too much.

"At that point," she turned to look at him, and Phil caught something in her eyes, something similar to the fire she'd displayed when she'd turned on Earl a few moments earlier, "one of two things will happen. Either the cold front moving down from the east will slow it and bump it toward the south," she traced a line that curved down toward the southern tip of Florida and off to the west, "or, if the cold front is too slow, or the storm has already gathered enough strength by the time the two fronts meet, it could shift north, or northeast."

"It could hit here, then," Phil said. It was a statement, not a question, but her smile widened for the first time.

"It could, but the odds are against it. Also, unless the storm grows a lot stronger than we believe it will, it would be weakened considerably by the time it reached this far inland. Probably it will strike on the eastern shore and bump up the coast."

"But not for certain," he persisted.

"It is never 'for certain,'" she answered. She held his gaze for a moment, and then turned back to the chart. "Nothing ever is. But this time you can be sure of one thing."

"What's that?" he asked.

"Well," she said, smiling more brightly, "unless I'm underestimating you and the average airspeed of a C-130, you have nothing to worry about. If the storm strengthens, it will slow down to fifteen, maybe eighteen miles per hour. As long as you keep far enough above it to avoid the wind, and close enough to it to deliver your cargo, you should be back with several hours to spare before the first of the winds and rain actually reach shore."

"Several hours?" Phil asked.

She nodded.

"That's a problem," he said, scratching his head and glancing down at the chart with a frown.

Now she looked confused.

"How can that be a problem, Captain?"

"Phil," he corrected her. "It's Phil, if you don't mind. The problem is Miss . . ."

"Andrea," she replied automatically, "Andrea Jamieson. I'm the senior consultant here."

"Andrea," he nodded, smiling. "The problem is with my dinner plans," he said, turning away sadly.

"But," she replied, following him around the chart table with a confused frown planted on her face, "I just told you, Capt . . . Phil. You'll be back in plenty of time for dinner. How will it spoil your plans?"

He turned back with a wink. "I don't have any yet," he said.

She stood, staring at him with her mouth open for just a second, and he grinned at her.

"You just get up there and drop that load of silver iodide on the storm for me, Captain Wicks," she said, reverting to his rank. He thought he caught the ghost of a smile on her lips, but he didn't wait to push his luck. "We have a storm brewing," she added.

Phil nodded and turned toward the door. On the way past Andrea's desk he caught sight of a colorful brochure. It rested on top of a pile of others just like it. Across the top of the front it said OPERATION STORMFURY in bright blue letters. He laid his hand on top of it and glanced at the paragraphs below.

"Take it, Captain," Angela called out. "It will give you something to read while you're working out those dinner plans."

Phil snatched the brochure and left the room. The questions about the storm had been important, but nothing he couldn't have gotten from the tower once he was in the air. It was the process he was after. The reason for the mission and the flight were unclear to him.

Phil had heard rumors, but he was trained for combat missions, and the reassignment to Operation Stormfury was not one he'd wanted. It was a crackpot program, one the government was ready to cancel on a moment's notice, but it had funding, and it had congressional backing, so here he was.

None of the other pilots could explain it to his satisfaction. Fly a bomber over a hurricane and drop a load of silver iodide into the storm, they said. Then, fly home and have a beer and take it easy until the next storm. It was his retirement assignment, he knew. You didn't draw assignments like Stormfury when there were hot spots of aggression all through Southeast Asia if they were planning on sending you back into battle.

As he made his way back down the same stairway he'd climbed, he thumbed through the brochure. It was meant for the press, he saw, nothing too confidential, but it was more than he'd been able to get out of any of his companions.

> *Operation Stormfury is dedicated to finding the Achilles' heel of hurricanes. Formed of a core group of meteorologists, engineers, and physicists working in partnership with the United States government and the four branches of the military, data are gathered from storms around the globe.*

There were drawings of boxes that were undoubtedly intended to be computers with arrows indicating the flow of data. It was childish and comical, but oddly compelling, and he read on. There was some technical information about the supercooled water in storms, water cooled below its freezing point. When a "seed crystal" like silver iodide was introduced, the water solidified around it. If this process could be introduced over a large enough area it could disrupt the structure of the storm, possibly weakening the eye, or causing it to fall apart completely.

There was more—a lot more—but Phil was having trouble concentrating on it. He'd wanted to know, but now that he did, it didn't seem as important. As he hurried back toward his plane, and his crew, he smiled.

He was thinking about dinner.

Chapter Seven

The air remained clear as Phil rolled down the runway and lifted off. There were four aircraft in all, and after their initial climb, they leveled off, tightened their formation, tipped their wings at the tower and banked off toward the Atlantic. It would take some time to reach the outer perimeter of the storm, and they intended to remain close until then. Phil wanted to maintain visual contact in case some trick of the hurricane's winds caused unforeseen problems.

The plan was to remain far enough above the storm that the winds wouldn't be a factor, but this was still a fairly new "science," and dropping silver iodide into clouds was not exactly the same as dropping explosive loads over enemy lines. True, there would be no one gunning for them, and no strafing fire or anti-aircraft barrage would impede their flight. This didn't mean they could relax. You could never do that if you wanted to live a long life, and Captain Phil Wicks intended to make it at least as far into the future as dinner.

"You okay, skipper?" Matt Schmidt, strapped in beside him, looked half-concerned, half-amused. "You look like you're flying in your sleep."

"Just thinking," Phil laughed. "Sorry. I took a hit from a pair of bright blue eyes a little while ago. Still trying to get my bearings."

Matt nodded and grinned. The two had flown together for a long time. Schmidt was a good pilot, but his specialty was communications. He'd been specially trained for this mission. They hadn't wanted to bring gunners to drop the "seed" loads, because the process was different. Rather than expecting men to unlearn perfectly good and useful combat skills, the decision had come down from above to train whoever was available. Despite the funding and the interest from Washington, Stormfury was not a priority.

In Matt's case, however, the man had wormed his way onto the team despite the ruling. He and Phil had flown together on hundreds of missions, and Matt considered the older pilot to be his mentor. Schmidt would be up for his own aircraft on his next assignment, and he could have had his choice of several active units, but he'd pulled some strings and called in some favors and gotten himself assigned, at least temporarily, to fly with his old partner.

Phil appreciated it, though he hoped that hitching his star to an old, nearly retired battlewagon like himself wouldn't hurt the kid's career down the road. If Phil were still in favor, he wouldn't be here in the first place.

"You mean the weather lady?"

Phil nodded.

Matt's grin widened. "She's a looker all right."

Phil banked the plane through the clouds and soared out over the Atlantic, using the motion of the plane to mask his own grin. "That she is," he whispered under his breath. "She surely is."

Andrea stood at the window and watched the four planes disappear into the clouds. Behind her the radar operators still called out coordinates, and the lieutenant at the chart table continued to plot the storm's course. Her legal pad lay forgotten across the top of her desk where she'd left it. Several more aborted attempts at the letter she'd been trying to draft had been crumpled and tossed, and she was no nearer to the words she wanted—that she *needed* to get her point across.

Beneath the other papers on her desk was a message from Washington DC. The funding for Operation Stormfury was going to be cut back to a small administrative load. The active branch of the program—her branch—would have their monies pulled. The government didn't see that further experimentation in cloud seeding would bring about any useful results, and with the war in Vietnam hitting high gear, they could ill afford the resources that had been allotted, particularly the planes and the radar.

On the runway, a fifth plane had taxied into position for takeoff. This one was an observation plane. It was fitted with cameras, microphones, gauges and dials that would transmit atmospheric and weather conditions through a high frequency transmitter to the receivers installed in a bank against the wall, just behind the radarscopes. The outputs of these receivers would feed facsimile printers, plotters, and a pair of large gray Teletype machines behind her desk. The equipment was state of the art, borrowed, stolen, and begged from a dozen other projects.

Once that data had been gathered and recorded, Andrea's real work began, as well as that of her closer associates. They checked the storm's strength and structure at every moment before, during, and after the seeding process. They checked water temperature, wind temperature, the atmospheric pressure on each side of the storm—in short, they would know all that there was to know about the conditions surrounding this particular storm.

If something happened on one front that caused a reaction on another, they would find it. Already they were able to predict which direction a storm might turn with some accuracy, and whether it would increase in strength. These things couldn't prevent the storm from hitting, but they could save lives, and for Andrea, that was what it all boiled down to.

She needed to find a way to make them see the importance of her work, the vital nature of the data they had already accumulated. While Washington continued to believe that their main purpose was to find a way to stop, or slow hurricanes, Andrea knew that the true value of the work lay in the enhanced understanding of tropical depressions and storms in general, and the ability to predict their actions with more accuracy.

To pit a few men and planes against the fury of such a storm, even a small one, was like sending a poodle out to herd elephants. No bomb ever dropped in aggression, not even those at Nagasaki or Hiroshima, had ever, or would be likely in the future to contain the explosive power of a single large hurricane.

"So," she asked herself quietly, "why are you standing here at the window watching that flyboy take off into the sky when you should be writing the letter?"

She didn't know the answer to that any more than she knew what she could say that would save Stormfury.

She stepped to the chart table and glanced down. The storm hadn't moved much since she had shown it to Captain Wicks, but it was no longer the only thing being plotted. The four seed craft had been added in, and the fifth, the observer, roared down the runway behind her. She heard the engines rev and felt the vibration, even from so far away, as the powerful thrumming shook the windows and walls gently.

Andrea shook off her concerns for the moment, and moved to one of the radar consoles. The young man seated in front of it looked up as she stepped near.

"Would you like a look, ma'am?" he asked politely.

Andrea nodded. She didn't think she should tell him she'd logged more time in front of one of these scopes than he had in his naval career. It wasn't important. What was important was that this be the day—the one time in all of the missions they'd planned, aborted, and flown—that they'd get the results they needed. In the end, it was the only real hope she had of continuing her work with Operation Stormfury. She might buy them some more time with an impassioned letter or two. She might be able to pull a few more strings, offer to fund a little more of the work herself if they extended their support, but this would be the last season.

If they didn't stop a hurricane before the end of the storm season this year, then this branch of the research was at its end, and it would be time for her to move on. She wasn't wholly unprepared for such an outcome, but it was frustrating.

She took the offered seat, and placed her forehead to the rubber hood that covered the radarscope. The screen itself was amber, backlit dimly. The surface was littered with bright dots and squiggled patterns. Some of it was clouds, some of it was just return from the ocean itself, but in the upper right of the screen, she saw it. The storm. It was larger than it had been the last time she'd looked, and much closer. It seemed to have picked up strength, as they had hoped. Maybe more than they had hoped.

She also saw the five aircraft, the four on a straight course for the storm, and the fifth slanting off to the near side and rising higher. She worked a control and placed a small circle over the lead seed plane. With a click of her finger, she brought up a set of rings. The rings showed distance from base. They were already well on their way, and it was hard, even though she knew it was true, to see the tiny yellow blips of light as men.

"We still have quite a while," the young man offered, trying to make conversation.

Andrea smiled, and was glad that the rubber hood hid the expression from him. They were all very helpful, but she knew that most of them, particularly the younger sailors, had a hard time figuring out how to handle working for a woman, particularly a younger and not unattractive woman. As often as not, they stumbled over themselves trying to be helpful.

"Yes," she said, rising. "Let's see if we can get the lead aircraft on the radio."

The boy nodded and returned to his seat. A small communications console flanked each of the radarscopes. The young man, Petty Officer Carlson was his name, flipped a toggle switch and depressed a large, square plastic button. He then picked up a headset, planted it firmly on his head and began to speak, issuing his own call sign and that of the aircraft.

"Sierra Papa One, Sierra Papa One, this is Sierra Foxtrot, over."

His voice crackled through the small speaker beside him, and when he released the key on the headset, his voice was replaced by steady static. He waited a moment, and then repeated his call. On the second try, a response came through, clear, but sounding very far away.

"Sierra Foxtrot, this is Sierra Papa One. Read you fivers, over."

Carlson turned to Andrea with a quizzical raise of his eyebrows.

"Tell him the storm has strengthened," she said. "And ask them to get as low over it as they can. This might be our last shot this year."

The boy quickly relayed her information, and her instructions.

"Is Miss Jamieson there, over?" came the tinny reply.

Andrea blushed, but nodded.

"Yes sir, right beside me, over."

"Tell her for a hamburger I'll drop to five thousand feet, but anything lower than that it's going to have to be steak. This is Sierra Poppa One, over, and out."

"Sierra Foxtrot, out," Carlson replied automatically, and then he broke into a huge grin.

Andrea blushed harder and turned away, but not before he caught her smiling in return. Without a word she returned to her desk. Instead of taking up her pad and paper again, she neatly stacked and filed all the loose work and cleared enough space for the readouts that had already begun spewing from the Teletype and the facsimile printer. They were initial reports from the observer craft, initial radar and aerial shots of the storm, as well as a set of "control" readings meant to help calibrate the transmitters and respective receivers.

From this point on there was nothing to do but to watch, and to wait. Now that the young radar operator was back in place behind his scope, the readings resumed, and the steady scratch of the stylus on the chart tracked the slow progress of the storm, and the quicker advance of the aircraft.

The amount of preparation, paperwork, and luck that went into planning such an experiment was incredible. Andrea had managed to get all of the pieces in place three or four times over the span of several years. There were only certain seasons of the year that tropical depressions formed in any great number, or with any strength. They traveled across warm water, down through the gulf, and without the proper meteorological conditions, a storm wasn't even possible.

Much of their research in preventing the storms from reaching shore involved an emulation of the conditions in nature during the off-season. It wasn't conceivable that they could stop a storm once it had reached its full fury, but if they could lessen it, or disrupt it, remove the path by which it would normally travel, or shake up the environmental conditions violently enough, they might cause the shift that would allow the storm to fizzle on its own.

One problem with this approach, of course, was that even if they succeeded, the reaction they caused would be almost identical to the course nature would eventually take herself, and that being the case, it was very difficult to convince others in her field, let alone generals and politicians, that the results they achieved were anything at all. They needed one storm to give them a radical shift, a shift that could reasonably be attributed to their program. So far, they'd caused only minor changes, and it was questionable whether those changes were happening because of the cloud seeding, or if they happened on their own.

Andrea knew she could go to the press. They were always around, and always available. The title of the project had leaked somehow, and anything with a name like Stormfury, even after years of producing nothing newsworthy, was worth watching. Who knew what the government might be hiding away in the dark recesses of buildings like this one? Another Area 51? Some new experimental aircraft?

The thing was, the press would take the information to the public, and the public was an even harder sell than the government. They would want immediate results, and after the first set of questions didn't net them anything spectacularly newsworthy, the press would start digging into the budget and the money being spent.

Taxpayers could ignore what they knew nothing about, but the minute you started telling them about some harebrained scheme to hunt hurricanes with their money backing it, they were all ears. Going public would just speed up the inevitable end.

She worked steadily through the readouts, making entries in a series of logbooks and marking charts. The storm had grown more quickly than they thought it would. It was nearly a Category Two now, and its breadth was enormous. Andrea frowned.

She didn't believe it posed any greater danger to the pilots, but if the storm got any bigger, the amount of silver iodide they had planned on would not be enough. It had barely been adequate, to her mind, for a tropical storm, let alone a hurricane, and nothing like the size of this one. Despite their greater understanding of hurricanes, they were as often wrong as right on the strength and direction of any given storm.

If it had happened any earlier, she probably would have called them back. There were two more small depressions forming, and there was still time to divert their resources to one of these before the end of the season, assuming the budgetary plug wasn't pulled immediately. They were committed, though, and the aircraft were nearly in place. Another hour, and the silver iodide pellets would be plummeting into the frothing, whirling mass of the storm.

Andrea wondered what it looked like from above. She'd seen pictures. There were aerial photographs, and the facsimile machine gave them a rough approximation of the storm, but she knew it would be different from the air. How could it not be? It would be the difference between holding a postcard of Niagara Falls in your hand, and standing on the precipice, staring over the edge to the crashing foam below.

The thought gave her a moment of vertigo, and she laid her head on her desk. The second her eyes closed, she saw the line stretching out over the waves. She saw and heard the water rushing beneath her and felt the change of pressure as the back window of her home burst inward and spewed glass and water and wind through the center of the kitchen and into the rear wall.

She heard the creaking, tearing groan of Muriel's house teetering over backward, and crashing into the water.

"Ma'am?"

A hand dropped lightly onto her shoulder and she released the memories with a rush of breath. She lifted her head and found the lieutenant standing over her desk, looking down at her in concern.

"I'm fine," she told him. "I just haven't been getting much sleep."

He nodded. Then he spoke. "The planes are in position," he told her. "They've begun their descent."

She rose quickly and followed him back to the chart table. She wanted to take over the radarscope again, but knew it was pointless. Petty Officer Carlson was well trained, and she'd learn more by listening to his steady reports than she would from watching the display herself.

She saw that the four aircraft were now plotted directly above the storm's position.

The radio crackled.

"Foxtrot Sierra, Foxtrot Sierra, this is Sierra Papa One, come in. Over."

The radar operator thumbed his switch and replied. "Sierra Papa One, this is Sierra Foxtrot, read you five by five, over."

"Foxtrot Sierra, read you same. Dropping altitude on my mark."

Slowly, the four planes fanned out and descended on the forward wall of the storm. Captain Wicks' steady voice droned over the speaker, dropping to twenty-five thousand feet, fifteen thousand feet, and on down. At six thousand feet his voice wavered. There was a roaring sound just for an instant, and a crackle of static.

The radar operator keyed his microphone. "Sierra Papa One, Sierra Papa One, repeat your last, you are breaking up, over."

There was nothing but static and silence. The speaker popped once then again, but that was all they heard. The radar operator tried again, but the result was the same.

He turned to the lieutenant, wild-eyed. "We've lost them, sir!"

"Keep trying," the lieutenant said, his voice calm, but his face pale. "Keep trying. The storm may have put up some interference. Try raising the observer and see if they can get through."

The boy flicked his toggle to the second channel and he spoke quickly. "Echo Sierra India, Echo Sierra India, this is Sierra Foxtrot, do you copy? Over."

After a slight delay, the pilot of the observation craft crackled over the line. The radar operator explained the communications loss.

"Sierra Foxtrot, that's a negative," the man replied. "We still have them on radar, but I get no response."

"Roger."

They kept at it, frantically shifting from frequency to frequency. Andrea gripped the edge of the chart table so hard that her knuckles turned white, and the lieutenant leaned close over his chart. He was not marking anything, but his head was cocked toward the speaker and his eyes were closed, as if in prayer.

Chapter Eight

Far above the cloud layer, it was difficult to believe that the storm existed. Phil kept a close watch on his instruments, knowing that the weather was unpredictable, but it was hard, from where he sat, not to enjoy the afternoon. It was bright, and the flight had been quick and pleasant. Matt had kept up a steady stream of banter about the upcoming World Series. The Dodgers would have Koufax on the mound, and the Twins were hot this year. It was going to be a series to remember, and Matt loved the game. You could see it in the twinkle in his eyes, and the animated way he swung his hands around when he spoke.

Phil liked baseball well enough, but he really didn't care who won. He was a Chicago Cubs fan, and his boys weren't in the running. He stared out over the clouds and thought about the load they were carrying.

They had trained for this. The drop was different than the bombs they would have released over a target in the war. These packages dispersed gradually, opening on a mechanism similar to those that first-time parachutists used. As the cylinders of silver iodide pellets rolled out and began their downward spiral into the heart of the storm, lines fastened to the aircraft would pull taut, just for a moment, and flip open compartments on the side of each load. This, along with the natural spiral as they dropped, would allow the cylinders to release their cargo in a pattern that spread out over the widest possible area. They would drop several in their run, then pull up and away and head back to base. The other three aircraft would spread along the near perimeter of the storm, punch in over the outer wall of the eye of the storm, and perform the same task.

It was a good enough plan, he supposed. The problem was, the plan had been conceived to seed the eye-wall of a storm seventy-five miles across. This one had grown astronomically. The last report he'd seen brought the winds almost to Category Two, and his radar, coupled with some reports from the observation craft, set the boundaries out around two hundred miles. A two-hundred-mile storm was going to take a hell of a lot more silver iodide to stop than what they had brought with them, at least if it was dropped from the five thousand feet originally planned.

It was possible that if they came in lower and concentrated their loads strategically along the way, that the effect, localized as it might be by such an action, would break the continuity of the storm's front.

He wished he could discuss this with someone who knew more than he did about storms, and this process in general, but there was no time. They were directly over the storm now, banking and turning, and all he had to go with was his very basic understanding of the process from a quick perusal of the brochure. Lifting his microphone, he called in to base.

"Foxtrot Sierra, Foxtrot Sierra, this is Sierra Papa One, come in. Over."

The response was quick and clear.

"Sierra Papa One, this is Sierra Foxtrot, read you five by five, over."

Phil smiled and keyed his microphone again. "Foxtrot Sierra, read you same. Dropping altitude on my mark."

Flipping channels, Phil called to the other aircraft. "Sierra Papa Squadron, this is Sierra Papa One. Over."

Three responses crackled quickly over the air.

"I'm going to drop down lower than planned," he said slowly. "Dropping load at thirty-five hundred feet, vice five thousand feet. Over."

"That's pretty low, Captain," a voice crackled back. Then, almost in afterthought, "Over."

"This storm is bigger than it's supposed to be," Phil said. "I want to concentrate our drops. If we release too high, the pellets will spread too quickly, and in a storm this size, we'll be spitting in the wind. If you feel turbulence, or things go south, pull up and regain altitude. I had a buddy flew over one of these puppies once—he said you could get down to three thousand safely."

He got three affirmatives, and smiled.

"I'll see you all on the other side of the storm," he said with finality. "This is Sierra Papa One, over and out."

The radio went silent, and Phil turned to Matt, who watched him carefully. "You sure about this, skipper?" the younger pilot asked. "I've never been that close over a hurricane before."

"Don't know if anyone has, other than that old buddy of mine," Phil replied. "We'll pull up at the first sign of trouble. I just don't want to be wasting our time out here."

Matt nodded, but he seemed anything but sure. "We lost comms with the base," he said. "I tried them a couple of times while you were telling the others. Nothing but static."

It was Phil's turn to nod. "Guess we're on our own then, partner." Then he grinned. "Let's do it."

They dropped out of the upper cloud cover, and Phil nearly pulled straight back up. The sight that met their eyes stole his breath and he felt a tingling, cold chill in the joints of his arms and caught at the base of his throat.

"Jesus," Matt said.

The storm spread out in all directions in a dark mass. They were near the eye; it was clearly visible, and an almost calm patch of sea. All about it, though, the wind howled at incredible velocity. They were buffeted, even at twenty-five thousand feet, and Phil clung to the controls grimly.

It wasn't like a storm at all from where they watched it. It was like some huge, demonic presence; sliding over the ocean like a sidewinder, ready to strike. Phil realized he was holding his breath and released it with a nervous laugh.

"Damn," he said. "Just for a minute there I was being quiet—I think I was afraid it would see us and turn."

Matt nodded. His gaze was riveted to the roiling, whirling mass of air, water, and clouds that spun out beneath them. The lower they dropped, the wider the storm grew, filling the horizon to either side. If anything went wrong now, they were statistics. No way around it, and the destructive force beneath them was awesome in its scope.

"You ready to drop this stuff off and get out of here?" Phil asked, forcing himself to break the silence. "I don't know about you, but that thing gives me the creeps. I can't shake the notion it knows we're here."

Matt turned to him, and Phil saw his own sudden understanding of what they were up against mirrored in the other man's eyes.

"I'm ready," Matt said. "Let's get this done."

Phil pressed gently forward on the controls and the aircraft's nose dropped slowly. The wind around them was rushing by at over a hundred miles per hour, but it was a steady, blowing force. Gusts could cause serious problems, but as they dropped into the hurricane's grip, the sustained wind did little to upset their flight. Phil watched the gauges nervously, all the same.

The wind chopped whitecaps from the waves and plowed a furrow across the surface of the ocean. You could see through in most places, like watching through a heavy fog, or driving rain, but at the same time it was a solid, focused entity, a single malevolent force of Mother Nature, grinding its way across the water.

"Keep your eye out for funnels," Phil said tersely. "This wind isn't a problem, but the closer we get to land, the more chance of turbulence."

Matt nodded. His hand hovered over the drop button, and the other gripped hard on the armrest of his seat. It wasn't likely the man would miss anything the way he was scanning the skies around them.

A gust shivered over and around them and the nose of the plane dropped suddenly. Phil held on and rode it out. He felt the craft shudder, then resume its smooth flight. He took a deep breath, pressed in again on the controls, and dropped lower.

"Thirty-five hundred feet," he called out.

Matt nodded. He flipped a toggle to activate his controls, and checked their position quickly. They had passed over the eye and were nearing the leading edge of the storm. As Phil banked slowly and ran them along that rim, Matt punched the first button. There was a low grinding whirr as hydraulic bay doors opened, another light jerk as the canister dropped away below them and the wire snapped open the door on its side. Phil got only a glimpse as he turned. The glittering silver cylinder dropped quickly, and behind it a shower of sparkling crystals floated for just a second, then whipped into the interior of the storm and were gone.

A few moments later, Matt depressed the second button,

but this time there was no way to watch the cylinder as it dropped away below them. They carried six loads, and they counted between the drops.

Phil's actions were almost automatic as the plane soared above the storm, and the canisters of silver oxide dropped away as before. Seeding the clouds—it had a magical sound to it, as if there was something that could be expected to grow from their actions. That wasn't the image that stuck with Phil, however. Phil was thinking about North Carolina, cotton fields, and a man named Bert.

Bert was a retired air force pilot. He'd had a little too much trouble with alcohol and discipline, so he'd left his military career behind and returned to buzz over the fields of North Carolina in a brand-spanking-new, brilliant yellow crop-duster. Phil had watched the man strafe cotton fields, fly too low over the road, taunt traffic, and perform tricks that would give some of Phil's own running mates heart seizures. Bert did all of this while drunk, and as often as not, while dropping a white mist of insecticide over the fields near Elizabeth City.

That's what this was like—crop-dusting. There were no hordes of insects to be poisoned or prevented, but there was much worse. The wind below could strip those same cotton fields bare in a matter of a few moments, and take the roof off the barn, and the barn itself if you weren't lucky. Tornadoes formed around the eye of the storm and removed entire city blocks, or a single tree, at their whim.

Phil had once seen a feather that a tornado had driven into the solid bark of a tree. His grandfather showed it to him, and it was a lesson he never forgot. The weather was not something that could be ignored, and it was not likely that they would ever control it. It would be good to understand it better, but often as not getting close enough to do that was not in your best interests.

The laws were getting stricter, and Phil figured if ol' Bert didn't mend his ways, he'd end up in jail eventually. If the man didn't perform such a valuable service, and better than any of the other local pilots, he'd have been grounded long before. Phil remembered because he'd gone to school with Bert's boy, Leon. Leon wanted to fly, like his daddy, but he didn't want to learn from Bert. He'd signed up for the U.S. Air Force the same day Phil had signed up for the Navy. More years than Phil wanted to think about, in fact, had passed since that day.

Matt pressed the final button and released the last of the cylinders to drop away, spinning into the maw of the storm. Phil concentrated on his instruments, and wondered briefly how things had gone for Leon in the military. The boy had already been well along the way to imitating his daddy's drinking problem, but maybe the boys in blue had straightened him out. Maybe not. Maybe it was Leon soaring over the Great Dismal Swamp with the barrels of insecticide strapped into place and a maniacal grin on his face these days.

As the final drop was completed, Phil eased back on the controls. The aircraft shuddered just once, caught in a crosswind, and then lifted gracefully. He was about to breathe a sigh of relief when Matt cried out.

"Three o'clock, skipper. Look out!"

Phil glanced to the side just in time to see a whirling, slashing funnel of water bear down on them. There were several of the huge waterspouts, like tornadoes, born of the crazed atmospheric conditions around the storm's edge. This one was huge, and though they would be above it, he knew they did not want to be caught in the drafts from that thing—not at this low altitude.

Phil glanced at the altimeter and grimaced. Thirty-eight hundred feet. Not rising fast enough. He didn't want to pull up too hard in this wind. It was steady for the moment, but more gusts could hit at any second, and if they caught him at the wrong angle they'd send the craft spinning away below, like the cylinders they'd dropped, to disappear into the choppy, foam-topped waves.

Easing the control to the left, he fought the rising panic that screamed at him to yank back and soar out of there. Phil banked away from the waterspout. They were still rising—four thousand feet—four thousand two hundred feet—very soon they would have enough altitude that the funnel would not matter.

It seemed impossible that their course would not intersect that of the swiftly moving spout. It snaked from side to side, and once again the impossible thought that the damned storm knew they were there invaded his mind. This—thing—this snake made out of water, whipped about with amazing speed, undulating unpredictably as though writhing in pain, or swaying from side to side like a cobra, trying to mesmerize them so it could strike. Phil pulled a little harder on the control and banked more sharply to his left. They picked up speed, and the plane spun off on an arc and dove back into the cloud cover above.

The spout was out of sight, and for a panicked moment, Phil thought they would hit it after all, that he would not be able to find it, or to avoid it, but then he saw the altimeter pass five thousand two hundred feet, and he released his breath. They'd made it. He flattened out and sharpened their angle of ascent, not leveling off until they reached fifteen thousand feet, well above any weather concerns.

"That was too close," Matt said. His face was still white, and his eyes had a glazed, faraway look that Phil didn't like.

The young pilot went on, not waiting for Phil to respond. "I swear it felt like that thing was some kind of big, hungry mouth, and it reached out to drag us in and swallow us whole. I've never seen anything like it."

Phil nodded. He picked up the microphone and called the other aircraft, one after the other. All responded within moments. Each had, it seemed, dropped only to about four thousand feet, and then pulled out. He couldn't blame them.

He flipped the toggle to the base frequency.

"Sierra Foxtrot, this is Sierra Papa One, over." He waited, and then repeated his message. On the second try he heard the eager young voice of the radar operator come back loud and clear.

"This is Sierra Foxtrot. We thought we'd lost you, Captain. Welcome back. Over."

"Sierra Foxtrot, this is Sierra Papa One, load delivered from thirty-five hundred feet. We have turned and are en route to base. Over."

"Sierra Papa One, This is Sierra Foxtrot, read you five by five. See you in a few hours."

"Sierra Foxtrot, this is Sierra Papa One, copy. Tell Miss Jamieson that will be steak. Over."

Flipping the channel back to cut off further conversation, he set a course for the airfield. The others fell in behind him.

He wondered what would come of it all. He'd seen the tiny pellets dropping into the rushing winds below, but he had no idea if they'd have the desired effect, or any effect at all. He knew, in fact, far too little about the storm they'd just faced off against. It had been a thrill to be so close, but at the same time the most terrifying experience of his life, including night flights through anti-aircraft fire. Nothing could have prepared him for it.

Phil had seen plenty of propaganda and training films about atomic weapons. He knew the stories of Hiroshima and Nagasaki, and he'd even been present for one remote test.

None of it had impacted him in the way the snaking, whirling wall of water trying to swat him out of the air had done. He knew he faced several long nights and dark dreams over this one, and he hoped it wouldn't be in vain.

He wasn't kidding himself. If the Navy thought it was a very important mission, he probably wouldn't have drawn the assignment. There was no way to know how the rules of promotion, and advancement in the upper echelon of the U.S. Navy would shift on a day-to-day basis, but barring some strange circumstance where he rescued the President's daughter from drowning and got an on-the-spot promotion, Phil knew his days as a Navy pilot were numbered.

This flight had given him back something he hadn't even noticed as it slipped away. He'd felt a spirit of purpose down there close to the storm, and he'd felt the same fire that accompanied battle. There was an enemy in the heart of that storm— maybe not a personal enemy, not yet—but he knew at least one person who was fighting it, and she owed him a steak.

Maybe, he thought, as the lights of shore glittered on the horizon, this assignment will work out after all.

Once the loads had been dropped, and the aircraft were safely up and away, Andrea and her people got down to the serious work. Two assistants arrived, their briefcases stuffed with printouts and maps, and ensconced themselves in the desks that flanked Andrea's own. There was Tracy Brown, a petite blonde meteorologist on loan from UNC, and Tom Briggs, a research specialist. He was the one they counted on to take what they brought in and organize it into something useful. He worked in one of the Navy's largest computer laboratories up in Norfolk, and once they had everything categorized, filed, and evaluated, he would take it and, along with his people, input it for further analysis.

The initial findings were positive, almost positive enough to put a smile back on Andrea's face. She was still on edge from the lost communication with the pilots, and she felt the memorandum weighing on her more heavily than she'd expected. She didn't want to see the program shut down. She had the resources to continue her research, with or without Stormfury, but access to the pilots, the radar equipment, all of the people who helped out with the various aspects of the research they were doing—all of this made a difference. It gave her stability and kept her focused—so she couldn't dwell in the past and get too angry at the storms, or go off half-cocked and cost someone their life. Andrea was well aware of her obsession with hurricanes, but she was also aware that others did not share it to the same degree. She had to compensate.

"It's slowed," Petty Officer Carlson called out from the radarscope. "The eye is getting a little ragged, and it seems to be just sitting there. Winds have dropped down to a sustained speed of ninety-two miles per hour. Does this mean . . ."

He stopped, and Andrea looked up from her paperwork. "That we stopped the hurricane?" she finished. She sat, thinking about the question for a moment, and shook her head slightly in frustration.

"I wish I could say yes, or even no," she replied. "From what I'm seeing here, the storm cut back about ten percent. That's a significant difference—it dropped back to a Category One, and even if it makes landfall now, it's the kind of storm that you can ride out.

"The problem is," she went on, "that it isn't a significant enough change in the storm for us to say that, without a doubt, this wouldn't have happened with the storm acting on its own. Storms grow, and others shrink. Some of them head straight in to land, picking up speed as they come, and others flounder, blow in circles, or head back out to sea. It happens all the time."

"But," the lieutenant glanced up from where he was plotting the latest report on the map, "this happened almost immediately after the silver iodide was dropped. Surely we can infer from this that we had an effect?"

Andrea smiled. It was funny how they all started out as men just assigned to this project, biding their time and waiting for the call back to war, or to home, and then, somewhere in the middle of each of these experiments, they bonded. Now it was "we" and not "you," or "you people," or "the project." It was we, and she felt it as surely as they did.

"We can infer what we like," she replied. "We can even believe it, and I'll be honest, the indications are pretty positive to me, but that doesn't mean that Washington is going to buy into it. In fact, even if they believed we were able to reduce that Category Two storm to a Category One and buy a little more time for the people on shore to evacuate, it might not really register. They might answer that the change was not 'significant.' Category Two storms hit often enough, and people weather them and move on. If we had dropped it back to a tropical storm, they might sit up and take notice."

"Maybe if it had stayed the size we expected," the lieutenant began.

Andrea cut him off with a tired, quiet tone in her voice. "I wish to God it had happened that way. We might have stopped a tropical storm, or a Category One, almost completely. They would have listened then."

"We'll get the next one," Briggs said, glancing up from his readouts. "It's only a matter of time, Andrea. We'll get one of the big whirling bastards and when we do, no one will be able to argue with the facts."

As if to emphasize his words, he shook his sheaf of computer printouts at her. The top one unfolded, and with a rippling motion, the whole stack unwound like a paper slinky, slipping over the front edge of his desk before he could catch it.

Everyone burst out laughing, but for Andrea the humor, and the moment were hollow. She didn't want to spoil it for the others, but she knew that this small success was not going to be enough to keep this particular branch of Operation Stormfury afloat.

Some of the experts would move on to NOAA, and no doubt they would offer her a position as well. Research, gathering storm data, predicting storms. It was fascinating, and the draw of their state-of-the-art equipment and nearly bottomless well of government resources was tempting. They would probably even keep much of the research under the Stormfury heading, though it would be a more passive, research-oriented operation.

She knew, however, that she would not go to NOAA. If Operation Stormfury faded, she would take up the fight on her own, move it into different battlegrounds and find support on different fronts. She had worked toward such a possibility for a long time. She had plans, and between the money her father had left her and what she'd earned through consultation and side-research, all socked away and invested carefully, she knew she could fund the beginnings of a very adequate storm center. She had just hoped she'd have longer to straighten out the details and to get her life on track before she was forced to play her hand.

Footsteps echoed in the hallway, and they all turned as Captain Wicks stuck his head around the corner to survey the room.

"Welcome back, Captain," Andrea said. "Good to see you in one piece."

He stepped into the room, and gave a quick wave to the rest of those gathered. "Did we do any good?" he asked.

Andrea started to give him a pat answer, but something in the seriousness of his tone brought her up short. Maybe, just maybe, he wasn't asking only to make conversation.

"There was about a ten percent drop in strength and speed," she said at last. "The storm is floundering, but it looks like it's going to make landfall in Florida sometime tomorrow afternoon."

"So," he replied, figuring quickly in his head, "we dropped it to a Category One?"

"For now," she agreed, smiling. "Actually, we haven't proven conclusively that 'we' did anything, but the storm is much weaker now than it was before you seeded it."

She saw him chew over all that was and was not said, and then his smile returned. "How long will you all stick with this?"

Andrea looked around the room. It was closing in on ten PM, and the storm was not going to hit land soon. There were others who would gather the tapes and film from the observation plane. It was time to shut down for the night.

"I think it's about time we called it a day," she said. "Lieutenant, can we wrap up that chart? I think we can say that any significant change we caused in the storm will show up in the data we've gathered. Anything from here on out is on Mother Nature, and she doesn't need us to babysit when she throws a tantrum."

The lieutenant nodded. He made some final marks on the chart and slid the folding arm to the side of the chart table. He pinned the map in place carefully and picked up a large, clear piece of Plexiglas from where it leaned against the side of the table. He spread this over the map to protect it and grabbed his hat.

"I don't care what they say," he told Andrea as he passed on his way to the door, Petty Officer Carlson in tow. "I believe we were behind that change. The timing, and the radical nature of the shift we saw don't fit as natural occurrence."

Andrea nodded. She believed he was right, and she appreciated the support. If she could get the same common sense attitude out of a couple of congressmen, or a general, she'd be able to stay in business until they had the damned hurricanes on leashes.

"See you tomorrow," she said. "We'll wrap this all up, gather the data, and take it back to the lab for analysis."

Turning to Briggs, she asked, "Did you get everything you need, Tom? I can have the rest of it ready by the end of the week."

"No hurry," Briggs assured her. "It's going to take time to sift through all of this, and I'm realigning the program a bit. I developed an algorithm that should allow us to cut out more of the interference. If I'm right, we'll be able to say with more clarity what we did, and did not cause. I'll have to reconfigure again, of course," he looked over at Phil and nodded. "I sure didn't expect them to take that load down so low. It was a good thought."

"I just didn't want to waste my time," Phil replied. "When we saw how much larger the storm had grown, I made the call to concentrate the loads instead of trying to fan out along the entire length. What we had would have been lost over two hundred miles of ocean, and I doubt we'd have any results to analyze."

"Like I said," Briggs replied with a smile, "good call."

"I'm going to do some calculations," Tracy Brown said. "I think we might want to reconsider the fanned out approach altogether. If the result we just saw allowed this much of a shift in a Category Two storm, then the problems we have faced in the past with much larger storms are changed as well. If we can concentrate on certain areas and not try to cover the entire storm, we might be able to take on one of the big boys."

"Let's hope we don't get a storm any time soon to test that theory on," Andrea replied with a frown. "I don't want to see a big one any time soon, if ever."

They all grew silent at this. Tracy and Tom gathered their things quickly and efficiently, and with their briefcases bulging, headed out the door, leaving Andrea and Phil standing alone in the empty office.

"It's kind of late for a steak," he said at last. "Could I interest you in a sandwich, and maybe a drink?"

Andrea hesitated. She had work to do, and she had to get home to her dog eventually. He was a very patient animal, but she knew he hated it when she was out too late.

His name was Buster. He was from the second generation of puppies left behind by Jake, who had died four years after the storm that brought the two of them together. Andrea's mother hadn't wanted the dog, but Andrea had put up such a fit that, in the end, Lilian Jamieson had given in.

"That would be nice," she said at last. "Let me get my things."

He watched her move about the office, straightening folders, turning off equipment, and packing a ridiculously thick stack of papers into her own briefcase. The thing was bulged like a cartoon suitcase primed to explode.

As they stepped into the hall together, she put it on the floor and turned to lock the door. Phil picked the case up without a word and carried it for her as they made their way to the elevator and outside. The TV van was long gone, and only the receding taillights of one of their companions' car could be seen, disappearing into the night.

The wind had picked up, but the sky was clear, and the

moon was bright. When the breeze teased a stray lock of Andrea's hair away from her face, Phil shivered. Just for a moment, he saw that storm again, and the whirling, furious snake of air slashing toward him through the sky.

Andrea caught his stare and started to ask what was wrong, but the moment passed, and Phil's smile returned full force.

"You'll have to tell me what it looked like up there," she said as they walked toward her car. "And then, if you like, I'll tell you what they look like from the shore."

Chapter Nine

Phil went up with Andrea while she dropped off her papers and fed the dog. Buster was bouncy and full of happy-to-see-her energy, and seeing the two of them together made Phil smile. He watched for a few moments, and then the dog came over to him, sniffed Phil's shoes suspiciously and wagged his tail hopefully, all at the same time. Phil knelt on the floor and scratched Buster's ears. The dog cocked his head to one side and thumped his tail hard on the carpet.

"Looks like you've made a new friend," Andrea observed. She put away the dog food and poured fresh water into Buster's bowl.

"Yeah," Phil agreed, giving Buster's ear a last scratch, "and the dog likes me too."

He rose and stepped toward the door, and she followed. She couldn't see his expression, so she missed the quick smile.

They ended up at a back table in a small pub nearby. The light was soft, the music softer. A candle flickered in the center of the table, creating a small circle of light around them. With the exception of the waitress, no one interrupted them.

"When we lost you on the radio," Andrea told him, "I was worried that we'd lost you altogether. It was brave of you to drop down so close to the storm, but foolish."

"I wouldn't have taken the aircraft, or my co-pilot, lower

than I believed was safe," Phil replied. He might have taken offense at her words, but he chose not to. She wasn't a pilot, so her reaction was understandable.

"I know others who have flown over hurricanes," he told her. "The danger really isn't from the storm, or its wind. It's the intangibles—the things you can't schedule around or predict. I thought it was a reasonable risk, but I'll tell you the truth—when Matt spotted that waterspout coming at us, I definitely had second thoughts. It's not the danger of flying that gets to a pilot, after a while. It's the factors you can't control. I guess it's the same with almost everything, driving a car, playing football—you can be the best there is, but there will always come a time when things shift and your ability is only a shield. There are things coming at you from more sides than you can block.

"You can drive carefully all your life, but eventually someone will pull out in front of you when you are thinking about your dinner plans, or some kid will bounce a ball where it shouldn't be. You can play football all the way through college and make it to the final game, only to have one of your own players fall on the back of your knee and ruin your leg. And you can get too cocky after flying through hell and back and start to take chances, just because it 'should' be okay.

"That's what happened today," he said. "I nearly lost a good man, and my aircraft, not to mention the rest of my life—and tonight." He smiled at her and took a sip from the beer the waitress had brought him. "And that couldn't have happened if I'd maintained the five thousand feet. I just didn't want the whole flight to be for nothing."

"What do you mean?" Andrea asked, finally cutting in.

"The storm was too big," he replied. "All of the planning I saw was to spread the silver iodide pellets over the entire eyewall of a large tropical storm. What we found when we got there was a two hundred mile wide Category Two hurricane, and the original plan was obviously not going to work. I could have just gone ahead with it, but I knew that wouldn't get you any useful results, so I improvised. It's a fault of mine, and this time that fault almost spilled over to hurt someone who trusted me."

"He wouldn't have agreed, or followed you, if he didn't think you were right," she admonished him, laying her hand across his gently. "And the other three pilots also released their loads at or near thirty-five hundred feet, on your orders. There was no way you could have anticipated the waterspout. It would have been worse over land, where the storm could have spawned tornadoes."

Phil nodded thoughtfully, but he didn't look up yet.

"That's not all there is to it," he said. "This is probably my last assignment. I knew it when they sent me here, and I was thinking about that when we took off this afternoon. I think maybe I was after one last hero call—flying into the face of danger, leading my boys on a daredevil mission. It was selfish. I'm glad it worked out," he added quickly, meeting her gaze at last. "I wanted to bring back something that would prove you were right, though I'm not sure why."

She smiled at him wanly and sipped slowly at her wine. Their sandwiches were slow in coming, but neither of them minded.

"I'm grateful for that," she said. "I'm afraid it might not matter much, but I am grateful."

Phil noticed that her smile had faded. "What's wrong?"

"They're going to close down my branch of the project," she replied. "We've made some progress, and today was a good indicator that we might be on the right track, but it isn't enough. Not for Washington to keep parting with the funding. They are giving all their attention to the war in

Southeast Asia, and I can't really blame them. For all the data we've gathered, and all the things we've learned about hurricanes, we can't really claim that there's much chance we can stop one."

"But what about today?" he asked her. "That storm fizzled. It was huge, and I saw it—the eye was very tight. What we did must have made a difference."

Andrea shook her head gently. "Probably it did," she said. "In fact, I'm very nearly certain that it did, but the change *could* have happened naturally. There are plenty of recorded cases where storms that looked like they might wipe Florida off the map have turned back to sea, or fallen apart. All it takes is the right environmental conditions—a shift in water temperature, a cold front blowing in from the right direction.

"We'll check all of those things, of course. We should even be able to prove that none of these conditions was present at the time the storm weakened, but it still won't be conclusive."

Phil was silent at this, and after another drink of her wine, Andrea went on.

"All our hope rested on that storm staying small," she said. "If it hadn't grown so large, and you'd made the same sort of difference that you did, you might have stopped it entirely."

"Can't we try it again?" he asked, frowning.

"I don't think we'll get the chance," she said. "Not with Operation Stormfury, anyway."

He thought about what she was saying, and then asked, "What do you mean? Are there other projects trying to do the same thing?"

"Not yet," she looked up at him and her face lit with a smile. "Not yet, but there will be, and soon. This is my life, Phil," she said. "It's what I've studied to do since I was a little girl, what I've based my education on. These storms can be stopped."

She fell silent, but not before Phil caught the short catch in her voice. "What happened?" he asked her gently, sliding his hand out from under hers and laying it on top.

She didn't speak at first, and Phil had just begun to wonder if he'd gone too far too quickly, or if he'd touched a nerve he hadn't been aware of. Eventually, she started speaking, but she didn't raise her eyes.

"I lost my father to a hurricane," she said. "It tore through my house, flooded everywhere near us. Daddy tried to rescue one of our neighbors, and her house collapsed into the flood."

"I'm sorry," he said, knowing how inadequate the words were.

She shook her head gently and went on. "It's okay. It was a long time ago. We moved inland then. My mother was never the same. I don't think she's gotten close enough to the ocean to hear the surf since the day we were rescued. She took me away from the ocean, and the beach. I didn't say anything to her then, but as I grew older, and the memories of that storm didn't fade away like everyone said they would, I knew I was going to have to take matters into my own hands. If no one else was going to do something about the storms, I knew that I had to try.

"I did well in high school and managed a scholarship to UNC. I studied meteorology at first, and some engineering. They thought I wanted to be a weather girl on some local television station, so at first they humored me. By the time I was ready to graduate with honors they had to take me seriously.

"Ever since then," she went on, "I've worked to increase my knowledge of hurricanes and tropical storms. I've been involved in several research programs. I patented two enhancements I suggested in the design of Doppler radar, as well as a design for home foundations more likely to resist the onslaught of storms. I've done pretty well for myself," she smiled at this, though Phil saw that she didn't put much humor behind it.

"So, you're rich *and* smart?" he asked, hoping to break the sudden gravity of the mood.

Instead, she just nodded. "I suppose I am," she replied. "But the money isn't for me. It never was. If they shut down Stormfury, I'll open my own center for storm research. There are at least a dozen other ideas that have never been tested that—in theory—could stop or weaken a hurricane. If even one family can be saved . . ."

The waitress arrived at that moment, and it gave Phil a chance to think. He smiled at the girl as she placed a steaming roast beef sandwich in front of him, and tuna salad in front of Andrea. He asked her to refresh their drinks, and when she was gone, he turned back to his companion.

"It sounds like you might need a pilot," he said without preamble.

She stared at him, and he held up a hand to stop her from speaking. "Hear me out first," he said, "and then we'll get back to our meal. I don't have much time left in the U.S. Navy, and I have no intention of being grounded by retirement. I could go and fly for one of the airlines, but somehow that doesn't appeal to me. I know you don't know what you will do, or need, at this point, but keep it in mind. If you open your storm center, and you need a pilot, I'm your man. I'll be honest—I've never lost anyone to a hurricane, but after what happened today, I'd sure like another crack at one.

"Besides," he grinned, "if I go back home the only work they'll have is crop-dusting, and I might be brave, but those guys are crazy."

Andrea laughed. She ate some of her sandwich in silence and watched him out of the corner of her eye. It was true. When she got things going at the center she *would* need a pilot, and a good one. Probably more than one. A single plane wasn't enough to seed even a small tropical storm, and as much as they spent their time studying the smaller hurricanes, what Andrea wanted was to find a way to strike back at the big ones.

"I may need more than a pilot," she said. Then, when he grinned at her and she realized why, she blushed hard and laughed.

"I *mean*," she corrected, "I will need someone to find and manage several pilots. Even as big as that storm got today, there are bigger ones, and those are the ones that need to be stopped. Those are the ones I'm after."

Phil just nodded. His sandwich was gone, and he was back to sipping his beer.

"If you are serious," he said at last, "I'm in. It's not going to be immediately. My tour is up in October, and I'll have some details to wrap up after that, but otherwise I'm free. I've been waffling over whether I'd let them put me behind a desk somewhere, or what I might do if they asked me to retire. The timing on this couldn't be better."

"It's settled then," Andrea said, and held out her hand.

Phil shook it solemnly, but there was a twinkle in his eye. "Don't think," he told her with a wink, "that being my boss is a way to get out of buying me a steak."

Andrea laughed, and it felt good. She'd left the base feeling down and discouraged, and somehow that had faded. It would be difficult to be on her own. Getting the equipment she needed would be expensive, and getting personnel qualified to operate it would be difficult. She could get any number of people familiar with the electronics or the meteorological aspects of her plan, but finding a group dedicated enough to share her vision was an entirely different story.

Still, what had seemed a daunting, impossible task moments before was beginning to look like a refreshing challenge. She lifted her glass and held it out to Phil, who raised his beer. "To new partnerships."

Phil smiled and nodded. "I'll drink to that," he said. "I will certainly drink to that."

They finished their drinks, rose, and made their way slowly to the door. They didn't hold hands, and when Andrea dropped Phil back off at the base to pick up his car, they didn't kiss goodbye, but the potential hung in the air between them, and they parted with a smile. The night had ended, but something else had begun, and they both felt like it was going to be big.

PART THREE

The Jamieson-Wicks
Complex—1976

Chapter Ten

About twenty miles inland from the North Carolina eastern shore, a complex of bunkers left over from the Second World War, centered by a low-slung, brick and glass office building, had been brought back to life. Vehicles of all types, sizes, and shapes rolled and roared around the various hangars and laboratories. The office building had been set up with its own generator, and a backup. The interior was gutted on the first floor and redesigned as a climate-controlled, dust-free computer laboratory. Behind thick, insulated windows, low banks of lights flickered. Enormous tape drives whirred as programs were read into memory and data was stored.

Along one wall, hanging by clips attached to the metal cans that protected them, row after row of these magnetic tapes hung, some waiting to see use, others archiving data and system backups. It was an impressive setup, and as Phil stepped through the front doors of the "Jamieson-Wicks Foundation" he stood for a moment and watched three or four technicians move efficiently around the computer bay. They all wore lab coats, but beneath these scuffed sandals and frayed blue jeans could be seen clearly. It was a far cry from the Navy, but Phil knew that these kids were experts in their chosen field. If they wanted to go work for IBM they could do so in a heartbeat, and they wouldn't hear a thing from their new bosses about their dress code.

The computer systems were partly funded by a grant for

the study of storm behavior. Several researchers and professors at UNC had access to the system, but for the most part it was controlled and run by Andrea's handpicked staff.

Phil skirted the computer bay and stepped into one of the old elevators. They'd kept the originals, with deep interiors for moving freight and huge, plastic buttons that lit up dimly with the floor number. Phil pressed five, the top floor, and leaned against the back wall of the elevator car as it lurched into motion. It was still early, but there was already a lot of activity outside.

The flight crews would not start for another half hour, and he didn't expect to see the pilots until nine or ten. There wasn't a lot for them to do between flights, and there hadn't been that many flights up to this point. That could change, he knew, and likely would change in the next few days. Hurricane season had begun the week before, and Andrea already had two tropical depressions charted. It was slow work. The government knew her, and they still made use of her expertise from time to time, but getting them to release information—even on the weather—was like pulling teeth. If it weren't for the extensive array of equipment Andrea had gathered, and the contacts they'd developed in the Caribbean, they wouldn't have anything better than the local weather stations.

As it was, those stations often came to Andrea for reports, and that was a good thing because, despite the steady flow of income from her patents, and a few new things the two of them had developed along the way, the Jamieson-Wicks Foundation was not a profitable endeavor by any stretch of the imagination.

Phil stepped into the hall and turned right, passed the first two doors, which were still dark, and knocked gently on the larger, center door before pressing it inward. A large reception area fronted Andrea's office, an expense Phil himself had insisted on. It lent an air of professionalism that was necessary when visitors entered their complex, and while this didn't happen very often, it was almost always a matter of money when it did.

A young woman smiled at him as he entered.

"Good morning, Mr. Wicks," she said brightly. "Andrea is expecting you. Mr. Scharf is expected at nine."

"Thanks, Lisa," he replied.

Lisa George was a short, energetic research assistant who had been with Andrea from the beginning. Before the keys had changed hands and Andrea had taken possession of this building and the grounds surrounding it, Lisa had worked with her on the maps and charts, organizing what data Andrea had managed to get out of the records of Operation Stormfury before the doors were closed, and helping to get it into a format that the new computers would recognize. She was efficient and exceptionally intelligent, and Phil was glad to know Lisa was nearby when Andrea needed her.

He himself could not help with the research end of what they did, other than to fly the observation craft now and again and bring back tapes and punch cards filled with data. He played his own part in the grand scheme of things. He ran the small fleet of aircraft that they actually owned, and handled the leasing of more when they were needed. Phil was good with business—a skill he hadn't known he possessed until he was forced to test it.

He knew he'd done wonders with what was available. He'd brought in ex-military mechanics and pilots, retirees for the most part who wanted their hands back into flying, but didn't want to sign on toward a second and less meaningful career with a civilian airline.

All of it was a wonder to Phil, and the center of that wonder was Andrea herself. He glanced down at his hand and smiled. He still wasn't used to the gold band that glittered there, or the thought that, after all the years he'd spent alone, wondering where his life was leading him, he'd found all the answers here, beyond the military, beyond wars and killing. He was well aware that most people could consider Andrea a crackpot and himself as the crazed sidekick, but what mattered was that he knew Andrea believed in what they were doing. It also mattered that even after thirteen years he could still see that waterspout whipping through the air at him and the rolling, grinding force of the hurricane he'd first flown over winding like a huge serpent across the waves.

Phil stepped past Lisa's desk and into Andrea's office. It was littered with folders and stacks of computer readouts rested on every available horizontal surface. Two chairs faced the front of her polished wooden desk, but they were as deeply buried as the rest of the room. Phil snorted in sudden laughter, and Andrea looked up, startled.

She frowned at him, but as he continued to grin and she swept her gaze over the surface of her desk, then the chairs and tables, she laughed.

"I never promised I was a good housekeeper, just a brilliant meteorologist."

"A *beautiful,* brilliant meteorologist," he corrected.

She stood up, and Phil walked around the desk and swept her into his arms. He picked her off the floor and spun her so his back was to the doorway and he could see out the large, tinted glass windows to the complex below.

After a long, lingering kiss, Andrea disentangled herself and stood beside him, staring down to where several large trucks were just arriving. They had a security gate with a guard, and he currently held a clipboard in his hand. He would be calling up in a few seconds, Andrea knew, to verify that this shipment was expected. It was.

"Is that the silver iodide?" Phil asked.

Andrea nodded. "More than I've ever set eyes on," she grinned. "You ready to do some crop-dusting?"

It had become a standing joke between them, the comparison between cloud seeding and crop-dusting. The complex wasn't far from Phil's home town, and he had taken her down on Highway 17 to watch the brightly colored planes in action, swooping out of the clouds, doing absolutely unnecessary barrel rolls and flips and diving so close to the fields that it seemed impossible they could miss all of the power lines and bridges. They never faltered, like birds in a flight pattern headed south for the winter. It wasn't the same kind of flying that Phil had trained to perform, but the courage behind it, and the spirit, called out to him on a deep level.

"Ready as I'll ever be," he replied. "Any news on those depressions? Do we have anything that looks like it might tighten up into a storm?"

She nodded. "One of them is pretty well formed already. It's still too early to tell, but it looks like it will be the first one to come down the gulf this year, and if it continues to grow like it has so far, it might be a big one."

Phil's heart lurched, just for a second. A lot depended on them finding the right storm to test their theories and processes on, but it didn't change the danger. The storm he and Matt had flown over had only been a Category Two, and there was a lot of room for growth above that. He knew he didn't want to think about what it would be like flying over one of the truly huge storms much prior to getting airborne. It didn't do any good to let your enemy know you were spooked—*or* your wife.

"Well, we'll have to watch that one close, then," he said,

giving her a quick, hard hug. "I hear Scharf is due to arrive this morning?"

Andrea nodded. He saw the spark jump instantly to her eyes, and knew that all niceties had come to an end. Keith Scharf was offering them a possible addition to their process, and any time that happened, Andrea was on fire with energy. It was an almost magical transformation—her features shifted from the soft, pretty woman he'd married to the intense, brilliant scientist as if she'd slipped a mask over her head while he wasn't looking.

"I think he may really have something, Phil," she said excitedly, turning back to her desk.

As she spoke she picked up the files littering the desk's surface. Phil moved to the chairs opposite and did the same. If they were going to have someone in here in less than an hour, they needed to be able, at the very least, to provide the guy a seat.

Andrea didn't stop talking as she worked, and Phil caught himself smiling again. He hid this in a pile of folders and turned toward the cabinets running along one wall. He didn't know which drawer was for what, but there was still some space on top where Andrea had trouble reaching, and he figured it was as good a place as any for temporary storage. Over the weekend, Lisa and a couple of her friends would come in and file it all, reorganizing what needed organizing and keeping Andrea on track—another job that Phil was glad was not his, as he was wholly unqualified for it.

"His theory is very simple," she continued, "though others have had similar thoughts before, and been ignored."

Her eyes flashed. Nothing irritated Andrea more than the attitude of most of her "colleagues" in the field of storm research and meteorology. They, for the most part, had taken the easy road and determined that there was nothing man could do to stop a hurricane. They went further than this, stating that there were ecological ramifications to interfering with storms, and that it wasn't something that should be attempted.

Andrea believed this was a way of shielding themselves from further mistakes and disappointments. If you just sat back and watched storms, you could learn a lot about them. You could warn people, help strengthen their homes, and give them more time to evacuate when things were about to be destroyed, but that was as far as it went. It was noble enough work, but it was timid.

While they might be timid in their approach, the scientists aligned against Andrea were less so when it came to protecting their turf. They made quick work of finding flaw with any new concept or theory involving hurricane or weather control, and this made it more difficult to find anyone with a sharp enough mind and quick enough wits willing to both develop such a theory, and to speak of it in public.

If Andrea hadn't been as prominent as she was, and her contributions to their science had not been so important, they would have treated her the same way. The quicker they disposed of "radicals," the more easily they could relax into their long careers of public "service" and retire—far away from hurricane territory. After all, Mother Nature controlled the storms, and who were they to interfere?

"What *is* his theory?" Phil asked, bringing her back from her thoughts.

Andrea shook her head to clear the mental cobwebs and went on. "He believes that if we were to apply an oil slick to the water directly in the hurricane's path, it would prevent the storm from being able to draw the moisture it needs from the ocean through evaporation. This was proposed several years ago, but at the time it was killed because of the impact on the environment. There are obvious problems with creating an oil slick on purpose."

"What makes Scharf's plan different?" Phil asked.

"He isn't proposing a petroleum oil slick," she said excitedly. "He believes the same end can be achieved using a biodegradable vegetable oil. To be more precise, given our location—he thinks he can stop a hurricane with peanut oil."

Phil stopped, holding a stack of files over his head precariously as he turned to gape at her. "Peanut oil?"

Andrea smiled and nodded. "There isn't any difference in the way peanut oil and petroleum oil coat the water, other than you won't find a lot of dead seagulls and fish coated in it when we're done. And the beauty is, there's plenty of it available locally—if he's right, we could have all we need in a very short amount of time."

"You believe it will work?" Phil asked, shoving the files into place and returning to sit in the chair he'd just cleared.

Andrea dropped into her own chair. "I'm not sure. I don't think that the oil alone will do it—and we've shown that, while we can control the moisture in the storm somewhat with the silver iodide and disrupt the storm wall, we may not be able to stop one completely, or weaken it below the danger point. But the two theories make an interesting partnership."

Phil nodded. He understood the basic concept behind how the silver iodide weakened the storm. If this new process could really prevent more water from evaporating into the hurricane, and the silver iodide seeding could work to remove what was already there, it just might be enough to do more than downgrade the winds by ten percent. It might be enough to bring the whole whirling churning mass of destruction to a halt.

"You see it," she said. It wasn't a question.

"If he's right," Phil nodded, "then it's the best news I've

heard since we started this. I still get calls from that woman, Pam Jones. You know, the one who thinks that we should go up with tug boats and haul a bunch of icebergs down so we can leave them in the hurricane's path?"

"I remember," she said, and laughed. "The last call I got from her, she'd given up on the tug boats and was convinced that if we used explosives to break loose large chunks of the arctic ice cap, they could be transported on slings between helicopters. That was her answer to my telling her the tug boats would arrive about a month after the storm had passed."

They laughed together. The world was full of people with great ideas for stopping hurricanes or controlling the weather. Most of them had no idea what caused the storms, and their ideas amounted to nonsense, but Andrea made a point of responding to every single input they received, or having one of her staff respond. If even one particle of useful knowledge escaped them because they ignored someone, it would be a bitter pill to swallow, particularly given the way the government had set her aside and ignored her research.

Lisa stepped into the doorway.

"Mr. Scharf is here," she said.

A stocky young man with curly black hair and a lopsided grin entered the office. Phil rose, shook hands with Scharf, and gestured to the chair he'd been sitting in.

"I'll clear the other one," he said.

Scharf nodded and stepped up to the desk. He shook Andrea's hand quickly and took the offered seat. He clutched a briefcase tightly to his chest, but he didn't move to open it.

"I'm glad to finally meet you," he said at last. "I've followed your work since I was a boy. I still have an Operation Stormfury T-shirt I made myself—a bunch of us had them. We were all going to be superheroes and control the weather."

The young man laughed nervously, and then went on. "I guess I'm the only one who ever really believed it."

Andrea smiled at him and leaned forward to put her hands on her desk. Her eyes were bright, and Phil knew she understood him completely.

"We could use a few more superheroes these days, Keith. We may not live in Gotham City, but there are plenty of dangers out there that men could protect themselves from. For the most part they do a poor job of it. Let's see what you've got."

Scharf nodded and placed his briefcase on the desk. While he arranged his papers and drew out some graphs and charts, Phil placed the stack of folders from the second chair on top of the high file cabinet beside the other pile he'd moved and took a seat.

"As you can see," Scharf began, "I've worked this out pretty carefully. I've never been in a position to test this in any more than a theoretical environment. We created a scenario at UNC—and we were able to use vegetable oil to almost completely cut off evaporation, but obviously those controlled conditions are not the ocean."

Andrea nodded. "We have some figures somewhere that were developed when they proposed the petroleum slick. I'll have Lisa dig them out later, if we need them."

"Very simply," Scharf continued, "I believe that a coating of no more than an inch over the proper amount of miles can stop a hurricane's forward progress cold. The biggest problem, as I see it, is that the storm will do what any force of nature does when confronted with an obstacle. It will take the path of least resistance. The fear is that this process will not actually stop a hurricane, but only divert it. If the new direction can be controlled, we can move the storm into cooler water and let nature take its course, but that's a pretty big if."

"We were just discussing this when you arrived," Andrea told him. "I agree with you, this is an incomplete and probably not altogether effective process. By itself, it would be risky at best. But we are still experimenting with silver iodide seeding. What I see in your idea is the chance of a two-pronged attack. If we reduce the moisture already available to the storm with the cloud seeding, and your slick can prevent it from drawing more from the ocean, we may be able to hold it in place until it self-destructs from lack of 'fuel.' At the very least we should shake up the structure quite a bit."

Scharf was nodding long before Andrea had finished speaking, and Phil saw with approval that the boy knew his stuff.

"It's just a matter of locating enough oil," he said at last, "and figuring out the best way to get it in the path of the storm."

Before they could go on a thin, nervous young man rushed into the room. He had a Teletype readout in his hand, the yellow paper flowing back over his shoulder giving the impression he was flying, his disheveled hair adding to the image.

He skidded to a stop when he saw that Andrea wasn't alone, and stood there, his jaw working nervously.

"What is it, Jon?" Andrea asked, biting back the laughter that nearly erupted. "You can speak in front of Mr. Scharf—Keith—I think he'll be working with us. What's that you've got?"

Jon Kotz handed the readout to Phil without even glancing at him and stepped closer to the desk. "It's happening," he said breathlessly. "The first of the storms has developed a solid eye, and is moving north, northeast pretty quickly. The winds aren't very strong yet, but it's a big storm, and very well formed. I think this one is going to be important."

Phil was up immediately and moving toward the door. "I'll get the radar up and running and see if I can contact the boys down in the islands. We should be able to get an HF link and see what they are seeing pretty quickly."

Andrea nodded, her eyes bright. Turning to Scharf, she said, "Well, Keith, you wanted to be a part of things. Are you ready to go to work?"

The young man rose, as Phil had done, and nodded eagerly. He moved so quickly that his charts and graphs tumbled from the desk, along with his briefcase.

"Yes, of course," he replied. "What can I do?"

"Get out there," Andrea said with a fierce grin, "and see if you can locate me two or three tanker trucks full of peanut oil."

Scharf goggled at her for a moment, and then, when he saw that she wasn't kidding, he gathered his papers quickly, fumbling with them like a nervous schoolboy.

Then Andrea did laugh. "Calm down, Keith. We have time. You can use the next office down—there's a phone there. Welcome aboard."

Without another word, Scharf clutched the mass of papers to his chest, gripped the briefcase in one hand, and headed for the door.

Jon, who had no idea what had just happened, stared after the retreating figure, and then looked back at Andrea in confusion.

"I think this is the one," she told him. "Let's go out and stop us a hurricane."

Chapter Eleven

The air was crisp and still cool in the pre-dawn hours. Phil Wicks stood just inside the door of the main hangar, watching for the sun to rise over the horizon. He half expected it to be red, like the sun Andrea had described to him so many times before, but when it finally came it was in trails of lavender and deep yellow, streaked colors washed over a pale blue sky. Phil stretched and grinned. It was a good sign. If he'd seen the red sky, he might have lost his nerve, but everything seemed as normal as it had the day before.

The storm had reached Category Two status the night before. It wiped out several small islands, leaving dozens of dead in its wake, but the crossing of land, even such a small surface as the islands had presented, had slowed its progress. Back over the open sea, the eye had formed more tightly, and Andrea expected that it could be as large as a Category Three by nightfall. They still had time. It would take days for such a storm to make landfall in the United States, and Phil expected to provide some problems for the storm before that was allowed to happen.

Keith Scharf had been as good as he seemed to be. He'd located the oil they needed quickly, and the trucks had arrived the previous day. The three of them, Phil, Keith, and Andrea, had met with their engineers and the brightest of their consultants, eating pizza and drinking black coffee late into the night, trying to finalize the how, where, and when of what was to come.

They had spared no expense; there wasn't time for it. Phil hoped they wouldn't regret the rashness of the decision over time, but it was too late to worry. He'd worked with several of the other pilots on a scheme for delivering the peanut oil. What they had devised was untested, but he saw no reason that it shouldn't work.

The oil had been transferred from the trucks into large rubber weather balloons. These were loaded carefully onto cargo planes and set to drop once the aircraft were in position. The impact of the balloons striking the water would be sufficient to rupture them and spread the oil over the surface, and if the pilots did their jobs, this would distribute the oil in a long strip about a quarter of a mile wide.

Phil hated the idea of going into an operation like this with an untested method, but then, how did you test something like this? Giant water balloons filled with peanut oil weren't run-of-the-mill equipment. The oil wasn't cheap, and the chartering of the aircraft on such short notice, and for such an oddball mission, had been difficult and extremely expensive. They could afford a one-time shot. If they failed, it would take them years to build up the funds to try again, assuming nothing went wrong, no one got hurt, and the government didn't shut them down.

The hardest part of it all was the timing. He knew the men he'd be flying with, and he knew what they were capable of. The others, though, the charter pilots who would be in charge of the oil, he knew little about. Would they hold their position in the face of the oncoming storm? They wouldn't be in any real danger—he'd explained this at length, and they seemed to accept it readily enough, but it was one thing to hear from someone that a thing is safe, and quite another to face it down and prove it.

Phil and the other "seed planes" would have to hold their

positions much longer. The path of the hurricane could only be predicted with a certain degree of accuracy. Once they were airborne, the cargo planes would have to fly out ahead of the storm wall. Phil and his pilots would take their position well above the storm, and the two groups would establish communications to fine-tune timing and delivery.

The slick had to be in place much sooner than the silver iodide could be dropped. The cargo planes had to be in and out prior to arrival of hurricane force winds, and that was the tricky part. How long would the slick remain in place on the water? Would it stick, or would the waves just spread it and wash it away? They had gone way over the initial estimate, providing what Scharf believed would spread to a slick at least two inches deep on the surface. It should hold together for a time, but would it be long enough?

They were counting on the fact that even if it wasn't as complete and all-encompassing as they hoped it would be, the effect of what remained by the time the storm wall reached it would be enough to significantly impact evaporation.

There was a lot of speculation involved. It was going to be a long flight, and Phil knew he should have slept in and rested for the hours to come. The aircraft they'd purchased were specially equipped for the drop—a better setup than they'd had with the C-130s in Operation Stormfury—but they didn't require a co-pilot. He would be on his own up there, and it wouldn't do to get sleepy and lose his concentration.

The others arrived slowly and made their way past him and into the lockers beyond. The flight crews had been working since daybreak. It had taken a lot of finagling of local authorities, and then a lot of hard, backbreaking work, but the old runway stretching out from the back of the main building had been cleared and the proper communications and radar equipment put into place, so that they could fly right out of the complex.

Originally he'd thought they would have to have everything moved and delivered to a local airfield, or to the military base above Elizabeth City, but Andrea had urged him to find another way if he could. She didn't want anyone catching wind of what they were doing before they had a chance to get off the ground. The media would be all over them, and likely as not the government would step in and either try to take control of the operation, or shut it down completely.

She was right, of course. Phil knew it as well as she did, maybe better. The last thing he wanted was for their operation, which had been a quiet, relaxed haven compared to the hectic world of a Navy pilot, to be shattered by a lot of media attention. It would be inevitable if they succeeded, but there was plenty of time to worry about that after the flight.

He turned away from the sunrise and into the interior of the hangar. He smelled the scent of fresh, hot coffee, and he wanted to see Andrea—maybe get some breakfast. It wasn't like he was going to be gone for days, but the two of them had seldom been apart for as much as a day since he'd retired and moved back to North Carolina. She was his anchor, and as the moment of truth arrived, he felt the need of a little anchoring.

They had scheduled a brief for all the pilots at ten AM. That was when they would get their final look at what was coming in over the weather facsimile and plan their most logical route to head the storm off. It would also be their last indication of how big the thing was likely to be when they finally reached it. Phil knew from experience this wasn't reliable, but they had planned for the worst. The amount of silver iodide he carried, and the amount of peanut oil being delivered, was calculated to be enough for a Category Five hurricane. If they ended up with only a Category Two, they should handle it easily, but if the thing shot through the roof and grew into a monster, they wouldn't be caught a second time with their pants down. Secretly, he hoped it would be about a Category Four—something significant enough to catch the world's attention, but not so large that the limits of their own planning were put to the test.

With the sound of ground equipment towing aircraft and the whirring of pneumatic drills ringing in his ears, he grabbed a cup of coffee from the mess and headed across the big inner lot toward the main building.

By the time all the pilots were seated, Phil and his boys on one side of the table and the three commercial pilots across from them, looking excited but a bit confused, it was nearly ten thirty. Andrea, looking tired, ran her hand back through her hopelessly disheveled hair, glanced around at them all before she began, studying their faces.

"We have the latest reports on the storm," she said at last. "It's a strong Category Three hurricane, at present, right on the verge of reaching Category Four. Sustained winds are around a hundred and twenty-nine miles per hour with gusts up into the hundred forty miles per hour range. The storm is moving north, northeast at about eighteen miles per hour."

"Where does that put it?" one of the commercial pilots asked.

Andrea smiled at him and held up a hand. "I'm getting to that. We've calculated it several times, and I believe that our best bet is to try and meet the storm about seventy-five miles off the coast of Bermuda. There are several reasons for this. One is that we have time to get there ahead of the storm, and for you three," she nodded at the cargo pilots, "that is very important. The other thing is that we believe this area will act as somewhat of a pocket—that it might help us to hold the continuity of the slick for a longer period of time. It's critical that we hit it just right, from the front and from above. If we drop the crystals too soon and the storm is able to draw up new moisture from the surface, we'll be wasting a lot of our strength, and the same thing is true of the oil. If we drop that too soon, the storm may hit it before the seeding has a chance to work. If that happens, we aren't sure what the effect might be, but it will almost certainly be very bad.

"One theory," she continued, "is that the storm will take the path of least resistance to try and get around the slick. That would mean it would go in the direction of the warmer water. I'm afraid that at this point in time it might divert the storm directly at the U.S. coastline. The very last thing we want to do, gentlemen," she placed her hands on the tabletop and leaned forward for emphasis, "is to send that thing this way. We are trying to prevent the loss of life and property. Equally bad would be sending it jumping off toward Bermuda. This is a tricky operation, and we have to be sure we're all on the same page when it goes down."

One of the cargo pilots, the one who'd spoken up, whistled. The others sat back and stared at Andrea, as if the importance of what they were about to attempt had just hit home.

"Now would be the time to back out, if you're going to do it," Phil said. "I can't ask any of you to take a risk like this unless you are certain it's what you want to do. I also can't risk the operation, or the safety of others, unless *I* am certain you're ready."

"Let's do it," the first guy said without hesitation. "I've seen what one of these things can do firsthand. I was lucky to get out alive." He glanced around at the rest of them with new energy. "If we have a chance at keeping one of them away, or stopping it completely, then I'm up for it."

The others nodded in quick agreement. Phil smiled. One thing he had found over the years was that most pilots tended to be a breed apart. They were as varied as any other group you might run across in life, but their hearts were strong, and they loved a challenge.

"All right, then," he said. "You three get out there and get airborne. Your loads are heavier, and you'll be longer getting across. We'll follow not too far behind, then veer slightly south and rise above the storm. Once we're ready I'll radio you my position. Give yourself about an hour's difference between your position and that of the storm when you start your run. That should give you plenty of time to get some altitude and get out of there, and at the same time it shouldn't leave too long of a time for the slick to hold. Once we hear from you that you're clear, we'll track as close as we can to the line and drop our loads."

The pilots stood and turned almost like a trained unit, and Phil smiled again. He called after them, "Good luck."

A few moments later he stood beside the table, watching the last of his own pilots file out the door and down toward the hangars and the airstrip. Andrea stepped up behind him and wrapped her arms around him tightly, laying her head on his shoulder.

"Are we doing the right thing, Phil?" she asked quietly. "Are we really?"

He laid his hand across her arm where it lay against his chest and nodded. "Yes ma'am," he said. Then he turned, hugged her tightly and gave her a deep, lingering kiss. "We'll be back before you know it. You still owe me a steak."

She laughed and swatted at him, but he'd already spun

131

away toward the door. The sun had risen high in the sky, and it was a beautiful day to fly.

Without a backward glance he left the briefing room and hit the stairs at a slow trot.

Andrea glanced over at the charts on her desk, and out the large window toward the sky and the ocean beyond. Then, with a quick cry, she dashed out the door.

"Phil!" she cried.

At first it seemed as if she'd missed him. She didn't slow when she hit the stairs, and she was halfway down, in danger of tumbling forward or crashing into one of the walls, when she saw that he'd stopped on the next landing to wait for her. He was smiling, but his brow had knit into lines of concern.

"What is it, princess?" he asked. He held his arms wide, and Andrea half ran, half fell into his embrace. Her jaw dropped at the sudden use of the pet name—a name no one but her father had ever used. Her mind shifted back over the years, and she saw that far-off porch. Heard the groan as boards released. She closed her eyes and when she opened them again, she was surprised to find she was shaking.

"Andrea," Phil said, "tell me what's wrong?"

"Nothing," she said. She hugged him, leaned up, and kissed him again. "I had something I wanted to give you—for luck. I forgot, and then you were out the door so fast . . ."

He grinned at her, waiting.

Andrea pulled a short length of nylon rope from her pocket. It was actually two short lengths tied together in the center. The knot looked a bit like a pretzel, and was carefully tied.

Andrea took the two ends in her hands, stared into his eyes, and yanked as hard as she could. The knot held, becoming tighter, but not slipping at all.

"What is it?" Phil asked.

"It's a sailor's knot," she said. "My father used this knot when he tied the line together for the arrow he shot . . . I . . . I had one of the other pilots show me how to tie it."

She held the rope out to him, and Phil took it. "What's it for?"

"This," Andrea touched one half of the rope, "is you. The other piece is me."

Phil stared at the rope, turned it over in his hands to examine it from all sides. "I know this knot," he said at last. "It won't slip. Unless someone cuts it, or unties it, these two pieces will never part."

Andrea felt hot tears threatening at the corners of her eyes, and she buried her face in Phil's chest to conceal it. "Be careful," she whispered. "Come back in one piece?"

"I promise," Phil said. He tucked the rope into his pocket carefully, and they stood on the stairs, holding one another close. The door below opened and closed with a loud bang and Phil pulled back. He leaned in, pecked her on the cheek, and turned toward the stairs again.

Andrea watched his retreating back, and smiled. The tears she'd fought moments before filled her eyes, and she brushed at them in irritation. "Steak it is, flyboy," she whispered. "Just come back ready to eat."

Chapter Twelve

The flight was smooth and uneventful. There was some light banter back and forth between Phil and the other pilots, but it was minimal. They all knew the seriousness of what they faced, and each man had his own way of readying for the trial to come. Of the four seed plane pilots, the only one who had been over a full-force hurricane was Phil himself. It wasn't the sort of experience you could prepare for by hearing stories over a beer in the evening.

They were good men. Phil had spent some time on their selection, finding ex-military pilots who showed a certain spark beyond the natural ability to fly a plane. It wasn't a cargo-hop job, or a guided tour flight they were embarked on. The danger was as real, and potentially more deadly than any campaign they had flown against enemy forces. The level of skill necessary to drop the aircraft down into the incredibly high-velocity winds of the storm and maintain that course without panicking had not been easily come by. The group he'd chosen was made up of seasoned veterans with thousands of flight hours under a variety of conditions.

There was Dan Satalino, who'd once been under serious consideration for the space program, Vance Richards, ex-Navy, like Phil himself, and Mike Pooler. Phil had interviewed a couple of dozen men and decided on these three. They were good, solid pilots, and they had the look of men who wouldn't back down when things got difficult. He was going to need that strength over the next few hours.

They were on a long, difficult flight. He wished, in retrospect, that he'd opted for slightly larger aircraft and co-pilots. Even a young or inexperienced second man might make the difference if things went to hell. For himself, though, he didn't want the pressure. He remembered the look on Matt Schmidt's face when the waterspout lashed out at them. He thought he could put himself back in danger like that, but he didn't want to see that look on another man's face again.

He was encouraged by the fact that, of the four planes that had flown that earlier mission, his was the only one that had met any form of danger. The waterspout had been a fluke— Mother Nature reaching out to slap him for his impudence. It wasn't, he reflected, the first time he'd been slapped, or the first time he'd managed to duck.

The other three pilots, those in the cargo planes, were a bigger question mark. The charter company had hired them. He had been as selective as he could be on which company to go with, but there just weren't that many companies willing to risk pilots and aircraft on such a "harebrained" project. He thought they'd seemed solid enough at the morning briefing, he just hoped they could follow orders. The timing was fairly critical if they didn't want to risk their lives and waste their time all at once.

Andrea seemed to believe that the peanut oil, without the seeding, could be a dangerous thing, having an effect far different from the one they hoped for. Phil didn't want something like that on his conscience. If the storm took a sudden jog toward the U.S., or even slashed out at Bermuda, he would never know for certain that he hadn't caused it to happen by his lack of planning, or by being too quick, or too slow to react. If they timed it all correctly, then at least he could share the blame with those who'd formed the original plan.

In some ways, he knew, he had the easiest part in all of it. They were all waiting for the same thing, but at least he was up in the air, flying and actively doing something. Back at the complex, all they could do was watch radarscopes, listen to radio communications, and hope they were as smart as they believed they were. That was a weight Phil could live without.

The miles flashed away beneath him, measured in streaks of brilliant white clouds that reflected the bright sunlight. It was a gorgeous day, and it was very difficult to convince himself that not too many miles distant the largest storm he'd ever seen waited for him. The contrast between the two images lent a surreal air to the flight, and Phil flew in silence.

It felt like there should be a soundtrack in the background, something classical and heroic, but the only sound was the drone of his engines, and the only things to be seen for miles around were the blanket of clouds beneath him, and his three companions, who were holding a good, tight formation around his lead.

Eventually the clouds below darkened. He saw, even from above, that they were moving more quickly. He knew he was nearing the outer edge of the storm. His radar showed it raging below, a giant monster of a thing so large it engulfed the entire screen. There were no edges.

Phil checked his chart. They were about forty-five minutes off of their target position.

"This is Sierra Papa One. All units find position and hold. Time is minus forty-five and counting. Over."

"Sierra Papa Two, Roger," was the immediate response, followed by three and four.

Phil sent his plane into a slow bank out over the center of the storm. The intent was to get the four of them in a line over the eye, and then turn to face the leading edge. From there they would sweep down in an arc, drop their loads, and break off to the side, gaining altitude as quickly as possible and putting distance between themselves and the hurricane with all possible speed. Phil would be the last to come through. He wanted to be in position to hear the others break away safely before he completed his run. That way he would know, as he pulled out himself, that his men were safe and on their way home. He wouldn't know for a long time after that what happened to the storm itself, but his immediate concern was to complete the mission, and then get back to North Carolina.

He switched channels on his radio and keyed the microphone again. "Oscar Sierra One, this is Sierra Papa One, over."

There was a quick burst of static, and then—faintly—he heard the call back from the lead cargo plane. "Got you, Sierra Papa One, this is Oscar Sierra One, how copy?"

"Weak, but readable," he replied. "We will be in position in," he glanced at his chronometer, then continued "minus thirty-eight minutes. I say again, minus thirty-eight minutes. Do you copy? Over."

"Sierra Papa One, this is Oscar Sierra One, understand in position in minus thirty-eight minutes."

"Roger," Phil answered. "We will begin our run in minus forty-five minutes. Do not drop your cargo until I give the call. Do you copy?"

"Roger," the cargo pilot replied. "We'll wait for your call, skipper. Good luck. Oscar Sierra One, out."

The reply was slightly weaker, but Phil understood it. He hoped that once they were all in position, the radio would be strong enough to reach the cargo planes. If not, things could get dicey.

He leaned back and studied his instruments carefully. He had to estimate his course based on the radar, and Andrea's estimates. He couldn't be certain from his current position just how wide the storm might be. A Category Five storm was huge, and the outlying edges could extend hundreds of miles, but all he wanted was the outer edge of the main storm wall. He wanted to start his run from the furthest edge, and he felt as if the chances of his signal reaching the cargo planes would be better if he was slightly offset from the main body of the storm.

As he soared high above the cloud cover, Phil tried not to think about the huge, prowling beast of a storm beneath him. He knew he was near the eye and passing over. The first of the other planes would be almost in position by now, and the second and third not far behind. Once he was in place he would send out the word—the others would pass it down the line, just in case the broadcast came through garbled, and they would dive down toward the storm wall. Just a few minutes, ten more, and he'd be ready. He banked again and glanced down at the smooth, rippling floor of white clouds beneath him.

The time passed, and he dipped slightly, leveled off and pointed the nose of the plane toward the front of the storm. He intended to come down on a straight line with it and turn gently and slowly once he was beneath the clouds. He had a stretch of storm that was his to seed, and he wanted plenty of maneuvering room on his approach. It was likely to be rough down there, with little room for error.

He grabbed his microphone, took a deep breath, and made the call. "This is Sierra Papa One," he said, speaking slowly and carefully. "In position and ready for approach. All units respond."

"Sierra Papa One, this is Sierra Papa Two, copy."

He also heard from Sierra Papa Three, but nothing from four. "Sierra Papa Four, do you copy, over?"

"Sierra Papa One, this is Sierra Papa Three. I've got him, skipper. All clear, over."

Phil nodded, though there was no one to see. "Roger. I'll see you boys on the other side of the storm. This is Sierra Papa One, out."

He flipped channels. "Oscar Sierra One, this is Sierra Papa One, over."

He waited a moment, and then repeated the call. Nothing. There was no answer, and beads of sweat formed instantly on his brow. He felt an odd prickle of fear run across his shoulders, but he held his voice steady and repeated his call. There was no more time to wait. He could only hope that his initial timing had been correct, and that the other pilots would make the right call.

Before he gave up, he sent a final call. "Oscar Sierra One, this is Sierra Papa One. Have no response, I repeat, have no response from your end. Commencing seed run."

There were a couple of pops, followed by a crackle of static. It might have been a response, but there was no way to know and in any case, there was no time left to worry over it. They would deliver their cargo, or they would abort. Either way, he was going in, and it was going to take all of his attention to pull off his own end of the bargain.

He dropped the nose and descended in a sweeping arc toward the clouds below, saying a quiet prayer under his breath.

James "Jamie" Bradshaw stared at his radio and counted the seconds. The allotted time had surely passed, though he couldn't say for sure. Something was wrong with his watch. Of all times for the damned thing to go crazy on him, here it was. One moment it had seemed as if there was a good half an hour left, and now it said less than two minutes. Wicks' last transmission had said thirty-eight minutes, and Jamie's watch had matched Wicks' at that time. Or had he not been concentrating? Wicks had also specified that he would call again, and that they should wait for his mark.

The thing was, conditions were not good. Out in front of the storm, which was where they would have to be to place the slick, the winds were stronger than anticipated. Rain-squalls had reached into that area, and it was going to be difficult, if not impossible, to maintain more than a few moments at that position before pulling out. Just enough time to open the cargo bay doors and drop load, and then get out. He also had the other two to think about. The other two pilots weren't going to back out on him, but he didn't think they were going to follow him to hell and back for the company, either.

He waited another minute. There was some static, but he couldn't be sure if it had been a transmission, or if it was the storm. He glanced at his watch, then whispered "To hell with it," under his breath.

"All units," he called, "this is Oscar Sierra One. Ready to deliver on my mark."

He knew they were spread out at intervals of about fifty miles. He would start delivering the huge balloons where he was, and they would deploy on timed drops across the first fifty-mile stretch. They hadn't had a chance to test this, but he had delivered enough troops during the war and dropped enough supplies behind unfriendly lines to know that the theory behind it was sound. The balloons would roll out, one after the other; if they fell as anticipated, they would burst on ~~~ct, and the oil would spread, each load catching the ⸍ the slick left by the last. Jamie didn't feel like betting any substantial amount of cash on the outcome, but he had a job to do, and he figured it was about time to make it happen, for good or ill.

"All units," he repeated, "this is Oscar Sierra One, deliver. I repeat, deliver cargo. Let's get this done and get out of here. Over."

The others responded quickly, and Jamie dropped into a slow dive. He knew he had to get as low as possible, but when he hit four thousand feet, the turbulence kicked up, and he started to lose visibility. It didn't take long to make up his mind. He studied the instruments, lined himself up as well as he could in front of the approaching wall of the storm, and hit the switch to open the hydraulic cargo bay doors. The balloons were strung on a sort of pulley; the weight of the first would pull them over, and each would fall a set amount of seconds behind the last.

The plane jerked slightly as the doors caught the wind, then he felt the thrumming vibration as the mechanism rolled, dragged the first balloon into place, and dropped it. He felt the weight shift and fought the controls doggedly, keeping his course in as straight a line as possible. He couldn't see a thing below or behind him, so he had no way to know how successful the drop was. All he could do was to keep on course until he had crossed his fifty-mile stretch, then pull up and get the hell out.

The wind buffeted him roughly, and once or twice he thought one engine was about to stall on him. The load lightened bit by bit, and in what seemed only seconds, he had crossed the fifty-mile stretch, and with a sigh of relief, he flipped the switch that closed the cargo bay and drew back on the controls. The sturdy, boxy cargo plane was sluggish, but it responded. When he climbed up and away from the storm and slipped off to the west, his control became more certain.

A moment later he broke through the clouds and rose above ten thousand feet. He leveled off and reached for his microphone.

"All units, this is Oscar Sierra One," he said breathlessly. "Cargo delivered, do you copy? Over."

"Oscar Sierra One, this is Oscar Sierra Two. I copy you five by five. What happened back there, Jamie? We still have fifteen minutes until the call. Did you get an update on orders? Over."

Jamie's heart sank. He glanced down at his watch. It had spun another thirty minutes. He frowned and shook his arm, but nothing changed. The second hand continued its smooth transition of the dial.

"Christ," he said into the microphone without thinking. Then he caught himself. "This is Oscar Sierra One, that's a negative. I seem to have a malfunction with my watch. The damned thing says we're already twenty minutes late, but I know that isn't right."

"Oscar Sierra One, this is Oscar Sierra Three. Roger that. My watch is FUBAR. According to it, we shouldn't even have started the trip. It was fine a while ago; what the hell happened? Over."

Jamie shook his head in bewilderment. "Damned if I know," he muttered to himself. "I don't know," he said out loud, keying the microphone. "Did you deliver?"

Both replies were affirmative. Jamie glanced back over his shoulder, but all he saw was the cloud cover. "I hope you're okay back there, Phil," he said under his breath. Into the microphone, he said, "This is Oscar Sierra One. Return to base, mission accomplished. Over, and out."

The other two copied his message quickly, and they ⌐ up, banking toward the U.S. coast and away from the ʦorm.

★ ★ ★ ★ ★

Several things happened more or less at once. The weather balloons of peanut oil struck and spread perfectly. The water was choppy, but the pressure from each balloon bursting on impact spread the contents until they joined and blended in either direction, and though the slick rolled up and down on the waves, it hung solid, forming a smooth, glistening wall on the water ahead of the storm wall. At least, along the central portion of the wall. The storm, larger than anticipated, stretched nearly three hundred and fifty miles. The slick managed to cover the path of the storm's center, and with a roar like a diesel engine, the hurricane struck that spot.

At that moment, Phil Wicks and the other seed pilots were only just making their initial turn and preparing to drop through the clouds and strafe the storm wall. They had no idea that the water far below and a bit in front of them was already coated in slick, glimmering peanut oil, or that the storm was making its first attempt to slip up and over that point.

At first the slick had no affect whatsoever on the storm. It took another five minutes, just long enough for Phil to give the final okay to his men, and for them to begin their runs on the storm wall. Just long enough for Phil to fail to contact three pilots who had already flown out of range of their already weak communications link. Just long enough for Phil to drop the nose of his aircraft through the clouds.

The storm sped up. The action of the wind at the eye of the storm tried to draw on the water in front of it. Super-cooled water and rushing winds worked to evaporate the surface moisture and failed. The harder the storm tried to evaporate the water in its path, the faster and tighter the eye wound, and still the slick held. The storm reached and stretched. Water rose to the left—the west—and in a long, sinuous roll that became the rush of a monstrous engine of destruction, the storm whipped to the side, bypassed and skipped around the oil and lunged toward the U.S. coast, just as Andrea had feared it might.

Phil didn't see this at first; he was concentrating on aligning himself with the storm wall. He leveled off at five thousand feet and stared down at the wild whitecaps below and the dark mass of the storm. His plane shivered, and he felt the strength of the storm in that touch. It wasn't like the other one, the smaller storm. This one you felt through the plane, through your seat and the flight suit, right to the marrow of your bones. It was a monster, and where the smaller hurricane had seemed malevolent and aware of him, this one was worse.

He was so insignificant in the face of so much power that he couldn't even credit that, if the storm *were* intelligent, it would pay him the slightest heed. Suddenly their balloons full of oil and their planes full of silver iodide seemed paltry—silly even. How in creation could they have believed, even for a moment, that they could face off against such a behemoth?

He considered dropping the extra thousand feet, then decided against it. They weren't trying to concentrate the crystals as they had the last time, but to spread them along the storm wall. He would be fine at five thousand feet, and he wasn't certain the aircraft would hold up if he went any lower. He considered calling the others to check their altitude, but there was nothing any of them could do to adjust at this point. They had to release their loads and get out, and the longer he cruised along the wall with the full force of the storm bearing down on him like a giant wave of water and wind, the more important that last became to him.

An image of Andrea, smiling at him, was all it took to gal- him into action. He leveled off and had his hand on eady to drop the silver iodide, when the world shifted. The roaring of the wind increased so quickly, and so sharply, that his breath was stolen. The aircraft shuddered, and he tilted to the right. The wind was too strong; it had caused one of the engines to simply quit—sucked the oxygen from within. He compensated without thinking and pulled up. Mission forgotten, he pulled back on the controls. The plane fought his control sluggishly and he felt the weight of the air streaming around him. He saw the storm wall, seething, not drawing closer, but rushing along on a tangent.

He gained altitude slowly, fighting for every inch. Sweat streamed down his back and into his eyes. He couldn't see, but he didn't need to. He was pulling up and that was all he needed to know, up and out of the grip of the storm—to safety. He felt the plane being dragged physically back to the storm, and he feared that he would be swallowed and forgotten, a gnat in that enormous, killing wind, but then he was free.

He burst through the clouds and with each foot he rose through the thinning air, the hold of the storm below diminished. He flipped the toggle for the dead engine once—twice—and on the third flip it roared back to life and stabilized his left wing, removing some of the pressure from his straining arms. He tried to breathe deeply, but it wouldn't come. Then he tried again and the air shuddered through his mask. So close, so fucking close.

Below he heard the monstrous roar of the wind.

"What happened?" he whispered. No one answered. Without hesitation, he turned toward the west and steadied the aircraft at fifteen thousand feet.

He didn't have much time to decide what to do, and if he was going to drop the silver iodide, it had to be soon.

"To hell with getting any lower than this," he said. The

storm screamed beneath him like a host of banshees, but he held steady on his course. He took a deep breath and glanced at his watch.

He tried the radio again, but neither the other seed plane pilots nor the cargo pilots responded. He heard nothing but static in return.

At the complex in North Carolina, Andrea stood, ashen-faced, and stared out the window into the growing gloom of late afternoon.

"What do you mean?" she asked the voice at the other end of the phone. She listened for a moment longer, and then let the phone's receiver drop from her hand. It swung down on its cord and crashed to the floor, but Andrea was already turning away from it, her eyes glazed.

"What is it?" Scharf asked, leaping out of his seat and rushing to steady her. "Andrea, what's wrong?"

"The storm," she replied. Her voice was very quiet, almost childish in its awe of the words being formed, "They said it's . . . they said . . . it's gone."

Scharf gaped at her. "Gone?" he asked. "We did that?"

Andrea shook her head. "They never dropped the silver iodide. Only three of the seed planes have reported in—Phil's missing. The cargo planes will be landing in about an hour. I don't know what happened, but the radar reading should be coming in soon. They said it strengthened, jerked to the west, and then . . . nothing."

"But . . ." Scharf could think of nothing to complete the sentence. He turned to the facsimile printer and watched as the green data light steadied, and the paper started to spit slowly from the machine. He watched, expecting that it was a bad joke, or a mistake, but as the map that represented the Atlantic slid past, rolling on toward the floor, there was no indication of a storm. Not a thunderstorm or cyclone, and definitely nothing that even remotely resembled a hurricane. It was as clean as it had been the day before.

He turned back to Andrea, but she'd walked to the window and was staring out at the sunset. Tears streamed down her cheeks, but he didn't know if it was because she thought that they had done it—or if she was worried about Phil—or both. He kept his silence. He stood beside her for a long time, until the shadows lengthened and deepened into night. Then, patting her gently on the shoulder to let her know he was leaving, he turned away to oversee the landing and docking of the planes. When he left the office, she still stood at the window, staring into the night sky.

Six planes returned. The three cargo planes landed with a bustle of excitement, and about an hour after that, three of the seed planes. There was less excitement at this. They all reported in, and Andrea listened to their stories distractedly, taking in the descriptions of how their watches had gone haywire, and how after pulling up at the first sign of the storm's going crazy, the seed planes had found themselves suddenly alone, in clear skies, but she never took her eyes off the skyline.

Eventually they left her alone again. She dropped into one of the chairs and laid her head on a desk, her face tilted toward the window, and dropped into a fitful sleep.

The fourth plane did not return.

Not that night.

Not ever.

The U.S. Navy and the Coast Guard searched for nearly a week. No debris turned up, or evidence that the plane, or the storm, had ever existed. They were just . . . gone. There was a period of a few days when the newspapers ran stories about other strange happenings off the coast of Bermuda. The pilots were interviewed and repeated their stories of watches gone askew and vanishing storms.

In the end, the storm, which had never gotten close enough to be a real threat, and the pilot lost trying to stop it, were forgotten as a thousand other distractions lured the world away.

That was the beginning.

PART FOUR

The Jamieson-Wicks Complex—2006

Chapter Thirteen

It was late, but Andrea felt only the slightest touch of drowsiness. As the years piled up behind her, sleep became more elusive. Time asleep was time wasted, and there was so precious little of it allotted to any one person. At her feet, curled in a huge lump of muscle and white and tan fur, the sixth generation of Muriel's long gone bulldog, Jake, lay curled into an impossibly tight ball. She had named him Elvis, though for the life of her she didn't know why. Maybe because they said the king wasn't dead, and Andrea could understand that kind of dream.

Her laptop was open on the desk before her, the screen lit up with a storm simulation program she'd developed a few years back—one of the many innovations her foundation had provided to the world. The software took the statistics at the beginning of a storm, queried the database on the HP mainframe computer on the first floor, and extrapolated the most likely strengthening, weakening, and path of a coming storm. It wasn't a hundred percent accurate—nothing was.

No matter how many storms she tracked or calculations she made, there was always something she had missed, or something that was slightly different than at any time before. The program was good, but like life, it had its flaws.

The storm whirling in slow circles on her screen moved jerkily. Each time the winds spun to simulate the motion surrounding the eye the image blinked and refreshed. The software could handle continuous motion, but the laptop, state-of-the-art though it was, lacked sufficient memory for all the data coursing through its electronic veins.

Across the bottom of the screen a bar graphed the sustained wind velocity, the maximum gusts, and the speed at which the storm traveled. Beside this, in a slightly larger banner, she saw her own name. Andrea. All storms had names these days, and when that practice had taken hold, she had programmed it into her software. This was the first simulation she'd created—her storm—and she'd named it Andrea. She didn't know, really, if she'd done this out of a personal connection with the storm, or out of simple guilt.

As their methods had improved, and the data poured in from all sides, the government and the weather stations, colleges, and universities participating and reaping the benefits of the software in return, the picture of what had happened so long ago had become clearer. She had no answers to her questions about where the storm had gone, or what had happened to Phil, because no answer was satisfactory in the face of the myriad questions. There *was* no explanation.

Storms don't implode—or no other storm ever had. They don't spin themselves into frenzied motion only to disappear. They don't, in short, do what her storm had done. Ever. For all the data she'd gathered, and all the wizardry she could pull out of her computer system to chart and predict what would come of each new tropical depression that formed, she couldn't even begin to guess what had happened to this one, tremendous storm, and of all the storms that had ever blown their way up the gulf, it was the only one she cared about.

She watched as the whirling mass on her screen ground its way toward Bermuda. She'd watched this scenario a thousand times. She'd input more data each time, twisted the conditions first one way, and then the next. None of it made any real difference. She'd seen the computer-generated storm wash over Bermuda, leveling everything in its path. She'd seen it spin in circles and die at sea. She'd seen it hit nearly every point on the eastern seaboard of the United States, but she had never—not once—seen it weaken, or disappear. It just wasn't possible.

Andrea's version of the software, what she ran on her laptop, had some modifications that the commercially available and government versions did not. She had built in modules that represented the silver iodide seed planes, and another that simulated the effect of different sizes and levels of oil slicks on the water in the storm's path. She even had a module, just for the hell of it, that involved the theoretical placement of an iceberg in the path of the storm. Thank you, Pam Jones, wherever you are.

If there was an answer to be found, she knew that it was in this extra data—the circumstances that most of the world had never been made fully aware of—that it would be found. The oil slick, which they had never reported to the government, had proven the most disturbing and confusing of all.

When she placed a slick approximately the size of Keith Scharf's peanut oil slick in the direct path of the storm, she got a variety of results, but they were all similar. Dependent on the temperature of the water, the air, the barometric pressure, and several other variables she could program into the system, the storm either slowed, or jerked to one side or the other. The few times she managed to get it to slow, the storm hesitated, weakened slightly, but held its course. Eventually the slick broke up, and the storm continued.

It was the other simulations that bothered her most. She knew from radar pictures of her storm that just before it dropped off radar, the wind speed increased dramatically, and the storm lurched to the southwest. It was a sharp motion, as if the huge, roiling behemoth of wind, rain, and death had slammed into a wall and slid down the side, picking up speed from the pressure exerted. What had resulted, for just a few minutes, was a storm beyond the bounds of any scale.

Technically, it was still a Category Five storm. Sustained winds of more than a hundred and fifty-six miles per hour, according to the Saffir-Simpson scale, were a Category Five. Of course, if the sustained winds reached nearly two hundred miles per hour, as they had in her storm—Hurricane Andrea—they were still considered Category Five winds. As you leaped up and off the charts with your numbers, the scale became silly. Categorizing something that improbable and out of proportion was arbitrary, and not really necessary in any sense but the most rudimentary and general.

In Andrea's world, the numbers were viewed for themselves, and the breaking down of those numbers into categories was useful more for explaining things in a context that laymen would understand than it was for any scientific purpose.

After Andrew, Hugo, and more recently, Isabel and Ivan, the average American was at least basically fluent in what statistical vernacular like Category One or Category Two meant in terms of damage, danger, and other basics. They didn't know what the central barometric pressure meant, or what effect hurricanes had on the environment. Most of them would be shocked to find that there was actually a purpose to the storms, that they drew warm water up from the gulf, and without the aeration they caused, biological cycles could be thrown off completely.

Andrea hadn't paid much attention to these facts either. Not a few years back, in any case. All she had wanted was to know how to stop them, to pay them back for stealing her father. What happened, instead, was that she had sacrificed another to her obsession, and though she was much closer to realizing her dream—actually controlling or stopping a storm completely—there were great, hollow caverns in her heart that she couldn't fill no matter how she tried.

The storm spun closer to Bermuda, and Andrea brought up the oil slick module. She thought back over the pilots' stories again, as she had so many times in the past, and searched for some word—some phrase she might have interpreted wrongly.

The thing they had never taken into account was the area itself. Bermuda—the Devil's Triangle. It had sounded silly at the time, stories to scare young sailors, or good ghost tales for telling around the fire, but nothing to worry about in a real-world scenario. Except that when the pilots had flown in front of that storm with their loads of peanut oil, their watches spun at different speeds. Their radios had not worked as well as they should. Things had gone horribly and completely wrong.

The slick had been dropped unevenly, and far too soon. The lead pilot, Bradshaw had been the man's name, had trusted his watch, and had lost his nerve somewhat in the face of the storm. Thinking about that—thinking about being in an airplane, soaring above the ocean, but directly in the path of something as huge as a hurricane, made Andrea's throat dry. She didn't know how any of them had done it. She never could have set foot in any aircraft going that close to the storm, so she didn't blame the pilots for their hurried, poorly thought-out actions. Still, the slick had reacted exactly as they had hoped that it would, spreading and coating the water directly in the central path of the storm.

But the silver iodide had not been in position to be dropped, and by the time it was dropped—at least three loads of the four, that she knew of—the storm had blown out of control. It hit the wall of the oil slick, sought the path of least resistance and warmest water, and lunged in that direction— straight at the U.S. coast.

It should have developed into the worst natural disaster in the country's history. It should have flooded the land with a tidal surge, battered the coast with winds that would have sheared homes and buildings from the ground and spit them at the heart of the country with contemptuous ease. It should have done all of these things, and if it *had* done them, it would have been Andrea's fault.

Yes, the slick was Scharf's idea. Yes, they were all involved in the program, the seeding and the slick were things they had discussed and worried to death in endless late night debates, but that changed nothing. When Operation Stormfury fell apart, it was Andrea who had obsessed. It was Andrea who had dragged them all along in her wake as she built her complex, fitted out the aircraft, and planned her assault on hurricanes, and it was Andrea they had all turned to for the final decision when they brought Scharf and his oil slick theory on board and decided to put it to the test.

The process intrigued them all, and they were all involved of their own accord, but the truth was very clear, and a bitter pill to swallow. Without Andrea as the catalyst to keep them all moving in the same direction, it never would have happened.

Yes, the storm, her storm, might still have turned. Yes, it might have hit the U.S. and caused a lot of damage. Yes, in the end, even their mistake had worked out—somehow. There had been no storm. In that much, they had succeeded, but it was such an empty sensation, such a hollow victory with no one to share it. Andrea knew this was a selfish way to view what, in some ways, had been a miracle, but she couldn't help it. Her capacity for belief in miracles had been dwindling since childhood.

On screen, the storm hit the makeshift lopsided slick she provided. She watched the statistics bar on the bottom of the screen. The storm hesitated, just for a moment. The wind speed dropped about ten miles per hour, and then, very suddenly, it accelerated. The white cloud that represented the storm wall jogged to the left. The wind speed leaped up over a hundred and fifty, then over a hundred and seventy, and leveled off at about two hundred and ten miles per hour. The storm spread out from the end of the slick as if squeezed from a tube. The size was incredible, and on its present course it would strike midway between North Carolina and Florida.

Andrea knew that by the manipulation of water temperature and cold fronts she could influence which direction the storm would take. She could even, if she worked hard enough at it, force the storm back out to sea and hold it there until it dissipated. The problem was, she could only do this on her computer screen.

The worst of it was that the oil slick could work. She still had no proof that the seeding would have mattered, but in about twenty percent of her simulations she was able to bring about an effect she called "The Coil." When a hurricane went into "The Coil," it tightened into a smaller, more compact mass of water and then, unable to sustain the evaporation that drew more moisture from the water, the storm simply devoured itself from within. It spun and spun until there was nothing left to fuel the energy, the storm wall broke, and the eye became ragged, then dissipated altogether. It was exactly the effect they had hoped for long ago, but it was too unpredictable.

The odds were as good that you would strengthen the storm as that it would reach "The Coil." Other than in simulations on the computer, the method had been scrapped altogether.

The storm on her screen, now so large that it blocked the coastline almost completely, spun closer and Andrea hit the pause button. She stared at the screen, the storm, and the numbers at the bottom of the screen for a long time. She traced her finger over the spot on the virtual map where her home on the Outer Banks had been. She touched the spot directly over where she now sat, twenty miles inland from the North Carolina coast. None of it would exist, she knew. If the storm were real, it would erase her home and her work, most of the people that still mattered to her, completely. Nothing would remain.

She closed her eyes and in that instant saw her father and Muriel, his strong arm around her bony shoulders and her arm held up to keep the birdcage from banging as they tried to leap through her doorway to the porch. Andrea saw the house drop, the churning water beneath, and the boat, dancing empty and forgotten beneath the porch. She saw Jake barking—could almost hear him—and as if in answer to that thought, Elvis stirred at her feet.

The dog brushed her hand with his wet, inquisitive nose and licked the blue-veined back of her hand. Andrea opened her eyes. She rubbed him behind the ear with one hand, and with the other she flipped her trackball, clicked the button, and reset the program. Then she pressed enter yet again, and the storm began its endless, conjectural dance across the screen. Andrea needed sleep, she knew, but it eluded her.

"Why can't I be like other people?" she asked Elvis, turning momentarily from the screen to gaze down into his huge, brown eyes. "Why can't I just count sheep?"

Chapter Fourteen

Andrea was up before dawn. Her apartment consisted of two rooms and an office converted to a kitchen on the top floor of the complex. She'd had a smaller place in Elizabeth City for a while, but the time spent commuting had seemed a waste of time to her, and as often as not she fell asleep at her desk, or in one of the padded leather chairs, staring out into the night sky.

The complex had grown by degrees. The hangars had been converted, one by one, until all but one of them had sprung up with steel reinforced walls and huge panes of triple-thick safety glass. If Andrea's calculations were correct, the buildings could withstand wind in excess of two hundred miles per hour without sustaining even minor damage. They were prototypes, examples of the design techniques and structural improvements she'd patented over the years.

One hangar still stood, shadowed and empty, near the main building. It was the hangar that had housed Captain Phillip Wicks' plane the day before he took off for his final flight. Andrea knew it was a horrible waste of resources, space, and money, but she had plenty, and she couldn't bear to touch it.

Phil had never been found. No wreckage had been found. There was no evidence that he crashed at sea in the storm, no more than there was that the storm had ever existed. She couldn't let go of the notion that one day he would fly over, call over the radio for clearance to land, and taxi into that old dilapidated building with a smile and a wave.

Keith Scharf was still with her, and he'd prodded her gently to do something about the hangar, but he didn't push too hard. She thought he was secretly afraid that if the hangar fell, she wouldn't be far behind it, and possibly that was right. There was damned little holding her together as it was. In her zeal to battle hurricanes, she'd lost sight of anything resembling a real life.

After walking Elvis and brewing strong, fresh coffee, Andrea opened the doors to her office wide and set about straightening things up. She hadn't gotten any better about filing over the years, though she had more assistance with it now, and less paper to deal with. Everything was electronic, CDs, DVDs, optical drives. Sometimes she grew nostalgic for the black screen monitors with their bright, glowing green letters and the huge, fan-fold reams of computer readouts that had all but buried her in the early days. Not often, though. It was nice to have all of the information at hand, and it was nice to have the computer do most of the work that had previously fallen to error-prone men and women.

Not long after eight o'clock, a string of large trucks wound their way down the long entrance road. Andrea stopped to watch as they showed their identification at the gate and were waved through. She'd known they would arrive early, returning from the latest experimental excursion. She also knew most of the results that they would bring with them, but she intended to wait and let Keith present them himself.

He had the right to be proud—he'd come a long way from the young researcher with stars in his eyes and peanut oil as his chosen weapon. After Phil's disappearance, Keith had been her strongest support. She loved her work, but a spark had been missing since she'd lost Phil. Keith Scharf had helped her to rebuild her confidence and her sense of purpose, if not to regain that spark.

She knew that, in his own, distracted way, Keith had fallen in love with her. She appreciated his love, but she couldn't return it, and after many years of quiet patience, Keith accepted that as well. He had been married only three years earlier, at the tender age of fifty-three, to one of their senior analysts, a lovely woman named Grace Purvis, and the two of them seemed very happy. Andrea had attended their wedding, and she felt genuine warmth for the two that must have been similar to the sensation of motherhood.

The first of the trucks rolled onto the grounds. There were loading docks in the rear of two of the larger buildings. The first story of each was a huge work bay, and she knew this was where the trucks were headed. Before rounding the corner, the lead truck stopped and Keith climbed down. His arms were full of folders. He waved and shouted something at the driver, and then turned toward the main complex.

Andrea set out two cups and poured the coffee into a carafe to keep it warm and fresh. She thought briefly of the old stainless steel urn they'd used when they first purchased the building, and she smiled. The Bunn-O-Matic drip coffee maker she now used was hooked directly into the water supply. You put the grounds in place—fresh from the companion coffee grinder—and pushed a button. Not everything about the good old days was good.

It took Keith a few minutes to make his way up the elevator and onto her floor, so Andrea returned to the window and watched the gates being locked behind the last of the trucks. As the vehicle turned around the side of the largest building, she saw that water dripped and sloshed out the back, running over the tires and splashing on the pavement.

Her buzzer rang, and she went to the door, pulling it wide with a smile. "Good morning, Keith," she said. "Good trip?"

Keith Scharf had aged well. He was still stout, and his dark hair still stuck out at an unruly angle, slightly gray above the ears, but full. He wore overalls and black work boots, and he looked every bit the foreman coming in off the loading bay to report.

"Very good," he replied, sweeping her into a hug.

Elvis hopped up then, nosing jealously between the two, and Keith laughed. "No worries, Elvis, you're still the king," he said, reaching down to pat the bulldog's glossy head.

"These are only the preliminary reports," he said, tossing the folders onto her table and smiling, "but I'm sure you already know that. It looks very positive."

"And with only three of the pumps," she replied. "Impressive. Better than we hoped, I think."

Keith nodded. "We were able to cut these three loose before they shipped out to the fish farm. I wanted to have new, fresh equipment when we tried this. It was still a little risky, but only to the machinery."

They both fell silent for a moment as the implication of what he'd said dropped over them. They knew full well why they would not risk personnel on these experiments, and there was no reason to speak the words out loud, but Andrea couldn't help glancing out the window at the empty hangar below.

The pumps he referred to were the newest in a long line of devices their company had researched and bought into. They served a dual purpose, which was a boon to the company financially, but everyone knew which of the two purposes their efforts were meant to support.

The first and least important, as far as Andrea was concerned, was the creation of highly oxygenated, mineral-rich, intensive biological zones, or fish-farm regions. There was a name for the effect when it occurred naturally, a St. Georges' Banks effect. These pumps could recreate the effect in regions of the ocean that were considered hopeless for food production—oceanic wastelands, or deserts. For purposes of re-mineralization, the air would need to be pumped down to near the bottom before release, allowing aeration and the breaking loose of minerals from the ocean floor.

Relatively small fish farms could be maintained privately by containing them within a set of nets with buoys and anchors, or within "bubble curtains" using the same effects as were used to screen Pacific harbors from submarine sonar during World War II. Larger-size fish farms could be "open," without containing nets, maintained by nations or private consortia or mixed public-and-private consortia for all to share in. It was a very noble project, and as far as it went, Andrea was happy to be part of the research.

For unknown reasons, government and scientific communities had largely ignored the apparatus. Keith had found it while cruising the Internet one evening in search of new theories on hurricanes. The likelihood had grown smaller over the years that they would run across someone with an idea they hadn't already explored, but Keith considered every avenue worth pursuing, and when his random search brought him to a page explaining the fish-farming device, and how it operated, he found that the inventor of the device had another possible use for it—stopping hurricanes.

Hurricanes require a path of warmer water to maintain a tight, well-formed eye and continue along their path. They are drawn up the Gulf Stream by the warmth of the water. The inventor of the fish farming pumps suggested that if enough of his devices, or large enough versions of his device, were placed in the path of seasonal storms, then run only a few days at a time, so that they didn't make a large disturbance in the eco-system, they might prevent the forming of the storms that ravaged the U.S. coastline before they even became an issue.

The pumps wouldn't have to operate in the same fashion as the fish-farming pumps. To reach water cool enough to change the surface temperature, the compressed air would only have to be forced down a few fathoms. The cold water would be displaced and rise to the top. These pumps, of course, required good, solid power sources, and would have to be large, or very widespread, but the theory behind the proposed system was sound, and it was enough to get both Keith and Andrea excited.

It wasn't really a process designed to stop a storm, but it was possible that it could. A large enough concentration of pumps could shift the water temperature over a large surface area of water dramatically in a very short amount of time, and if they were placed in the path of a hurricane, or tropical cyclone, they might cause enough of a shift in temperature to slow or stop the storm. Certainly they would be disruptive, and sometimes that was all that was necessary. An unexpected front, or a shift in barometric pressure, could shatter the continuity of a storm. Hurricanes, for all their power, were fragile things, and once the eye had been disrupted, they often fizzled out or died into thunderstorms and rainsqualls.

Of course, it would take more than a few of the pumps to bring about a noticeable affect on a very large storm. The smaller units designed for fish farming wouldn't do. You'd need hundreds of them, and it wasn't feasible to place them across the entire storm wall of a hurricane. The cost would be high, and the pumps would certainly be lost, along with whatever anchored them in place. The initial estimate, in fact, was one pump in place for every one-third of a mile of ocean space to cover the storm wall of a hurricane.

Then the real work began. First Keith and Andrea had scaled the pumps exactly as they appeared on the 'Net, and they'd funded a couple of small, experimental fish farms. The initial results were unimpressive, but with some fine-tuning, and after bringing in a few experts, they were able to create a stable, healthy environment in a previously unproductive expanse of the ocean. Keith immediately funded a dozen more small operations and started the wheels turning to apply for government grants to sustain them. The food they produced was donated charitably, and they quickly caught the attention of several large companies.

Meanwhile, Andrea and Keith took the design in an entirely different direction. The pumps used for the fish farms were too small for their purpose. They weren't much bigger than those used to run a simple jackhammer, and while they worked fine for what they'd been designed to do, they wouldn't be powerful enough to displace enough super-cooled water in a short enough time to effect changes in a storm. They needed something more powerful, and what they latched onto was what Keith called "The Barge."

"The Barge" was, basically, just what it sounded like. They started with long, flat ocean barges, modified so that each had five very large compressed air pumps attached along the waterline one side, and three more on the opposite side. They designed the barges to be towed into place and anchored at either end. The barges themselves hadn't cost much—there were plenty of craft of that sort in mothballs, available through the defense re-utilization system, and since they were funded for research on larger fish farms, it hadn't been that difficult to arrange for purchase.

The pumps had been more difficult, but Andrea was a

wealthy woman. Between her own funds and those of the corporation, the cost of the equipment had been absorbed.

Now the fruits of their labor sat on the table before her. A small tropical depression had formed a week earlier, and they had gone quietly into action. Keith oversaw the placement of three of their barges in the path of what was quickly forming into a tight tropical storm. When the storm reached the supercooled water displaced by the pumps, the storm broke up. There had been minor damage to two of the three barges, but they had stopped the storm in its tracks, and they had lost no equipment. It was the first concrete success in all the years they'd been together. It was a huge step forward in storm research, and if they could add just a little more to the file, Andrea was poised to approach the government with the culmination of her life's work.

She wanted to bring Operation Stormfury back on line, not as a group considered to be staffed by idealistic crackpots fighting impossible odds, but with real direction and proven solutions. Her research had moved ahead by leaps and bounds. She had improved the structures of buildings in the paths of storms, decreased the revenue lost by insurance companies and government grants for the rebuilding of ruined cities, improved the accuracy and range of Doppler radar systems, and provided her simulation program for the prediction of the habits of hurricanes. Now she wanted to provide the basis for a network of the compressed air pumps that could be run at infrequent intervals to prevent the danger of hurricanes to the United States altogether. There was a lot of research involved. There were ecological concerns, but she believed that, at the very least, the threat of huge hurricanes could be limited and possibly eliminated.

Altogether they managed to outfit twenty-five of the barges. They had the ability to drag five of them at a time via ocean-going tug boats. Five of the barges were anchored off the coast of Bermuda, another five off the Cayman Islands, and two were still being fitted in the shipyards in Norfolk, Virginia. The rest were docked along the North Carolina coast. They had kept the purpose of the craft to themselves, giving vague answers involving fish farms and keeping the core group of scientists, engineers, and technicians under tight rein.

Andrea felt the years weigh heavily on her shoulders. She didn't have that long to find the key to her dreams, and she felt the ghosts of her father and Phil hovering in the air just out of reach, watching her and waiting for redemption. If she failed, her father would not be avenged, and Phil would have died in vain. She knew both of these assertions were wrong, but she couldn't shake them, and had long since given up trying.

"I think we have it this time, Andrea," Keith said, drinking the last of his coffee. "I really think we have it."

She turned back from the window and smiled at him, nodding. "I think so too," she replied. "All we need now is a larger storm, and a chance to get the equipment into place. I want to put everyone on alert as of now."

Keith frowned just for a moment. He'd just returned, and Andrea could see that the idea of heading back out immediately didn't much appeal to him.

"We have to, Keith," she said. "The season is almost over. If we hold off much longer, we won't be able to do anything until next year."

Keith's features softened, and he rose, stepped closer and took her hands in his. "I know," he said. "I'll pass the word along, and I'll get messages out to the islands to keep all the barges and boats on standby. We can get moving pretty quickly once we have a reason."

Andrea gripped his hands, then turned back to the window. "Call me tonight, when they're ready," she said. "I'll sleep better."

Keith watched her for a moment, and then turned toward the door. "Will do," he said as he stepped into the hall. "And don't worry," he added. "There will still be something this year. We have almost a month."

Andrea didn't answer, and after a few moments Keith's footsteps faded as he reached the end of the hall and stepped into the elevator.

Elvis lifted his head, waited until the elevator door slid closed, then looked at Andrea with his head cocked. He whined softly, but when he got no response, he laid his head back on his paws and stared up at her.

At the window, Andrea stared down at the empty hangar. Tears streamed unheeded down her cheeks, but the corners of her lips were turned up in a grim smile.

Chapter Fifteen

Andrea sat by the big window that evening and stared down at the complex, her phone cradled against her shoulder and her feet up on the concrete window ledge. She smiled, and with her free hand she twirled the ends of her hair almost girlishly. It had been a very good day, and she was enjoying the conversation.

On the other end of the line, Gabrielle Martinez was discoursing on the miracle of the contained fish farm. Gabrielle was as enthused by her work as Andrea was consumed by her own; the other woman's stories of pumps and compressors, nets and buoys, and the inherent problems of coordinating all of these elements with mostly natives to assist her had lightened Andrea's mood considerably.

"Really, Andrea," Gabrielle said, "it is working out very well. We have three farms here now, spaced along the outer range of coral reefs that were dead or dying, and they are *producing*. You should see the looks on the faces of some of the older fishermen, men who spent long patient hours watching as we got everything into place, and longer hours still explaining to me that there were no fish to be caught where we were setting up, and that they would guide me to where the fish could still be found, if I would pay them.

"Just the other day I invited two of them out. They were so solemn. One of them brought me in his boat, as if our own craft weren't safe, or we didn't have the skill to get to our own installation. I let them into the area with the nets, and Jason—you remember Jason?"

Andrea nodded, realized Gabrielle couldn't see it, and replied, "Yes, we met last time I came down to look things over."

Gabrielle went on so quickly that Andrea realized the question about Jason had been rhetorical. "Jason hauled in a couple of the nets. They overflowed. Those fishermen had never seen a catch like that, and I thought they would dive over the side of their boats when Jason released the net and dropped his catch back into the water.

"It took me a while to convince the men that the fish weren't going anywhere, and that more would come as we continued the process. I showed them the pumps, and I explained what the equipment did, but I don't think much of it was absorbed. All they could talk about after we pulled back through the nets and headed for shore was the nets and the fish. I'm half-convinced they think it's magic, and that Jason is some sort of sorcerer."

"That's wonderful, Gabrielle," Andrea said. Her smile was deep and genuine. She liked Gabrielle, and had been happy to add the woman to their staff the previous year. So many great minds who could do so many wonderful things for the world were buried every year in bureaucracy, red tape, and poorly funded programs that it was one of the joys of her life that she could afford, now and then, to rescue one of them and put them to work. Despite her own agenda with the hurricanes and tropical cyclones, Andrea was proud to be part of the fish farming research. If it panned out, so to speak, it could actually make a significant impact on world hunger.

"Hey," Gabrielle said suddenly, "the wind is picking up here. Looks like we've got some rain on the way, so I'd better hang up and get in to shore. I love this job, but I don't want to be caught out here in one of your storms."

"No fear of that just now," Andrea replied with a short laugh. "We have a couple of small cells forming, but nothing close to you at the moment."

"That's good to know," Gabrielle replied, her voice suddenly echoing as if from very far away. The connection was weakening. "I think I'll head in all the same. It's really choppy out here, and darker than it should be. Even a good thunderstorm can be dangerous if you get caught out on one of the farms."

"Be safe," Andrea replied. She clicked the button that closed the connection and tapped the antenna on her chin thoughtfully.

She rose and walked past her desk and her laptop to a larger monitor screen that hung from one wall. She grabbed a remote from the couch and flipped the on button. She clicked past the networks and cable channels and into the private network they'd set up for use within the building. She could take feeds straight off the computers if she got tired of the laptop's small screen, or she could tap into the radars.

The screen lit up with colored patches and a map. The default map was small, scaled to show the United States coastline and on through the Midwest, as well as the entire Gulf Stream storm track. She saw that the two small storm cells she'd mentioned to Gabrielle were right about where she'd expected to see them. There was no other significant activity. Over Bermuda, where Gabrielle and her fish farms were anchored, the sky was mottled with brilliant green. Rain. There was plenty of rain there, and no doubt some winds that would seem pretty wild out riding on a small craft by the fish farm, but nothing to get excited about—at least not if you were hunting hurricanes.

Andrea felt something nibbling at the back of her mind, but she couldn't get it to latch on. She shrugged, turned off the television, and sat at her desk, staring at the laptop. Almost without conscious thought, she brought up the simulation software. They had added a new module, and with the data that had been extracted from Keith's report, it would be possible to bring it into the simulation for the first time.

She brought her storm on screen, Hurricane Andrea. At the beginning of the simulation it was still far up the gulf, significantly smaller, but moving quickly. Next, she loaded in the new module—the barges. She had the capability of using from one to twenty-five barges. Currently they didn't have the funds to allocate any more, and if their calculations were correct, and they were able to prove their findings to the government, there would be no need for any further construction. Andrea felt the years bunched at her back, ready to spring.

Even if the government took the program over and brought back Operation Stormfury, she would not be the one to lead it. She had been doing this for too long, fighting the storms, watching them wash over Florida and North Carolina, Ivan—heading north, and then cutting back south and then north again, washing over Louisiana while southern Florida was slammed by storm after storm. It was time for her to get one in the win column, and then settle down.

She pulled up all twenty-five of the barges. The experiment had given them good, solid numbers on the temperature difference that the units could create, and how long it took to make such a difference. Keith's people had input the data that morning, so it was all ready for her to manipulate and study. They also had good data on how long it took to get the units towed into place and operational.

These had been the only figures necessary to complete the

simulation module that allowed her to test them against the real thing. With the software she could pit the barges against the biggest, baddest storm she'd ever seen, and she could change the variables and adjust that simulation until she had it exactly right. She might never see another storm like Andrea—prayed that she did not—but whatever storm she did come up against, she wanted to be sure that it came out the clear loser.

She attached the barges in fives to a series of large, ocean-going tugboats, two groups of five leaving from near the complex in North Carolina, one from Bermuda, where it was staged, and the other two groups of five barges from the Norfolk area—though two of these barges were still dry-docked, she used the full force for this initial test. Once she had them on course and moving into place, and their positions fixed in her mind, there was nothing left to do but to wait.

Andrea knew how warm the water had been off Bermuda that day so long ago. She knew how fast the wind had been blowing, and how far beyond the outer wall of the storm the weather problems spread. There were few details of the storm she couldn't recite like a child's poem. She had studied that storm for so long it had become a part of her.

It wouldn't be easy to get the barges into position, but it was not impossible. The last thing she sent out was a pair of very fast cutters that trailed behind the main group. Once the units were in place, detached and anchored, these smaller, faster craft would pick up the crews from the barges and hightail it out of there, heading off at a right angle from the storm and shooting for clear, open water.

They would be cutting it close, but Andrea believed the two boats would have time to get everyone on board and get out before the worst of the storm could hit. They only needed to get far enough away that the boats would not be swamped.

Her crews were experienced and fearless—she'd picked them partially for these qualities. Once they were away from the main wall of the storm, they would turn into whatever weather they were too slow to evade and ride it out.

In the case of the simulation before her, it wouldn't matter. All of the boats would escape on the Bermuda side, and the storm itself, once it reached the slick of glittering peanut oil, would move to the left—to the southwest. Once they had convinced the experts that their data was supportable in a real world scenario, and the government was on board, and the units were deployed on a more permanent basis, running part of each month to create a temperature barrier against hurricanes, when they were in season, escape wouldn't be a problem. The units could very likely be automated, and in any case, they would have a lot more lead-time. She was giving this test the worst-case scenario, as she saw it.

The barges moved slowly. She'd sped up the time scale considerably because she didn't want to spend days sitting in front of her computer screen for each simulation, but it was still a lengthy process. The tugboats and barges ground their way slowly across the screen, turning well west and a little south of the storm and stretching out in a long line. She had set them to drop at fifteen-mile intervals. It might not be close enough, but she thought that it would. With the huge compressors in operation, five to a barge, the amount of cold water displaced from the depths would be staggering. There might not be a solid wall of cold in the hurricane's path, but what there was would be intense and concentrated near each barge and would spread outward, mostly in the direction of the storm.

The barges were placed with the five-pump side facing the storm, and the three pumps on the opposite side spreading the wall of chilled water further along the storm's path. If it managed to retain its strength past the beginnings of the "wall," it would have to cross past the point where the far-side pumps effect ended.

As the tugs passed each point on the screen where she had placed a marker, a barge dropped free of one of the chains and a small timer appeared on its deck. This represented the expected amount of time it would take to anchor the barge and get the pumps running. This time, like the transit time, had been accelerated. Andrea knew that it would take, on average, about two hours for all the equipment to be in place and activated once it was on site. It might take considerably less, but that was the least amount of time she felt comfortable allotting the process. It would take a little longer for the cutters to tie up to each barge and take the five crewmembers off of each platform.

Her fingers shook, and she rose, turning toward the coffee. She wouldn't do the program or the test any good by sitting and staring at it, no matter how hard she might wish she could. Trying to ignore the screen as it flickered and shifted behind her, Andrea rinsed out her coffee cup, dropped in two spoonfuls of sugar and a small packet of creamer.

She didn't have to be sitting in front of the simulation to see it. She took her cup and moved to her favored spot and stared out over the complex from the huge front window. The heat from her coffee caused a momentary spot of fog on the thick glass. She knew that the cell had fully formed by this point. She could see the outer curls stutter flashing across the screen, as if the eye of a hurricane was like a human heart, pulsing and beating, pouring its strength into the wind and the rain and churning up the waves with unseen appendages below.

Andrea didn't know who'd coined the term "eye" of the hurricane, but she thought that whoever it had been should have been able to watch the storm on her computer simulation before making the call. If they'd seen what she saw, day in and day out, they would have called it the heart of the hurricane, not the eye. The storm was blind in its fury. If it could see, it wasted no compassion or interest on what it found in its path.

She turned away from the window and returned to her seat. The barges were lined up in a semi-circle just to the left of and below the approaching storm. She initialized the oil slick and watched the glittering graphic representation spread across the waves. She could have programmed in aircraft and dropped the oil in balloons as they had done so long ago, but that would have led to the temptation to create authentic looking seed planes as well, and one of those planes would not make it home from the simulation. It was hard enough to relive her failure time and time again without adding the pain of cartoon versions of her husband dropping into the ocean and disappearing forever to the show.

It wasn't important how the slick got onto the water, or how the silver iodide was introduced into the storm. The seeding had not been a factor, as far as they knew. The slick had been placed so far ahead of schedule, thanks to the malfunctioning timepieces, that most of what had happened—whatever that might have been—was over before the three planes she knew had delivered their seed packages were in position. She assumed that Phil had been in position as well, and further assumed that his silver iodide pellets had been dropped into the suddenly—and impossibly—larger storm.

Either way, she didn't believe that it would make much of a difference. In fact, she'd run the simulation a number of times without including the silver iodide with little visible difference in the outcome. There just wasn't enough useful data to attribute major changes to that portion of their operation.

She wouldn't have included the seeding at all, but she wanted everything to be portrayed as accurately as possible.

Below the storm, the small boats filled with the teams who would light off the barge equipment pulled away at an angle down past the lower edge of Cuba and out to sea. The devices themselves blinked from their original orange color to bright yellow, signifying they had come on line. The first of them had been live for some minutes—the last came to life shortly after the boats pulsed away.

Andrea glanced at the figures tabulated at the bottom of the screen. She knew what the water temperature had been when she began, a balmy seventy-eight degrees. She watched closely, and slowly—almost imperceptibly at first, and then as the computer performed its algorithmic calculations on the volume of displaced water and the amount of heat exchanged during the process, the number dipped. Seventy-seven—a long pause—then seventy-six and seventy-five in rapid progression.

The storm drew closer, nearly ready to collide with the slick and take its kamikaze lunge at the U.S. coastline, but before it could do so the barges kicked into high gear. The speed of the temperature drop increased, and in a moment it held steady at just under sixty-two degrees. The devices—if the calculations were correct, and she believed that they were close, if not perfect—could drop the temperature of the water sixteen degrees in a matter of only a few moments. She knew the temperature would continue to decrease slowly as more and more of the warmer upper layers were dispersed or replaced with the cold, deep water forced up by the compressed air pumps.

The storm crashed into the wall of the oil slick and spun hard. Wind speed increased dramatically, and with a familiar and gut-wrenching whipping motion, it shot down the length of the sparkling patch that depicted the oil and curled off away from Bermuda on a northwest course. It was heading straight into the path she had known it would take. This foreknowledge was an advantage she would not have with a natural storm, but this was a simulation, and she needed to know what would happen if she got everything exactly right, not what might happen if a rogue storm canted off course and made a beeline for the Cayman Islands.

The temperature had continued to drop, and was approaching fifty-eight degrees. A shift of nearly twenty degrees in such a short period of time was more significant than she had expected. Her mind worked at a similar speed to that of the computer, but she was able to slip off on odd vectors when her imagination dragged her. It was the heat exchange that had eluded her in her initial estimate. She had not accounted for how much more quickly the change could be spread once the water being displaced and the water displacing it had a chance to approach one another's temperature.

It took less energy to drop the temperature of water at sixty degrees than it did to drop the temperature of water at seventy-eight degrees, and the same amount of energy was being expended. It hurried the process. The only thing in question now was—would it be enough? Would *anything* be enough?

She watched the graphic of small particles dropping over the storm wall flash. The silver iodide had been delivered. The storm gained in strength so quickly and to such an impossible level, that Andrea had the urge—as she always did—to press back away from the computer, as if it might explode from within and drive shards of plastic into her skin with its force. The winds soared to a sustained speed of over two hundred miles per hour, and the entire mass of the hurricane picked up speed, traveling across the water at around twenty-five miles per hour.

The temperature near the barges had dropped to fifty-five degrees and held. It was unlikely it would drop further before the storm reached that point, but it should be more than enough. Fifty-five degrees was well below the temperature the storm needed to maintain a tight "eye," and without the eye even the most powerful of storms was just a bunch of rain clouds blowing over the water. It would falter, fizzle, and die out before it ever made landfall. That, at least, is what she hoped would happen.

On her screen, the storm reached the outer edges of the temperature controlled water. She had developed the barge module so that it colored the water that had been affected in shades of light blue, the coldest point being almost white, centered around the devices themselves, while the cold that radiated out from that point was shaded in gradations of darker and dark blue until the point beyond the range of the barge's influence, where the water was such a dark blue it was almost black.

The storm passed out of the dark water and into the first layer of lighter blue without hesitation. There was no noticeable slowing of wind speed, and no effect on the eye. With the high-speed rendering capability of the simulation controlling things, Andrea watched in fascination as the storm rolled up and over the cold front. The outer reaches of the storm swirled over the barges, and at that point all that was visible were the numbers at the bottom of her screen, and the eye itself.

She thought it was going to slide right over the barges, swallow them whole, and continue on its course, but it did not. As the eye neared the cold zone, she saw the outer wall thinning. A break in the wall of the eye itself appeared, and then another. The storm, rather than continuing forward, hesitated. She was reminded of a huge spider, stopping and drawing back on its haunches, seeking in every direction and looking for a target at which to strike.

The storm slid over and past the area where the barges were anchored. Though the eye was destabilized, it fought to reform. She watched, bit her tongue sharply and tasted blood. Her hands gripped the arms of her seat so tightly her knuckles went bloodless and pale from the strain. The storm slowed. The mass of clouds still moved toward the U.S. coastline, but not as rapidly as before.

It had dropped from twenty-five miles per hour down to about twelve, and showed signs of further slowing. The eye, which had been a tight, pulsing black whole in the center of it all, spread into a vaguely oval shape and grew ragged around its edges. Wind speed dropped quickly to a hundred and fifty miles per hour, and then fell away drastically. There were still huge, wild gusts of air, but the storm was disintegrating.

As it passed over the area where the barges had been placed, Andrea watched the screen carefully. In the very center, there was nothing. The barges that had blinked bright yellow after activation were simply not there at all. That was two. On the upper end, toward the north end of the line, two groups of five barges still floated. One was still bright yellow; half of the others had returned to their original orange color, indicating they were no longer likely to be active. The barges had been rated for the amount of damage, the height and severity of waves and the strength of wind they could withstand. She'd been resigned to losing all, or most of the equipment, but as the last wisps of what had been the largest Category Five hurricane in history—albeit for a very brief span of time—passed over that line, she saw that three of the five groups were still in place, and one was still active, pumping away. It had been enough. Her wall of cold water had ruined the storm's continuity, shredding it like soft cotton caught on barbed wire.

Andrea leaned back in her chair, laid her head against the top, and stared at the ceiling as green traces of rain and thunderstorms made landfall on her computer screen. She stayed that way for a while, then sat up, halted the simulation, and saved the results. With the patience of long obsession, she reset the controls and restarted the simulation. She varied conditions and locations slightly and let the program run, rising and walking back to her place by the window.

Gazing down at the empty hangar, she placed her hand on the chilly glass and laid her forehead against it. Closing her eyes, she whispered. "Send me a storm, Phil. Send me a storm so I can rest."

No one answered from the shadowy complex, and after a few minutes she dimmed the lights and lay back on her bed. Elvis leaped up onto the mattress and curled in beside her, lifted her arm with his cold, wet nose and insinuated himself beneath with a soft "Whuff." Andrea smiled, scratched his ear, and drifted off to sleep as the laptop continued to cycle the storm silently across its screen.

Chapter Sixteen

Andrea awakened out of a dead sleep into darkness. Flashing lights strobed through the windows, and Elvis was up, paws on the sill, staring into the night. He let out a short bark, almost a growl, and ran to the next window, where he repeated his action.

Andrea thought her alarm was ringing, but even as she reached out to grope for the clock and stop it, she knew that wasn't right. Her alarm was set for daybreak, and that was hours away. The sound she heard was the phone. She swung her legs off the side of her bed, closed her eyes, blinked to clear her thoughts, and grabbed the receiver off its hook.

"This is Andrea," she said groggily. "Who is this? What . . ."

"It's Keith." The reply had no inflection at all. It was terse, as if the words had been bitten from something and clamped between his jaws. Then he went on. "I'm in the control center. Get down here."

The line went dead, and Andrea sat, staring at it. A low siren rose to join the flashing lights below. Her first thought was fire, or the police, but she dismissed these quickly. The flashing light was green. That was an internal alarm meant to awaken the staff and put them on alert.

It didn't take long for her to slip into jeans, sneakers, a T-shirt, and her lab coat. She didn't even bother looking into a mirror; there was no time to tame her unruly hair, or to stop and wash the sleep from her eyes. She wasn't sure how she knew this, but she did. Keith had never once, in all the years she had known him, spoken to her as he had on the phone, and what she'd heard in the tone of his voice had both thrilled and terrified her.

Elvis trotted at her heel, glancing up and down the passageway as they went, and pausing for a second to sniff the elevator before stepping in at her side. The dog sensed something. Andrea sensed it too—electricity in the air that she'd never felt before.

"What is it, boy?" she asked, reaching down to pat the bulldog's head. "What in the hell is it?"

Elvis had no answer for her, and the elevator doors opened on the first floor with a soft whoosh. There were small groups of technicians and engineers gathered in different corners of the main lobby, and Andrea thought this strange. They had a night shift, but it wasn't this populous. Most of those gathered held coffee cups cupped between both hands and looked, as she knew she must look, as if they'd been dragged straight out of their beds and placed here on display.

Andrea barely nodded at the others as she passed through their midst and pressed the button to open the computer room. Though the equipment had come a long way over the years, some habits died hard. The room was climate controlled and, as much as possible, they kept it dust-free as well. The equipment housed inside—computers, radar consoles, and communications sets—was not as delicate as earlier models had been, but the extra precautions made Andrea feel better, and seemed to please their insurance company as well.

She walked quickly down the center aisle to the control center at the far wall. This was a slightly raised portion of the floor lined with monitors; radarscopes, radio consoles, and a confusing array of computer control panels and tape drive units. In the center was a table, similar to a U.S. Navy chart table, but computerized. The mechanical arm that stretched out across the surface of the map moved slowly, scribing something onto the paper's surface, but Andrea didn't notice.

As she drew closer, she saw that Keith and two others were gathered around a large monitor screen. On the screen was the same radar image that Andrea had checked just before going to bed, the Atlantic, just off the coast of Bermuda. It was the same, that is, with one glaring exception. Where Andrea had seen only bright green patches of rain, the screen was white. White and pulsing with that familiar, hungry heartbeat centered on a tight core so dark it seemed to draw her forward the last few steps.

Andrea pushed through the others, slipped around Keith, and laid her fingers directly on the screen. It was the storm—her storm—Andrea. It was exactly as it had been, exactly where it had been. She glanced down at the dials and gasped breath into her lungs so quickly and harshly that her head spun and she reeled, nearly fainting. The dial was set for the live radar feed—it was no simulation.

The storm had taken the expected lurch toward the coast. There was no slick of peanut oil on that water, as if it were coming back *after* it hit the slick, jumping back through time.

"I . . ." she tried to speak, but nothing came out. She knew she should be breathing, but that was beyond her as well.

Keith and one of the technicians grabbed her by her arms, supported her and dragged her back so that she fell heavily into one of the padded leather chairs. Her eyes never left the screen, and it was taking too long to get her breath. Finally it came in a startled gasp, and she sucked the air quickly. Leaning forward, she lowered her head, just for a moment, and forced her mind to clear and her heart to function normally. She had to think.

"That's not all," Keith said, leaning close with one hand on her shoulder.

Andrea raised her head and turned her uncomprehending face toward his. "What do you mean?"

"We've been in contact with the Navy and the Air Force," Keith replied. "They have been tracking this almost as long as we have, and they've picked up something our radar has not.

"There's an unidentified aircraft coming in about five thousand feet over the storm. They've tried to raise it on the radio, but have had no luck. They are sending out intercept craft, but I told them I thought they might have better luck with their radio if they dropped back to an older frequency. They're trying that now."

Andrea's eyes grew wide. She turned and stared at the screen.

"Get the other radar image up," she said, suddenly regaining control of her mind and her body. "Overlay it onto the storm image. Find that plane."

"Already on it," one of the assistants, a tall girl named Alicia Kotz called out. "We aren't really set up to do it any longer—not since we cancelled the seeding program."

"Just get it on the screen," Andrea replied, knowing she was being too curt and absolutely unable to control it.

Tears threatened to spill out the corners of her eyes, and she gripped the arms of her chair too tightly. Her heart was working too hard, and she knew she had to get a grip on herself. There was no way to be certain—yet—what had been spotted, but there were things to do—things that had to be done, and she couldn't do any of them if she was carted off into an ambulance and taken away.

"How long do we have?" Andrea asked quickly. She already knew the answer, but getting the others thinking and moving was vital.

"Two, maybe three days before it's too late," Keith answered at once. They had both seen the simulation run so many times that it played in their dreams.

Andrea had lost Phil, but it was Keith whose theory had placed that slick in the storm's path. If it had not disappeared all those years in the past, it was Keith who felt responsible for the disaster that followed, and now that disaster had come back to haunt him—to haunt them both.

"I mobilized all teams," Keith told her. "I knew you'd do the same, but even the extra half an hour it saved us may make all the difference."

"Can we get all twenty-five barges into place?" Andrea asked him. "Is it possible?"

Keith shook his head. "The two in dry dock aren't ready. We couldn't even get them out and floating in time, let alone operational. That leaves us with twenty-three. Of those, I'm ninety-nine percent certain of eighteen. If we could get them all underway this minute, it would be one thing, but if we hold up the tug in the Caymans until all five of his are gathered, he might not have time to make the transit. The storm is moving . . ."

"At twenty-five miles per hour," Andrea finished. "I know. God . . . I know."

She studied the bottom of the screen. The readouts were very similar to those that displayed at the bottom of her simulation program screen. The wind speed of the storm was incredible. It was well over two hundred miles per hour, and showed signs of increasing.

"The water temperature is lower than it should be," she said, thinking out loud.

"This year has been cooler, overall," Keith agreed. "That

should work in our favor. The damned thing may have pounded its way back through some weird, psychic wall in the air, but it didn't bring the ocean with it. The water is still warm enough, though—warm enough to sustain a storm."

Andrea nodded distractedly. Eighteen. They were only going to get eighteen of the barges into place in time—assuming that they were in time at all, and that her simulation was more than a clever video game for old storm-obsessed women with nothing better to do than play God. Her mind shifted back to the night before. Twenty-five were enough, according to the simulation, but how much of reality did that really cover? How much of what they thought they knew did they really know?

People respected storms after the past year, but they didn't understand how deep that respect should go. They didn't understand, on the average, that a Category Two hurricane made the destructive force that hit Hiroshima look like a child's antique tin toy hammer stacked up against a twenty-pound sledge. Mostly the world got lucky.

The coast of the United States was famous for dodging direct hits, and even those that had not been dodged could always have been worse. There had never been a threat like this, and once the word spread out through the weather networks, NOAA, and the unstable, inefficient official channels of the government, the entire east coast was going to be in panic.

Andrea held up her hand to silence anything any of the others might be about to say. "Two things," she said calmly. "We have got to get our people moving faster than they have ever moved before, and we have got to convince the government to call for an evacuation. They won't want to do it. They'll want to look, and stand around with their thumbs up their noses and stare at readouts—check on the weather channel—a million other things than getting on their phones, radios, and faxes and getting the truth out about this storm.

"We can tell them that truth. I have a hundred saved simulations of this storm striking the coast. At least a hundred," she mused, thinking for a second. "We need to get these out there and into the hands of the people that can make things happen. We have to show them and we have to *convince* them—and we have to get them moving. That is going to be the hardest thing we face.

"Our people know what to do. I have no doubt we will get our equipment where it needs to be, and that brave men and women will race out there to risk their lives for this . . . battle." Her voice broke, suddenly, and her eyes filled with tears. "I know this," she went on, clearing her throat and brushing the tears away impatiently. "I also know that as ready as we are for this, the rest of the world is going to be equally stubborn in ignoring it. People are going to die. The TV is going to start spitting nonsense about duct taping windows and buying a lot of bottled water and they are *not* going to understand, or believe, what is coming, unless we force them."

Andrea spun to Keith. "I want you to be the one to do that, Keith," she said. Then she continued, speaking quickly and still holding up her hand to forestall his reply. "I know. I know you want to be on that first tugboat out of here, and I know you want to be on site to manage the setup. You could do it, I know you could, and you hate this storm almost as much as I do.

"But this one is on me. I don't have a lot of boat cruises left in me, but I have enough left for this one. If I stayed behind to try and convince the government what was about to happen . . ." Her voice trailed off.

"Keith," she turned to him and took his hands, "I have to be the one to go. If that's Phil up there," she nodded toward the screen, where the storm now had been joined by a pulsing radar blip—an aircraft, "then I can't be here when he lands. If he lands. I can't trust that I'll do what needs to be done, or that I'll even care."

Andrea's hands shook and she willed them to stop. She kept her voice as calm as possible. "You will get the work done here as well as I could, and I will get the barges into place. If it works out that we both make it through whatever is to come, I'll be able to face him then."

Keith wanted to protest, she saw it in his eyes, but in the end he must have seen something in hers as well. He nodded at last. "The tug leaving from here is already being fueled," he said gruffly. "The barges we brought in yesterday are being staged and should be back at the harbor within a couple of hours. There are some minor repairs needed, but I've ordered all the equipment, and a couple of extra men, so that the repairs can be made en route. We can't afford to leave even a single pump behind."

"I'll be ready to leave in under an hour," she told him. Then, as if just remembering he was there, she leaned down and patted Elvis on the head.

"You're going to have to stay with Keith," she told him. "But I'll be back."

The dog gazed up at her, his head cocked and his eyes bright. If someone had told her in that instant that he understood every word she said, she would have believed. She could still hear his ancestor, Jake, barking at the storm, barking at the house collapsing over his mistress, and her father. She still felt his cold, damp fur pressed against her under the wool blanket on the Coast Guard cutter that had saved them that long ago day. She could even smell the wet dog smell that had filled her nostrils for days afterward—long, confused days that blurred together in her memory.

"I know," she said, her eyes blurry with tears and burning. She knelt and hugged the dog tightly, and he licked salty tears from her cheeks and whined low in his throat. "I know, buddy, but it's going to be all right."

Then she was up and moving, striding as quickly down the center aisle of the computer banks as her wobbly legs would carry her. She didn't look back, and she hoped to God that either Elvis would sit tight, or Keith would grab the dog's collar. She had used up all the emotional energy available to her, and she had very little strength of any other kind to get her through the next few hours. There would be time to rest once they were underway, but not before then.

She wanted desperately to rush to her room and set up the simulation with only eighteen of the barges, but she knew there was no time. It wouldn't matter anyway. The most powerful software program in the world, running on the fastest computer, could not replace reality, or reproduce it. Random chance played too large a factor to be accounted for by simple logic.

Andrea exited the clean area and headed straight for the elevators. All the others who had stood around drinking coffee a few moments before had disappeared. She saw groups of men working quickly out on the lot, and the lights above the equipment bays glowed brightly through the high windows of the two outbuildings where the barges had been taken just the day before. She hoped that the repairs necessary were as minor as Keith had said. They were already going to be operating on too few pumps, and this storm was no tropical depression, it was a rampaging monster. The barges would have to be at full capacity to handle the beating they were about to have administered to them.

The elevator slid open, and she stepped inside. When it opened on her floor she hurried to her office and apartment, already going over what she would need to bring with her and trying to anticipate what she might forget and regret. As she entered the office, though, the window caught her attention. Maybe it was just the flashing green lights below, or the sound of some of the equipment. Maybe she'd caught a reflection from truck headlights winking off the glass.

Whatever it had been, it drew her without any hope of denial. She stepped to the glass, planted both of her palms against it and stared off into the darkened sky. The very first glimmer of daylight rimmed the horizon, and as her eyes adjusted, she saw that there were clouds overhead. They didn't coat the sky, but were scattered across it in long, thin strips.

She strained her eyes and scanned the distance, but there was nothing to see. She didn't know why she had thought there would be, but something had tugged at her heart. He was up there—she knew it, though she couldn't have told why. He was up there, maybe dropping a load of silver iodide pellets into a monster. He would bank away from that storm, if he could, and he would fly home. He had always been flying home. She wished she could be there to greet him.

At that instant, she almost wavered and called Keith. She could stay with Elvis. The building was designed to handle a storm exactly like the one that was coming, and even if everything went wrong, and they failed, as they were as likely to do as not, she could ride it out. She could be there when that plane cut over the horizon and came in low, looking for a landing field that was overgrown now and planted with gardens. She could be on the radio with him, guiding him to a safe landing somewhere nearby, and be there to greet him when he climbed down from the cockpit.

The clouds glowed, and the sun peeked into view. The

sky, which had been a light rosy pink, ran slowly to a deep, bloody red. Andrea closed her tear-filled eyes and turned away. She had to pack, and she had to get moving. If she'd doubted it, God had sent her a quick note, written in dripping ink across a brightening morning sky.

She hoped that she wasn't too late.

Chapter Seventeen

In a small wooden building far too close to the beach in Bermuda, Gabrielle Martinez hunkered down beneath the frame of a window, her arms wrapped around her knees. The wind outside howled with a force that drove the breath from her, and she knew from the way the walls shuddered at each fresh gust that the building wouldn't take much more.

They'd long since lost power, and Jason, who had been sitting with her over evening tea, had crawled into the next room to try and locate a radio. They kept some old military surplus communications devices tucked away for emergencies, and he was determined that he would use what he had to contact someone who could help.

Gabrielle let him go, despite her sure and certain knowledge that his efforts would make no difference. No radio signal was going to get through this storm, and if it did, just who in hell would they call? Still, it kept the younger man occupied, and that was better than having him sitting beside her, talking too much and working himself into a panic.

The wind hadn't built gradually, as Gabrielle had known storms to do in the past. One moment there had been a light evening rain falling, they'd had the BBC on the radio, and the most important thing the two of them had had to discuss was how to market the fish they were producing most effectively. As much as they, and Andrea, wanted to do their part to end world hunger, things like artificial fish farms were not cheap.

The business had to turn enough profit not only to stay in operation, but also to grow and to attract the sort of support and personnel that could make a success of it.

Charity was well and good, but you had too little control over where the actual food ended up, and it didn't really help to pay the bills, unless you counted the tax cut it provided.

Then the world caved in on them. The wind slashed out of nowhere and nearly ripped the roof off over their heads. Gabrielle had never heard such a roar, and a quick glance out the window before she'd hit the floor and cowered against the wall had shown her smaller buildings that were not faring as well as her own. The laboratory and dormitory they lived in had been designed along specifications that Andrea had developed over many years of study. The building was meant to withstand hurricane force winds better than any that had come before, and so far it seemed to be living up to expectations, but this was no ordinary hurricane.

In fact, unless all the rules Gabrielle knew about hurricanes were hogwash, it should not be there at all. Storms don't just blow up out of the air. Tornadoes could form that quickly, but this wasn't a tornado. The winds were sustained, and they covered the land as far as she could see.

Jason crawled back around the corner. Just as he did, a huge gust of wind shook the windows in their frames, and Gabrielle was certain they would be yanked physically from the wall and thrown across the room. Jason put his head down, covered it with his arms, and let out a strangled cry, but the window held. A moment later, when he realized he was going to live at least a few seconds longer, Jason lifted his head and scurried across the remaining space as quickly as he could, dragging a green metal box behind him by a strap.

As Jason's back came to rest beside hers against the wall, Gabrielle glanced down at the green case in curiosity. Jason flipped open several heavy metal catches on the sides. When the final catch released there was a quick hiss of escaping air, and Gabrielle realized the case was airtight and sealed.

Inside was a small rectangular radio. There was also a long, folding green antenna, a microphone on its coiled cord, and another piece of metal that appeared to be an end-cap of some sort. After Jason had the unit out of its box and had begun fiddling with it, Gabrielle realized this last piece was the battery. She hoped that Jason, or someone, had taken the time to charge that battery. Then, catching herself, she almost smiled. No one was going to hear the transmission anyway, so what did the strength of the battery matter?

But something had changed. Jason sensed it too, and glanced up at her. The wind was still strong, but not *as* strong. The walls shook with each succeeding gust, but not as they had shaken before. The sense that the building and everything in it was about to be ripped up and thrown aside was passing.

Jason turned quickly back to the radio and screwed in the antenna. Next he clipped the battery unit to the rear of the radio and flipped the power to on. There were several bands on the radio—crystals installed inside the radio itself determined the frequencies.

This radio had been tuned for emergency channels, and for one channel they used among themselves. Each of the fish farms had a remote transceiver installed in a weather-sealed compartment on one of its buoys. Jason flipped through the channels. All they heard at first was static. There were quick popping bursts of sound that broke through, but none of it seemed to be actual traffic. He tried three emergency channels one after the other, but either no one was broadcasting yet, or no one close enough to do so still had the capability.

The wind died down further, and Gabrielle risked pulling herself up to look out the window.

Everything in sight had been flattened. Everything. Trees lay down across the ground, some of them as big around as the trunk of her body. There had been several outlying buildings around them, small places where they kept things like coiled rope and lawn tools. Now, there was nothing. No foundations, no walls, and certainly no lawn tools. Gabrielle fervently hoped that none of what had blown away from outside her place had harmed anyone in another place.

"We should have tied it all down, or put it away," she said.

Jason looked up from the radio, where he'd just made his third circuit of the frequency switch without finding anything but static. "We should have tied down what?"

Gabrielle made a vague gesture toward the yard beyond the walls. "Our things. Our buildings, the tools—all of it. When there's a hurricane coming, you're supposed to . . ."

"Are you nuts?" he asked her, maybe a little too bluntly. His eyes were very wide, and he stared at her in amazement. "There was never any time when this hurricane was coming. We didn't hear about it on the news and decide not to evacuate. One minute it was raining, and the next the big bad wolf was at the door threatening to blow it in. Just like that. When do you suppose we would have tied things down?"

Gabrielle knew he was right, but it didn't change her fervent prayer that the shed no longer holding her rake or the small riding lawnmower, had not sheared off some poor, unfortunate man or woman's head, or crushed them with the weight of the storm bearing down from behind. She shook her head and watched as the winds died away to a steady breeze. Rain drummed the roof again, and spattered hard against the window, but if it hadn't been for the destruction surrounding them, and the dim, lightless interior of the room, there would have been no indication that the storm had ever existed.

"What just happened?" she asked. "What in God's name just happened, Jason? What was that?"

He only grunted in answer. Then there was a crackle slightly louder than the static they'd been listening to, and a voice came faintly over the radio.

"Bermuda Station, this is Sierra Foxtrot One, over."

The voice was familiar. It was Andrea's voice, crackling over their private frequency.

Jason gripped the microphone hard and replied. "Sierra Foxtrot One, this is Bermuda Station. You are not going to believe what just happened here, over."

Andrea's reply was clear, but weighted with concern and weariness. "Bermuda Station, we know what happened, over. No time now, more later. Get your people to the barges and get that tug underway. Will contact you once you are at sea. And hurry. For God's sake, hurry. Over."

Jason stared at the microphone in his hand in disbelief. He glanced at Gabrielle, who waved her hand impatiently at the radio. He turned back and keyed the microphone. "Sierra Foxtrot One, this is Bermuda Station. We have heavy damage here, I repeat, heavy damage."

"I know," Andrea replied. Now she sounded impatient, and either irritated or frustrated. "Believe me," she said, ignoring protocol, "I know. I need you out here, Gabrielle, if you're there. I need all of you out here, and quickly. We may already be too late."

Still staring at the microphone in his hand, Jason shook his head. Gabrielle caught the motion and stepped closer, taking the microphone out of his startled hand.

"Andrea, we will be there if we can. We're leaving now. Bermuda Station, out."

She flipped the radio off and held out her hand to Jason, who was staring at her in slack-jawed amazement.

"Get up," she said, grabbing a jacket off of the wall, and pulling her cap down over her eyes. "We have to see if we can find a jeep that will still run, and we have to get to the others. The tug should be safe; it's harbored on the far side of the island. The barges are there as well, to keep them safe. You know that as well as I do."

"But, what about," Jason waved his hands around to indicate the building, the yard with its missing hardware and outbuildings, the power that didn't function.

"It will be here when we get back," Gabrielle replied tersely. "Andrea paid for all of that, if you recall. We aren't likely to keep it at all if we don't get out there and help her do whatever it is she intends to do."

They both knew what Andrea intended. There was only one thing Andrea had ever intended to do, for all her grand talk about world hunger and fish farms. They were going to fight a storm—probably the one that had just brushed past them with such maddening force.

The two bundled their jackets around themselves tightly and stepped out into the rain swept night.

At exactly 11:48 P.M., a large tugboat, the *Santa Muriel*, pulled out of a harbor near downtown Norfolk, Virginia. It had arrived less than a week before with five barges in tow, but it was leaving with only three. The other two remained at the shipyard, up in huge metal dry-docks, where the hulls were being scoured and painted and the pumps were being overhauled, cleaned, and tested.

It was late, but those bustling about the big tug's deck moved with the surety and ease of long practice. Captain Jay Greenwood had his cap tipped back on his head and his hand on the wheel. The tide would only be high enough for their exit for another hour, and with the heavy load they towed, their progress was anything but swift. The *Santa Muriel* was a strong craft, the strongest of its type available, but the barges weren't light.

Just before he'd left port, three teams had embarked on the barges, swarming over the dark surfaces and stowing their gear in the berthing compartments at one end of each barge. The compartments included a small labyrinth of chambers below the main deck; there were bunks, a small kitchenette, and little else. This was no pleasure cruise they were on.

Captain Jay was glad he had his own cabin on the tug itself. It was a hell of a lot more comfortable. He had a ten man crew for this trip; they'd be taking double shifts and sleeping when they could. The call to get underway had come on incredibly short notice, but he'd been warned long before that it might happen just like this. They didn't make many voyages, and when they did, they weren't too taxing, so he didn't mind earning his pay this time.

The rest of it worried him, though. That storm, if it was as big as they said it was, and moving as quickly as they said it was, was going to be trouble. As good a craft as the *Santa Muriel* was, it was not what you wanted to be riding if you got caught in such a storm. The barges were worse still, but he knew the plan as well as any. Once he'd towed them into place they would take over, and he would hightail it for the far side of Bermuda.

The two cutters were fueling, and their crews were being recalled. They would leave the following morning and catch up along the way. Once the barges were operational, the two fast, light boats would pick up the crews, one by one, and get the hell out of Dodge. It made sense, and in theory it would be just fine, but Jay knew theories and trusted them about as far as he could hand-toss the *Santa Muriel.*

He glanced at the small plastic Jesus that dangled from his ship-to-shore radio, and for just a second, he closed his eyes in silent prayer. If he'd had a Saint Christopher's medal, he'd have rubbed it for luck, but all he had was a headache and black coffee, and he figured that was going to have to do. The sun would be up soon, and they had a lot of miles to cover before they could get these barges into position.

Behind him on the barges, pumps were checked over and lubricated. Men and women scurried over each barge's damp, salty deck, moving with smooth, efficient ease. They had practiced for this moment since the first day the barges hit the water. They might not be the answer to the coming storm, but they were ready to find out—and if Andrea had been there, watching them, she'd have to have admitted it was all she could really ask for—and then some. It was going to be a long trip.

Andrea stepped out the front door of the complex as the helicopter touched down. She waited as it settled and the blades began to turn more slowly. They weren't going to stop. When it was safe, a man in a flight suit and helmet motioned to her, and she ran to his side. Over her back she'd slung a canvas knapsack filled with warm clothes and everything she could fit in such a small package that she might conceivably need at sea. In her other hand she carried a heavy briefcase with her laptop, some notes, and a few other odds and ends that hadn't fit in the knapsack.

Reports had been coming in all morning. The storm had veered away from Bermuda. Heavy damage had been sustained from the wind, and there had been a small storm surge, but overall the island had come through okay. Gabrielle's people were working their way across to where their tug and their five barges lay in wait, and the supplemental crews, including those who would pilot the tugboat, were on alert to be on station.

All that remained was for her to reach her own crew, get on board, and get underway. The helicopter would drop her near the docks, and she expected to be on the ocean and moving within the hour. She took a last glance up at the sky through the whirling helicopter blades, and then she looked away before the tears could return. The time for that was past—and still to come. For now she had to focus.

She climbed into the helo, and they shut the door behind her as she strapped in for the ride.

The race was on.

Chapter Eighteen

The wind speed above the storm was greater than Phil had ever encountered, or dreamed possible. He knew that if he tried to turn too rapidly in either direction he'd be caught in the grip of that rushing air and dashed to his death. Visibility was short, and though they seemed to be functioning, his instruments were a little off. He didn't trust the altimeter at all. It fluctuated randomly, and once or twice it spun completely around. Phil figured the sensor had been damaged, and reflected that he was damned lucky if that was all that was damaged. He was able to keep his wings level, and the controls continued to respond normally, and that was enough. It had to be.

He'd lost all radio contact. He knew the time must be long past for seeding the storm wall, but he knew, also, that he couldn't trust his perception of time or distance well enough in such a situation to be certain. With a quick, silent prayer, he flipped the toggles that released the silver iodide pellets. He knew they were trailing off behind him into the wind, swallowed up instantly and dragged into the whirling vortex of air beneath him. He wished he could watch their glittering descent, just to see it with his own eyes and be certain they'd reached the storm's wall, as he intended, but there was nothing to see below, or above.

Phil had flown blind plenty of times. The instruments were as much a part of his senses as his hearing or his eyesight. Without the altimeter, though, he couldn't shake the image of the storm. With visibility so low, it was impossible to judge if he was drifting up, or down, and the thought of getting too low and being sucked into the storm ate at his concentration. It took less than two minutes to drop the entire load of silver iodide, but it might as well have been two years.

The vibration of the aircraft communicated with him through pings and groans, and each time he felt a new flutter, or heard a sound he'd not heard before, he was certain something vital had been dislodged—something had given under the relentless pressure of the wind, and that his life stretched before him measured only in seconds.

The plane held, and his courage held, and at last he was able to reverse the toggles and close off the release mechanism. He breathed a sigh of relief, but only allowed himself that one moment of ease. What came next was going to be tricky—maybe the trickiest bit of flying he'd ever pulled off. He was flying blind and he had to start pulling up and away. He had to stay with the wind, keep himself as level as possible and get to a safe altitude, preferably far above the upper cloud layer where he couldn't even see the damned hurricane, and he had to do it immediately. Even if the plane could withstand more of this, his mind could not.

Slowly, and very carefully, he pulled back on the controls. At first he wasn't sure that the flaps were responding. Was it possible for the wind to move so fast that they didn't have the force to shift? Then he felt the nose rise. He compensated immediately, afraid that if he let the aircraft get too far off level, the wind would catch under the nose and flip him like a pancake. There was a brief shudder, and the turbulence shook him through to the bone, but he felt the familiar lift in his stomach, and knew he was gaining altitude.

What followed was another long, excruciating period of

emptiness. There was nothing to see, nothing, really, to judge his altitude by. The steady grind of his engines was solid and comforting, but the roar of the wind and the storm competed with it, and the balance was nerve-wracking. Then he noted that the clouds above and in front of him were a lighter shade of gray, and a moment later he broke through, soaring above the clouds. The late afternoon sunlight glittered and almost blinded him. Phil closed his eyes, blinked slowly, and leveled off.

He glanced at the instruments and noted that the altimeter read seventeen thousand feet, and seemed to be steady. It might not be totally accurate, but it was close, and it no longer fluctuated or slapped back and forth. This time the relief was immediate and all consuming. He checked his gauges and fuel and found that he was well prepared for his return flight. The turbulence and winds were much less difficult at seventeen thousand feet, and just to be sure he pulled up a little more before dipping his wing and turning toward home.

He still had a couple of hours' flight, and he didn't want to waste any time celebrating his escape from the storm. It was bad luck to celebrate before your wheels struck tarmac and, in fact, Phil wasn't feeling very energetic.

He pulled the Thermos from where he'd stowed it behind his seat. After a few moments of careful maneuvering, he managed to pour himself a fresh cup—still hot—and took a long sip. He didn't exactly feel sleepy, which was good, but he did feel weak. He knew it was probably just an aftershock of the stress of being caught down in that storm out of contact with the world, but it never paid to take chances.

He waited until his cup was empty before he grabbed the microphone. He hoped the other aircraft were on ahead of him, closer to home base and already thinking about a cold beer, or a good dinner. He knew they were all good men, and exceptional pilots, but this had not been any normal flight. It also worried him that he'd lost contact so soon with the cargo planes. Something hadn't been right about the whole mission. The gauges whirling, his watch seeming to lag behind what his mind told him was the correct time, and the communications equipment fritzing out over such a short distance— all of those things were exceedingly strange.

Without communications, it was impossible for him to judge what effect, if any, they'd had. One thing was certain. As he turned and headed for the coast, he saw no indication that the storm had been stopped. In fact, starting just before he'd released his load and pulled up and away, the thing had strengthened. He knew this could just be "The Coil"—the effect that Andrea had explained might be caused by contact with the slick on the ocean's surface. If that were the case, the storm should spin itself right out of existence somewhere behind him.

If not, however, then it was just possible he'd be flying in barely ahead of the damn thing, and that they'd be riding it out together and testing the storm proofing that had been accomplished on the complex itself over the years. That was fine with Phil.

In fact, he had to shake his head and reach for the coffee again. The thought of sitting with Andrea, curled up on a couch, or a bed, waiting out the storm of the century had made him drowsy. He was surprised when, as he started to unscrew the lid of the Thermos, his hand shook.

He set the coffee aside and reached for the microphone on his radio. There would be time enough to pour a fresh cup after he found out what the status was. If there was good news, even coffee would do for an impromptu toast, and he found that he very suddenly wanted it over with if the news was bad. Three other pilots had come up here under his direct supervision, and three others he had hired had risked their lives as well. As he keyed the microphone, he tried to comprehend why he'd just been flying along, his mind drifting, without trying to raise the others.

"This is Sierra Papa One, all units respond. I repeat, this is Sierra Papa One, over."

The radio crackled a couple of times, as if there were signals too distant to be picked up, but there was no response. He tried again, repeating his call, but there was no answer. He thought briefly of the other men, Satalino, Richards, and Pooler, three good pilots, but he didn't allow himself to dwell on the images their names brought to mind. He had no evidence that there was anything wrong. For all he knew his own radio, or the antenna it was attached to, was damaged and not working at all.

Phil flipped the channel and called out again. "Oscar Sierra One, this is Sierra Papa One, please respond, over."

Again his call was met with dead silence. Phil shook his head. He felt weak, and it would be a while before he was in sight of shore, let alone ready to come in for a landing in North Carolina. He knew he had to get his mind focused and cleared, and do it quick.

He flipped the switch one last time, and called out to the other three seed plane pilots. No answer. The cargo planes should have been out of there well ahead of his own men, so he wasn't as surprised not to hear from them, but how long must he have been in that storm? If he'd remained far enough behind the others, paying attention to his malfunctioning watch, had they gone on without him and put enough distance between themselves and the storm that he couldn't reach them? It seemed unlikely, but the radio continued to spit reality at him in short bursts of incoherent static.

If they were out there, they weren't answering. If they

weren't out there, where the hell were they? He wouldn't consider the possibility they were all lost. One, maybe; he knew it hadn't been simple pulling down so close to that monster, and maybe one of them might have lost concentration, or nerve, or even run into one of those waterspouts that had come so close to removing him from the game years before. It was not conceivable to him that the same fate might have met all of the others. They were top-notch pilots in state-of-the-art aircraft. They were trained for this, and they knew what to expect. It had to be his radio.

He reached for the coffee again and ignored the shaking in his fingers. What he could not ignore was the blue veins that crossed the back of that hand, or the deep wrinkles etching his skin.

"Holy mother of God," he whispered.

He turned his attention back to the Thermos, and the cup. Without regard to the hot liquid splashing onto his skin, he filled the plastic cup. The controls were set on auto, and they would hold steady enough—steadier than his hands, or the trip-hammer beat of his heart. He set the cup down on the floor beside him and re-stoppered the Thermos carefully. Spilling the hot coffee on his hands was one thing, if he got it down into his flight suit, or onto some of the controls, he might find himself with even greater troubles.

But was it possible to have greater troubles than looking down at your hand and finding that it was shriveling before your eyes? Could it get worse than to take off in perfect health and find that you could no longer hold your fingers in front of your face without them shaking, and that—by the way—your hand no longer resembled your hand at all, and if it wasn't wearing your U.S. Naval Academy ring and the wrist wasn't encircled by the watch Andrea had given you for your last birthday, it would be difficult to credit it as your own hand at all, even though it moved every time you thought it should, and appeared to extend from the sleeve of your flight suit?

Phil didn't think so. He knew he could glance into the window beside him and catch a glimpse of his face, but he wasn't going to do that. Not now. Not with the ocean beneath him and the controls of this aircraft gripped in his increasingly weak hands, or with the skyline blurring at the edges in ways it had never done before. He didn't want to see gray hair and busy, out-of-control eyebrows. He didn't want to see red veins or cataracts where his clear blue eyes had been. So he didn't look. He stared straight ahead, sipped his coffee, and he flew.

Every five minutes he picked up the microphone and called out. "This is Sierra Papa One, any units in area please respond."

No one answered. He considered going to the emergency frequency, but decided against it. If it turned out he was having some sort of delusion brought on by stress, he might endanger his license, and despite all the sudden physical discomforts, he could still fly. He'd get the plane on the ground, get to Andrea, and there would be time after that to sort out whatever was happening to him. He just needed to get home.

At Norfolk Naval Air Station, there was a flurry of activity. The storm had sent units scurrying in all directions, some trying to get ships underway and out of the possible path of the storm, others working to secure aircraft, or to get them fueled and out of the area before they could be caught on the open tarmac by the hurricane's winds.

There had never been a storm like this one. Meetings were held in barracks, squadrons, detachments, and all of them concerned the same thing. Get out. The base would normally shut down to "essential personnel" but this time there was no staying behind. The hurricane headed their way was huge— beyond the scope of anything they had any experience with, and the immediate concern was to get as much equipment, and as many people out as quickly as possible.

In the tower, however, there was another problem.

Lieutenant Mariner stood, staring out over the crowded runways, wishing he were anywhere else. He had to get his home boarded up. He had sent his wife, Tabitha, and their two children ahead on the road. Getting out ahead of the rush had seemed the best bet, and he knew he'd have to be one of the last out of the base. He didn't mind that, really, except that Tabby would worry.

The airfield was a madhouse, and he felt the tension crackling in the air of the tower more than at any other place— more than at any other time in his life. They were all worried about a thousand other things, personal things, loved ones, homes, and boats—but they had a job to do, and today, of all days, they could not slip. There was too much at stake, and far too much traffic, for distractions.

So fate, of course, had provided one.

"You still have that guy Scharf on the line?" he asked.

The young woman behind and to his left, Petty Officer First Class Hill, had a headset on—pulled back out of the way—and a phone receiver in her hand. She nodded. "Yes sir," she said. "He says that unidentified aircraft will answer if we change frequency. He also says it will answer to the call sign Sierra Papa One, but he doesn't say how he knows this."

Lieutenant Mariner nodded absently. He was staring down at where a truck, one he'd just told to hold its position on the far side of a runway, pulled out and started forward. A P3 Orion, barreling down the runway on its takeoff run, pulled up early and soared just over the top of the truck, which suddenly lurched forward, spinning rubber.

"Get that idiot up here," Mariner barked.

Then, turning to Petty Officer Hill, he said, "Get someone on one of the old VHF sets and tune in that frequency. Get that guy out there on the horn and direct him here. I don't know how we're going to fit him into the pattern, but he can't land down where he's headed. There's a thunderstorm front there already, ahead of the storm. Visibility is next to nothing, and there are some pretty serious wind gusts.

"We may have to arrest him later, when the time comes, but for now we have to get him, and every other pilot out there, down, fueled, and out of here before this storm hits."

"What about Mr. Scharf?" she asked him.

"Tell him we'll do what we can."

Petty Officer Hill nodded, repeated what she'd been told, and hung up the phone. Then she rose, exited the tower and headed down to the radio room below to find someone who could get the old, out-of-date frequency tuned in. Their sets in the tower were patched into radios that were kept in racks below. The radios each had assigned frequencies, and this was not one she was familiar with. It would take a few minutes she knew, but that was okay. The tower was insane, and any time spent away from it was a wonderful break.

The aircraft they were trying to reach had shown up on radar about an hour before. The first reports were from two ships. They reported it as having U.S. markings, very old, propeller driven, and not answering to calls on any frequency. The pilot was keeping it steady at about seventeen thousand feet, and it was coming from the direction of the storm.

They knew nothing of the flight. There was no flight plan filed anywhere, she had checked personally, and the airfield that the caller, Scharf, had told her the pilot was headed for had not been operational in over a decade. None of it made any sense, and Scharf had been just evasive enough on the phone to make her nervous. The last thing they needed in the middle of all the chaos the storm had brought was some lunatic terrorist in an antique plane thrown into the mix.

She didn't like the way that was the first thing she thought of, but in the past few years there had just been too many bad incidents for her to shake the possibility free from her mind. What good would it do a terrorist to attack in the face of a hurricane? Even if they caused damage, the odds were it would all be erased in the coming disaster, and in any case it would take second fiddle to the storm in the news.

She stepped to the door of the radio room and buzzed. Access was controlled, and she had to wait until someone opened the window in the center of the door and peered out at her before she could be let in. She knew most of the techs, and they were usually happy to see her, but she saw immediately that things were no less tense here than they were at the top of the tower.

The guy who let her in, Petty Officer First Class Howe, smiled quickly, but was moving away almost as soon as his hand left the doorknob.

"We've had some systems go down," he explained as he walked. "I have to finish this alignment or we'll lose 121.5."

She nodded. The frequency was one of the standard air-control frequencies, and she knew how critical it was. She watched as he stepped onto a short stool, stuck a long, very thin screwdriver into a hole on top of one of the receiver's electronic modules, and turned it slowly. He watched a meter that was built into the rack carefully. The needle swung up, back down, and then, eventually evened out on the large zero in the center. With a grunt of satisfaction, he stepped down, released the catches on the rails that held the receiver and slid it back into the rack, fastening the screws on either sides with quick twists of his thumbs and forefingers.

"How can I help you, Katie?" he asked, turning back.

The two had known one another for a long time, and suddenly it felt good to be in the presence of someone she didn't have to worry so much about upsetting. "Lieutenant Mariner wants this frequency dialed up on anything you've got available for it," she said, handing over the sheet of paper. "He wants you to patch it through as soon as possible."

He took the paper; glanced at it, then back up at her. "Now?" he asked dubiously.

She nodded. "We have a crazy guy out there in some kind of antique plane. He was supposed to be landing down in North Carolina—at least that's what we've been told. The only thing is, there's no active airport at the place he's headed for—hasn't been for nearly twenty years, and we can't get this guy on the radio."

"So why this frequency?" Howe asked. "This is old. I remember it from training, but we haven't used this actively for years. They might still use it in Europe somewhere, or NATO, but . . ."

"That's what's weird about it," she nodded agreement. "But the guy who called us with that frequency—Scharf was his name—was patched through from Washington. General Lynch himself authorized it and told Lieutenant Hill to do anything we can to help them, and to get this plane on the ground safely. It's all weird, and this is the worst time in the world for it—you know?"

Howe nodded and smiled at her. "You holding up okay?"

"I'm fine," she replied, "just nervous is all. You know me. Can you get that tuned for me?"

"It will take a few minutes. I'll give you a call when it's live."

"Thanks, Jack," she said. Then, seeing that he was already moving and already distracted by the banks of transceivers, receivers, and other equipment, she turned away and slipped out the door and up the stairs to her desk. It was going to be a long, long day.

Phil blinked at the clouds below and frowned. There was no way to deny it; his eyesight was not what it had been that morning. He could see the clouds, but they blurred at the edges. He had to squint at the gauges on his control panel to make them out in detail, and he was tired. He was, in fact, more tired than he could ever remember being, and the drone of the engines threatened to drive him over the edge into sleep.

He was tempted to drop down a few thousand feet. The coast would be in view shortly, and he very much wanted to see it, but he was afraid. It was almost a superstitious fear, like a few moments earlier when he hadn't wanted to look at his own reflection.

What if he dropped down and couldn't see land? What if he was within fifty miles of the shoreline, but his eyes could no longer make it out? He could still see the instruments, and if he had to, he knew he could land with those alone. He'd done so many times before, but never when he was so physically exhausted, and never with both of his hands shaking as if they'd contracted a sudden palsy.

Then, out of the blue, his radio crackled, and a female voice rose above the static.

"Sierra Papa One, this is Norfolk Naval Air Station, do you copy, over?"

He stared at the radio in disbelief. Why would the air station be calling him? Where was Andrea, and how in hell did they know his call sign?

The call was repeated, and this time he picked up his microphone, keyed it with his thumb, and replied. "This is Sierra Papa One, en route to North Carolina. Read you five by five, over."

There was a momentary silence, and then another voice came on line, masculine, and tinged with—what, anger? "Sierra Papa One, this is Norfolk Naval Air Station Tower. Request you abandon course. Reroute to our position and remain on frequency. We will talk you in."

Phil stared at the radio. He glanced at his fuel gauge. He had plenty to make Norfolk, but he had the image of Andrea's face clearly planted in his mind, and it was the force that kept him alert and moving. He was so weary he didn't think he could fly an extra mile.

"Norfolk Naval Air Station, this is Sierra Papa One, not sure I can comply, over. I'm—ill—very weak. I have enough fuel, but request permission to continue on course to North Carolina. I need to set this bird down, over."

"Sierra Papa One," the radio crackled back, "that is negative. There is nowhere to land on your current course. Weather is too violent. Your people contacted us and advised us you needed to be brought in. Repeat, reroute to Norfolk."

Phil shrugged, though there was no one to see the gesture. If he had to make it to Norfolk to see Andrea, at least the fact that she'd contacted Norfolk meant they were probably okay.

"Roger, Norfolk," he repeated. "Send me the coordinates, and I will comply. Repeat, I will comply."

"Roger, Sierra Papa One, we'll be waiting for you. You might want to hurry—there's one hell of a storm riding your tail. Norfolk Naval Air Station, out."

Phil chuckled. If they only knew. He blinked into the bright sun one last time and banked to his right. He skimmed far above clouds and coast alike. It would take about twenty minutes to reach Norfolk Naval, and he'd made that approach so many times before that he could do it in his sleep. He thought that was a very good thing, because he had an idea if he didn't hurry, that was exactly what he'd be doing.

As he soared over the Great Dismal Swamp, Phil dipped through the clouds and banked in over Virginia. His suddenly dimmed eyes did not immediately notice anything different, but the bright lights of Hampton Roads stretched out beneath him like a glowing carpet, too blurred to be anything but some sort of fever.

The shifts should have changed over, but not all personnel were available, and when the late afternoon sun started to dip beyond the horizon, dripping lavender and gold onto the waves, Lieutenant Mariner still stood watch at the big plate glass window of the tower. The flights had slowed some. Most of those that were trying to get out ahead of the storm had already pulled out. They had two squadrons fueling and in final maintenance checks. These would be the last before they began the meticulous evacuation of the base, locking things down as tightly as possible, getting final computer system backup tapes into lockboxes and dragging them to waiting trucks. It was going to be a very long night for a great many people, but Lieutenant Mariner wasn't thinking about any of it.

About a mile out he could make out the lights of the approaching plane. The pilot, Wicks was his name—he'd learned that over the course of the past few hours—was all but asleep at the wheel. They had controllers taking turns chattering in the man's ear, keeping the radio live so that he wouldn't just pass out and drop out of the sky on them, and it was nerve-wracking.

They had cleared off one runway, and the few inbound

and outbound flights that were scheduled adjacent to that runway had been put on hold. All of the emergency equipment they had the manpower to put on the field had been activated and was standing by, just in case. This could be extremely ugly, he knew, but he was hoping this pilot would surprise him and hold it together.

Lieutenant Mariner had great respect for anyone who could still get a plane like the one incoming up in the air, and he figured that should count for something. The guy was no amateur, but something was wrong. Something was very wrong indeed. The voice of the man they'd been communicating with had changed slowly over the course of the conversation. It was probably just that the man was sick, but if Mariner had been asked and not given time to think about it, he'd have to have said it sounded as if they were talking to an old man.

"Lieutenant?"

He turned and saw that it was Petty Officer Hill. Her shift was also over, but she'd chosen to stay with them to the last. The Navy was providing a truck to get them out, and her belongings had been packed that morning. It was an advantage to living in the barracks—you could travel light. She held a small sheaf of papers in her hands.

"What is it?" he asked her, turning reluctantly from the window.

"We just got this in," she replied. Her voice had a tentative quality, as if she wasn't sure she should even speak the words. He held out his hand impatiently and took the papers.

"It seems, sir," she said, "that the last time there was a flight plan filed for this aircraft was thirty years ago. It was on a flight near Bermuda, dropping silver iodide crystals into a hurricane."

Lieutenant Mariner glanced up at her sharply, and she finished in a flurry of words.

"The plane never returned, sir. It's been missing ever since. The pilot, Phillip Wicks, retired Navy, would be eighty-four-years-old."

He stared at her. His hands gripped the papers so tightly that they crumbled, but he paid no attention to them. He whirled to the window and called out. "Get this damned plane down, and do it now. I've had enough of this. We have an evacuation to complete, and this . . ." He shook the papers in the air, then tossed them over his shoulder and stalked to the window.

No one spoke, but the radio squawked, and Phil Wicks' voice crackled weakly over the speaker.

"This is Sierra Papa One on final approach. Landing gear is down. Coming in low. The wind is starting to pick up and I'll be damned if I can make out the numbers on the runway from higher up. I . . ."

Silence followed, and they all stared out the large window into the gathering gloom. The lights on the wings of Phil's plane glimmered. They watched, horrified, as the wings dipped, first one way, then the other. The aircraft settled, and just at the last moment, it leveled out. The wheels touched, bounced roughly, touched again and held. The plane barreled down the runway, and then it began to slow. The left wing dipped and the craft skidded, shifting onto one side and coming down hard on the opposite wing, but it was nearly stopped, and a few moments later it halted with bright flashing lights and sirens all around. The wind had picked up, but the skies were still clear.

Lieutenant Mariner stared out at the plane for a moment longer, then shook his head as if clearing it of unwanted thoughts, or a tangle of cobwebs. He turned to his right and issued orders rapidly, working to clear that plane off his runway and get standard traffic patterns rolling. They didn't have a lot of time left to get this place cleared, and he'd spent all the time he could spare plus quite a bit extra on this odd-ball plane and whatever sort of game or hoax it entailed.

Phil grew more and more confused as he neared the ground. The voices of those he'd been speaking with were cheerful and full of confidence, but he knew what they were doing. They were trying to talk him down with a minimum of damage to their airfield, their schedule, and himself—in that order. The storm couldn't be more than a couple of days behind him, unless it hit down south and worked its way north, and they must have plenty to keep them busy without talking in a civilian craft with a sick pilot.

There was no time left to think, or worry over it. He held the controls so tightly in his hands that he was afraid his fingers would snap. Despite this, he barely had the strength to keep the craft level, or the wits to keep the nose up and to work the flaps. He knew he was still moving too fast when he bounced the first time, and when he dropped again, he reached for the throttle and backed it off more quickly than he should have. He wanted to get the speed down quickly, forget the rules. He didn't know if he could keep the damned thing on the runway, slow or fast, but if he could reduce the speed enough he might minimize the damage to himself and the plane. He didn't know what was wrong with him, but he knew that if he didn't concentrate, he'd never find out.

And that wasn't all he would lose. He wanted to see Andrea. He wanted to know what happened to Dan Satalino, Vance Richards, and Mike Pooler in the other seed planes, and the pilots of the cargo planes. He wanted to know what happened with the storm, if they'd stopped it, angered it, whatever. What he knew was that it couldn't end in the plane, bouncing down the runway and out of control because he was too feeble to bring it to a stop.

As the engines throttled back, groaning, he stomped the brakes. The plane lurched, and with his one hand on the throttle, the other could not maintain control. The plane slipped to the side, skidded, and then slowed. He saw the lights of the tower pass in front of him as the plane spun to the side, felt the controls yanked from his hand and the whole world shift to the right, and then, blessedly, he sank into darkness, and it was no longer his concern. His last vision was of flashing lights, and he thought he heard a loud, distant siren, lulling him to sleep.

The emergency vehicles surrounded the plane quickly. Fire equipment was ready, their foam nozzles aimed at the old aircraft. A man in a protective suit approached slowly. The engines had stalled, and one of the wings had dug itself into the edge of the runway, not causing a lot of damage to the tarmac, but cutting into the grass alongside. The lights still flashed, but on close examination, the hull of the aircraft was pocked and corroded. It looked like it should have been in a junk heap somewhere, not flying seventeen thousand feet above the ocean, and the closer the man got, the slower he walked.

"Be careful in there," a voice squawked unnecessarily through his headset. Petty Officer Bob Barnett didn't have to be told twice. Not this time. The closer he got to the old aircraft, the less he wanted to climb up on that wing and open the cockpit.

In the background, Barnett heard more sirens. The ambulance was approaching, and this got him moving again. Whatever the condition of the plane, it *had* been up there, and now it was here, and it was his job to get it open, check on the pilot, and get him out of there. Any further questions or concerns would have to wait. He heard boots scrape on tarmac behind him and knew that Bill Purvis was moving in behind, backing him up.

Barnett clambered up on the wing of the old plane, fighting for a moment to keep his balance. It was tilted toward the far side at a good angle. He took the three steps up the wing quickly and went to work on the catches that would allow him to flip up the glass and get to the man inside. There was no movement, and there was no way to tell from out where he stood just how badly injured the pilot might be.

He worked for a few moments, and just as Purvis stepped closer, as if he was going to hop up on the wing and help, the last catch sprang free, and he lifted the window up and away. Barnett stumbled back in surprise, nearly tumbling off the wing.

"What is it?" Purvis called up. "What's wrong?"

When Barnett didn't answer, Bill Purvis clambered up past him and looked into the pilot's seat.

Behind the controls, his head lolling to the side and his eyes closed, whether dead or passed out, Purvis couldn't tell, was an old man. The pilot had a shock of white hair and looked to be in his late seventies, or even older. He was slumped in the seat. On the other seat was an antique Thermos of some sort. The upholstery of the seats was ragged, like you'd see in a very old car, or a theater seat in a movie house past its prime. The control panels had paint chipped off of them, more of it flaking away as Purvis watched. The man's flight suit might have come out of a closet where they forgot to include mothballs.

Then the man let out a snort, a very loud snoring sound, and Purvis turned to Barnett.

"Christ," he said. "The old bastard scared me half to death."

Behind them the ambulance pulled up, and without another word the two reached in and unstrapped Phil from his seat. They gripped him under his arms and lifted, and he woke then, startled and very groggy. A moment later they were able to help him out of the plane and onto the wing.

As he stepped down, the ambulance attendants took charge of him, and the rest of the crew began righting the plane and hooking it up for tow.

They didn't say much—but there would be plenty said later. As they started away, it rocked and nearly teetered again. One of the tires on the right side went flat. The rubber flapped as the wheel turned, and tore away as they dragged it free of the flight path. The tire had rotted off, and they scurried about picking up the debris.

Standing at his window and overlooking the mess, Lieutenant Mariner could not begin to guess what he'd just witnessed. He saw the ambulance roar off into the distance, and considered, just for a moment, trying to reach their dispatch on the phone and find out what the hell they'd learned. The moment passed as the radios came to life. He had two squadrons to get into the air, and personnel to get the hell out of Dodge.

Phil's plane was towed off the main part of the runway and tied down on the main airfield. There was no place for it currently in the hangars, and there had been no orders on how to handle it, so they did the simplest and least intrusive thing they could do. They parked it, secured it against the storm, and ignored it.

In a car, rushing up Highway 17 from the complex, Keith Scharf's mind raced. He wanted to be at the complex, monitoring the calls coming in from Andrea and the other crews, but there had been no one else he could send on this trip. No one with the connections or authority that might get him in and out of the naval base with the proper answers, and no one who could have answered the questions he was sure he was about to face in any way that would be taken seriously. Keith intended to get in, get Phil, and lie as thoroughly as he needed to to make it happen. He intended to call in every remaining favor he had in Washington. Whatever it took.

If Phil Wicks was sitting somewhere in Norfolk, Virginia, thirty years after his plane disappeared over Bermuda, confused and trying to get back to Andrea, well, Keith was going to make sure he made it.

He only hoped that Phil was okay, that he'd be on time, that Andrea would return safely, and that he could make it all happen before that damned storm made it all a ridiculous waste of time. He needed a miracle, and as he roared out the end of the swamp road and rolled up the entrance ramp onto Interstate 64, he gave a silent prayer to whatever God rules hurricanes that just this once, it wasn't too much to ask.

Chapter Nineteen

Phil was aware when they lifted him from the aircraft, but only peripherally. He couldn't seem to focus. He was very tired, and, he suddenly realized he was hungry as hell. They were fairly gentle with him, and he did his best to help them when he was on the ground, sort of tottering along between two of the ambulance attendants toward the strangest medical vehicle he had ever seen, but he knew he was likely hindering as much as aiding their progress.

It didn't help that everything looked wrong. The tower was a sleek, glass-fronted building with gleaming walls. The emergency vehicles and equipment were unfamiliar to him. The ambulance itself looked like something Captain Kirk might have driven out of his shuttle bay.

He tried to make sense of it all. He listened to the voices of those around him. He answered the questions they asked him. His name. What day it was, and several more. Phil was mildly irritated when they repeated several of these, and snapped his answers when he was forced to repeat himself. He understood the worry over concussion or dementia of some sort, but he knew perfectly well what the date was, and he hadn't yet forgotten his name.

They half led, half carried him to a gurney that had been rolled out of the space-age-looking ambulance, and despite his mild protests, they had him laid back on the soft, padded surface and strapped into place in moments. The efficiency of it made him slightly dizzy, and the feeling of disorientation deepened the murk surrounding his thoughts.

He tried to ask about the storm, and about Andrea, but they shushed him gently and closed the doors behind him. A young attendant sat in back with him, her hand resting on his arm.

The vehicle was moving in what seemed only seconds, and the siren's wail prevented Phil from trying again to voice his questions and concerns. He laid back, smiled weakly at the girl beside him, and closed his eyes. If he couldn't talk, then he would sleep. Surely they'd answer his questions when he woke up—and God he hoped they'd have food.

Keith wasted fifteen minutes he didn't have with the guards at the gate, only to learn that Phil had already been moved. It took a call straight to the commander of the base to get him past the front desk of the Sewell's Point Medical Clinic.

The clinic was just outside the fence surrounding the naval station itself, and it was to here, according to the last call he'd gotten through, that Phil Wicks—if it was, in fact, Phil Wicks who had landed that plane (Keith knew it must be, but it was easier for his already over-worked mind to keep the impossible stuff buried as deeply as possible until it was absolutely necessary to deal with it)—had been brought. He fumed as the hospital corpsman at the check-in desk made the calls, watched the young man's face shift and the color drain.

"This way," he said quickly, after placing the receiver back on its hook. "We have him mildly sedated. At his age, he shouldn't have been flying anything but Delta, you know?"

Keith didn't say anything. He was thinking about the last time he'd seen Phil Wicks, the day they'd sent the pilot and the others out to do battle with a hurricane. All of the other pilots had made it back. They'd lost no one else in the storm, which was a miracle, but the search for Phil or evidence of his aircraft had been long, painful, and futile. Nothing had ever turned up.

Now, as he climbed the short flight of tiled steps, breathing the medicine-scented air and feeling the almost tangible antiseptic cleanliness of the place drip off the walls and stick to the soles of his shoes, he didn't know if he was anxious or terrified to see what their actions had wrought.

The young corpsman led him down the second story hall, through swinging double doors and up to a desk. At the desk, an older, matronly looking woman in green scrubs sat watching a tiny black and white television. It was tuned to the news, and reports of the incoming storm were splashed across the screen.

"Edna," the corpsman said softly.

The woman turned, and the young man gestured at Keith. "This man needs to see the old man who was brought in. The pilot? It's been cleared all the way to the commander of the base."

The woman glanced back at her television screen for a moment, and then nodded. She rose and stepped around the counter, holding out a hand to Keith. "I'm glad to see someone come in for that poor man," she said, shaking her head. "He's talking like he's crazy. They say that he flew a plane into the air terminal, but I don't see how that's possible. His eyesight isn't that good—probably lost his glasses somewhere—and he thinks it's still some time in the 1960s. I thought he'd never quit going on about the ambulance they brought him in. And he keeps asking for a woman—Andrea?"

Keith nodded. "Can you take me to him?"

She nodded, hesitating to see if he was going to offer any

further comment. When Keith remained silent, she waved the corpsman off and turned on her heel. "Follow me, Mister—"

"Scharf," he replied. "Keith Scharf. I'm an old friend of Phil's—I think he'll be glad to see me."

The corpsman watched them hurry off down the hall, then turned and returned to the front desk. Most of the patients had been evacuated earlier, moved to facilities further inland, but some of those who were more mobile still required evacuation, and he had a lot to coordinate before the end of his shift. He knew the entire facility would be closed the following day, and he didn't want to forget something that could come back to haunt him. Somehow the look in Mr. Scharf's eyes reminded him this was possible.

Phil was asleep when they entered the room. The nurse, Edna, moved very quietly, and she swung the door to the room open with practiced ease, making only the slightest of clicks when she turned the knob. She followed Keith into the room, and he didn't object. It was going to be one hell of a strange conversation, but he didn't see any harm in having it overheard. Likely she'd leave with the impression that both he and Phil were insane, but that was fine as well. The important thing was to be certain Phil was okay, and if possible to get him out of here and back to the compound with as little fanfare as possible.

Keith didn't want to be caught on Highway 17 through the Dismal Swamp when the first winds from the hurricane hit— the road was dangerous enough without a storm. It was the only one he'd seen in his life with a warning sign at one end proclaiming the number of deaths on the road over a period of years. A sort of I-told-you-so to motorists with a macabre flair.

He stepped to the side of the bed slowly. At first he

thought it was a mistake. The face of the man on the pillow was old. A shock of brilliantly white hair shot off at a jaunty angle from the top of his head, and a gray stubble of beard framed the man's weathered face. Then Phil opened his eyes, those brilliant, blue eyes, and there was no doubt.

"Oh my God," Keith said. "It's you."

Phil blinked once. He squinted up at Keith, obviously having trouble placing the face. Then, as his mind grappled with the problem and began to put things into perspective, his eyes widened, and he raised himself on his elbows. "Keith?" he whispered. "Keith Scharf?"

Keith nodded, reached out and laid his hand gently on Phil's arm. "We've got a lot to talk about, Phil," he said. "Do you think you're well enough to travel?"

They turned and looked at Edna, who was watching them carefully, waiting for something—she didn't know what—to make sense of the moment. When she didn't speak up immediately, Keith took the initiative.

"I need to get Mr. Wicks back to our facility in North Carolina," he said. "I need to be certain he's able to travel—healthy enough, I mean. We don't have much time before that storm hits."

Edna shook her head slowly, and then stopped. It wasn't normal policy to release a patient who was under observation so quickly, but this was different, wasn't it? They were all going to be evacuated, and if this man had people to care for him and a place to go and ride out the storm, it would certainly be better than whatever overcrowded spot the Navy would find for him.

"I'm not sure I'm authorized to make that call," she said at last. "All of his vital signs are normal. He was dehydrated, and starving, but he's eaten a little and his heartbeat and breathing are stable. I suppose, under the circumstances . . ."

"I knew you'd understand," Keith pressed his advantage. "If you could just find his clothes?"

Edna nodded. She returned in just a moment to find Phil sitting up on the bed, staring down at his own hands as if he'd never seen them before. She knew there were more questions she'd like to have answers for, but knew as well it was unlikely she would get them. In her arms she carried Phil's flight suit. Keith took the bundle from her gratefully, and Edna turned away.

"You stop by and check out with me," she said over her shoulder.

No one answered her, and once the door swung closed behind her, Phil started to dress at once.

"I don't think I'm in Kansas anymore," he commented dryly, as he carefully worked his stiff legs into the canvas flight suit. Most of the equipment had been removed, and that was fine. The one-piece, zip-up-the-front outfit was just the thing for someone who suddenly found that his body didn't function the way it had the last time he'd been fully aware of his surroundings.

Keith laughed. "It's still Kansas, but boy has the wizard been up to some tricks. You get dressed, we'll get on the road, pick up a hotdog and some coffee, and I'll try to explain things to you as best I can."

"Andrea?" Phil said.

"She's fine—or was the last time I spoke with her. I'll fill you in on the way back to North Carolina."

Phil nodded. He zipped up the flight suit, looked around quickly to see if there was anything of his in the room that he shouldn't leave behind, and then shrugged. If there *was* anything, the U.S. Navy could have it. Keith held the door for him, and he stepped out into the hall. He was having trouble getting his muscles to respond, adjusting to—what—age? If he had aged, and Keith had aged—how many years had passed? What had he lost—and had they gained anything by the effort?

Phil shook his head and followed Keith to the nurse's station. It was going to be a long, messed up day—already had been—and the only three things he'd heard that changed that even a little were the words hot dog and coffee, and the news that Andrea was all right. He might feel like hell, but if Andrea was okay then there was a chance everything would work out.

They waved to the corpsman below, who looked as if he wanted to delay them and ask some questions, but then caught sight of the black and white television he'd been watching, and thought better of it. He didn't return their wave, but they were out the door and into the parking lot in moments, and a couple more brought them to Keith's car.

Keith held the door open for Phil, but Phil stood on the sidewalk and stared down at the car. It was sleek. There were none of the boxy lines he was familiar with. The headlights and taillights seemed just part of the surface of the vehicle. Finally, he bent and carefully worked his way into the passenger seat. When Keith closed the door Phil let out a startled bark, and then bit it off, and a moment later he was laughing. Keith slipped into the driver's seat and turned, smiling quizzically.

"What's so damn funny?" he asked.

Phil couldn't speak through the laughter, so he just grabbed the shoulder strap of the seat belt and pulled it away from his chest. The passive restraint system had caught him completely by surprise, slipping back to lock him in place.

"This thing scared me half to death," he said at last. "Jesus, last time I heard people were still arguing that these things were more of a restraining danger to safety than a help. Now . . ."

He stopped. His laughter cut off, and Phil leaned back heavily, staring up and out of the windshield, into the darkening sky.

"When is . . . now?" he whispered. "Jesus, Keith, what the hell happened to me . . . to you?" He turned to stare at the slightly younger man who was now so much older. "What happened to the world?"

Keith started the engine, backed out of the parking place, and thought about his answer. "It moved on," he said at last. "The world moved a long way since you last saw it, Phil. Hell, I don't even know where to start."

Of course, the start and the finish had been quite a bit alike. In the beginning, Phil had disappeared, along with the storm, and in the end it had come back, and he had followed. The in between held a lot of fascinating stories, a lot of innovations, gadgets, studies, presidents, and culture that was of no real importance to either of them at the moment.

What was important was that the storm was back, and that Andrea had gone this time, leaving the two of them behind to worry, and to wonder. This time she wasn't the general, viewing and controlling things from some hideaway bunker. She was the field general, and this time the battle was for keeps.

"I don't suppose we could get lucky and the damned thing would just phase back into—wherever," Phil asked when Keith had brought him as far up to speed as possible in a short amount of time. "It's been gone a very long time," he glanced down at his hands, as if to try and measure that time, "it seems like maybe it could get sucked back into that other place. It existed there longer than it did here, after all."

"I hope it doesn't work like that," Keith answered. "For one thing, it's good to have you back. For another, what if it took all those boats and barges with it? What if it disappeared again and Andrea, the crews, and all those pumps we've spent so long perfecting just disappeared?

"If she came back in another thirty years, she'd die. We'd already be dead, and the storm? Something tells me that unless we put that damn thing out of commission ourselves, and soon, it's going to keep going on until it reaches its goal."

"You talk about it like it has a mind and thoughts," Phil replied. "It's just a storm, Keith. For all we did to it, all we may, or may not have caused, it's just a lot of wind and rain, feeding off itself and the warmth in the water. Let's hope you've been a little more clever in the last few decades, and that these pumps of yours are up to the challenge."

They drove the last twenty miles in silence. Phil stared out the window of the smooth-riding BMW—that's what Keith told him it was—and marveled at the glow from Elizabeth City. There hadn't been so many lights the last time he'd been here. There hadn't been all that much of anything. He couldn't process all of the changes, and decided it didn't matter. If one thing was still the same, or near to the same, it would be enough. If Andrea made it back to him, and he didn't keep getting older, get feeble, and die on her before she had a chance, that would be grand, he thought.

"Shouldn't we be evacuating with everyone else?" he asked, just before they pulled up to the gate of the compound. "Won't the storm hit here if the pumps don't work?"

"It will hit here, all right," Keith replied, "but if there's one building on the entire east coast that can withstand this hurricane, you're about to return to it. I don't expect you'll recognize much."

Keith kept talking as they pulled through the gate. The

guard stared in past him at Phil, and it was obvious that rumors had spread quickly. The young man knew exactly who Phil was, and wasn't surprised to see him. They were waved through quickly.

None of it mattered in the next few seconds. Phil took in the gleaming central building and the looming factory-like structures that flanked it, but they didn't catch, or hold his attention. He was staring at the hangar. It stood, just as it had stood so many years—wasn't it just hours?—before. She hadn't changed a thing. The paint had been replaced over the years to preserve it, but the hangar waited like a long-lost friend, and tears streamed from the corners of Phil's eyes as he watched it pass in the BMW's side windows, then turned and craned his neck to stare a little longer after they'd rolled past.

Keith stopped in front of the main doors and got out quickly. He came around and helped Phil out to stand beside him, and the two stared at the old hangar together.

"She wouldn't let anyone touch it," Keith said simply. "It's been waiting just like this, as if she knew you would return, since the day you rolled onto the airfield out back and took off. The field is long gone, all our flights go through a local airfield now, but she kept the hangar. I've argued with her over it, but now—now I'm glad she's a bullheaded old thing. Damned if I'm not."

Phil couldn't speak. The weight of all that had happened was finally dropping onto his shoulders, and he swayed on tired legs. Keith grabbed his arm to support him, but he shrugged this off and took a tentative step toward the old hangar, and his memories.

"There will be plenty of time for that later," Keith said, "but we have work to do now, Phil. We have to check on Andrea, see if there are any reports. If she calls in and needs anything now, the only ones who can help her are all in this building behind us. We need to join them."

Phil tottered, took another half step forward, and then shook his head. "Let's go," he said, turning abruptly toward the now-unfamiliar central building. "Show me the new magic, and let's see if we have any tricks up our sleeve that can do some good."

Keith slapped him on the back lightly and led the old pilot through the main doors and into the new-and-improved computer room.

The screen was fancier, and all of the colors took some getting used to, but the radarscope image looked familiar enough to Phil's trained eyes. The storm was monstrous. There was literally no scale in existence that accounted for a hurricane of this strength. To call it a Category Five was like calling Mohammed Ali a boxer. He was—or had been last time Phil checked—the heavyweight champion of the world. This storm was his counterpart, and it packed a much deadlier punch.

Keith brought up the simulation program. It still displayed the results from the last test that Andrea had run.

"It worked?" Phil asked incredulously. "You ran—Andrea ran a simulation and these pumps actually stopped the storm?"

"I wish it were that simple," Keith replied, "but in a nutshell, that's exactly what happened. There are always factors you can't account for, random factors like sudden weather fronts we didn't foresee, but the output of the program is a scenario that, should all of our postulations prove true, is the most likely outcome."

"But still," Phil repeated obstinately, "she stopped it."

"Yes," Keith admitted, "but look here."

He changed screens back to the radar map, and then added the overlay that included the currently plotted locations of the boats, barges, and equipment. "That simulation was run with a perfect formation of all twenty-five of the barges we created, all in place and operational with five large pumps apiece. Here . . ." he stopped for a moment and indicated a grouping of smaller blips on the screen, "are the barges. Andrea should be on the last one." Again, he pointed at the screen.

Phil stared at the point that marked her location and his heart lurched. That small blip on the screen was so small, so insignificant in the face of the approaching storm, that he nearly cried out in fear. Instead he held himself in check and listened carefully.

"Andrea left here in time and if nothing goes wrong they should be able to have all of the pumps they have with them in place and running. These other markers," he pressed his finger to the screen where two small blips, moving quickly enough to show motion on the screen, were headed straight at the barge wall, and into the face of the approaching storm, "are the cutters that will get them out. They'll be shooting off around the near side of Bermuda and out into the open sea.

"There is always a chance that the storm will turn that direction, but we don't believe it will. One thing in our favor is that this storm may be a bit confused, so to speak. It departed under perfect hurricane conditions, but it has returned into an unseasonable cold front. This could work in our favor, though I believe that a storm this size will find a way across. We can't take for granted that the weather conditions alone will cause the eye to break up. We have to go after it."

"How many?" Phil asked without looking away from the map.

Not catching his old friend's drift, Keith started to go on, then stopped. "How many what?" he asked.

"How many barges do they have—the pumps that stopped the storm in Andrea's simulation—you said there were twenty-five barges, all working properly? That was enough. How much do we have? How close are we to a hundred percent operability?"

"Three barges left Norfolk last night, and ten from here yesterday—Andrea flew out to make the crossing with those. On Bermuda we have another ocean-going tug with five more barges. That makes eighteen. The last set of five is too far away to make it safely into play, so—eighteen."

"Is that enough?" Phil asked, turning sharply. "Do we even know?"

Keith shook his head, but met Phil's eyes steadily. "If it can be done," he said, "we both know that the one who can make it happen is on that boat. She's no spring chicken, but I think you'll find the years have been very kind to Andrea. She's got a lot of fight in her."

"No amount of fight will help her against that storm," Phil replied.

"You're right on that," Keith agreed, nodding. "On that we're just going to have to pray."

Phil stared at the screen as Keith flipped it back to the radar image. He couldn't quit thinking about it, rearranging the barges from the simulation screen to a tighter area, or leaving large gaps at one point or another, and trying to see her face— her older, wiser face—as the storm bore down on the barges, and the woman he loved, threatening to wipe her away as cleanly as fate had removed the last thirty years of his life.

Phil Wicks wasn't a religious man, but as he watched, his lips moved, and he whispered his prayers into the dark, empty night.

Chapter Twenty

Andrea gripped the rail tightly and stared out over the choppy waves. It wasn't too rough yet, but she knew what they were experiencing was the veritable calm before the storm. Her two boats, with the tug out of Norfolk, had formed a ragged flotilla that made its slow passage toward Bermuda at a steady pace. Her calculations put them well ahead of the hurricane, and radar reports backed her up, but there was something about the gray of the sky that would not allow her heart—or those around her—a moment's peace.

It was like staring into a vast gray expanse and wondering if you were moving toward it, or if it was moving toward you. The sky might have been a huge wall of water, disguised only by the fact that it stretched so impossibly high that it broke through the clouds and you couldn't make out the whitecaps riding the top of the wave.

Andrea knew the sensation. She'd felt it once or twice in movies, sharing the adventures of some ill-fated group just before the arrival of a desert sandstorm, or the avalanche that dropped half a mountain of ice and snow down on their heads. She'd seen it in the eyes of those waiting for the monster they knew was out there, poised in the dark and ready to leap onto their backs and steal their lives. She knew she had seen it at least once in her father's eyes, after he'd come home from the wars. She'd woken him up early one Saturday—her stomach had hurt, and his side of the bed was closest to the door.

Without thinking, young Andrea had stepped close and laid her hand timidly on her father's cheek. He had come out of his sleep so quickly, and so completely, grabbing her wrist painfully and lashing out, that she'd barely managed to turn to the side and avoid the blow. In seconds he was himself again, pulling her close and whispering to her that it was going to be all right, but in that moment she'd seen stark terror and absolute rage warring behind his eyes, and after that she knew they were there.

This was like that. She saw the calm, gray sky, so heavy with moisture and covered in clouds that it seemed nothing could penetrate its gloom. Behind that, her storm waited, pacing back and forth like a caged animal, whirling in and in and in to the perfect circular eye in the center. She knew that eye, had met its gaze a thousand times on her computer screen. It was watching them, and—and it was hungry.

Still, they were making good time. Andrea swept her gaze over the tightly formed group, over the tugs and their crews, either standing as she was at the rails, or bustling over the decks. She had Phil's old Navy peacoat wrapped tightly around her, the collar flaps up. It wasn't really cold, but it wasn't warm either, and the spray from the waves gave her chills wherever it struck her skin. It should have been bright and sunny, but the sun was temporarily lost to them, and she wondered how many of them would ever see it again.

Then she shook those thoughts from her head and turned back toward the cabin. Before she reached the doors, a loud THWUP! THWUP! rose, and she spun wildly, afraid the storm was on them without warning. She turned around completely, growing dizzy. Before she could stumble, Jay Greenwood, the captain of the tug, came up behind her and steadied her. Then, raising an arm, he pointed into the sky to their left.

An orange and white United States Coast Guard helo hovered in the air, chopping whitecaps from the waves as it came down low over the water. A man in an orange flight suit stood in the open door holding a bullhorn.

"Turn back to shore," he called out. "There is a storm ahead, you cannot ride it out, turn aside."

Andrea covered her eyes by flattening the palm of her hand in a sort of salute and stared up at the man. She'd expected this. She hadn't gotten clearance for what she was attempting, but she knew they had no way to force her little navy back into port, other than by threat of the storm itself.

She waved.

The man repeated his warning, a bit more loudly. This time he added, "This is the United States Coast Guard. You are ordered back to land. I repeat, there is a storm ahead—you cannot ride this out."

Andrea shrugged, and for a moment, she was afraid that the helo would hover directly over their boat and lower a man to the deck. Then Captain Greenwood returned to her side and thrust a bullhorn into her hand.

"Let them know we have no intention of turning back," he told her. "They'll argue, but they won't waste much time on us—they have a sweep to make, and they have to get back in, refuel, and get themselves to safety."

Andrea nodded. "This is Andrea Jamieson of Operation Stormfury," she called out. "We know about the storm, we are out here to try and stop it."

There was silence after this, and she saw the man repeating her message to those inside the helicopter. She could imagine the stunned responses. Then the man was in the doorway again.

"We have no authorization for your operation. Stand down, and return to port."

"I'm afraid we can't do that," Andrea replied. "We know the risks. If you have others to warn, you'd better get going." Then, as an afterthought, she added, "We'll be fine. We know what we're doing."

As she spoke the words, she wondered if any bigger lie had ever been spoken in all of human history. She knew what they were *trying* to do. She knew what they hoped would happen, and she really believed that they would probably be all right. She let none of her doubt taint the conviction in her voice.

The young man clung to the door of the helo and watched her for a long moment. Then, with a shrug of his own, he brought the bullhorn back to his lips. "Good luck, then. God knows, you're going to need it."

Andrea didn't respond, only waved, and the helicopter door slid closed. A moment later it rotated and dipped its nose, rising and gaining speed rapidly, swinging back to a parallel course with the shoreline. Captain Greenwood had been right, there were others to warn, and they had plenty of miles to cross before they'd be able to think of their own safety.

Andrea wrapped her arms across her chest to pull the peacoat tighter, then turned and stepped into the boat's cabin and out of the weather.

There was a smaller version of the chart tables she'd grown accustomed to over the years in one corner. Near it was the equipment she'd had installed after leasing the tugs several years earlier. There were two radio sets, a satellite cellular phone with Internet capabilities, and a UHF receiver set up to relay radar information from the compound. They could pick the storm up on their own equipment, but it wasn't long-range, and it wasn't intended for something of the scope that this hurricane presented. Andrea shrugged out of the heavy wool coat and slid into the chair.

Their signals had been strong so far. One of the boat's crew, a seaman named Seth, was at the helm. He watched an array of dials and indicators, watching his speed and course and being careful to keep steady tension as he towed the barges through the choppy water. His movements were quick and confident, and Andrea smiled.

"The other boats checked in on the hour, ma'am," he called over his shoulder without taking his eyes off of the ocean or the gauges. "They had a small problem with one guide wire on number two, but they've gotten it under control. We're dead on course and about an hour ahead of schedule."

"Thanks," Andrea replied, "we'll need every minute we can get, I'm afraid. We'll be ahead of the storm, but who knows what kind of surge, or waves might run out in front? Best we're in and out of there as quickly as possible."

"Yes ma'am," the young man agreed. "That's what we're aiming for."

She turned to her laptop and settled the mouse's pointer over the icon that would link her to the satellite. She knew this was a luxury they would lose, eventually, as their proximity to the storm began to distort and wipe out their signals. Andrea intended to check the charts, and to get an updated map of the storm's progress, but in the back of her mind she knew what she truly wanted. She wanted to get to her e-mail and see if there was anything there from Keith. She wanted to know about Phil.

The last communication she'd seen had told her that Phil's plane was on final approach to Norfolk Naval Air Station. Keith had been on the phone all day trying to get through, to get information and to get clearance, once the plane was on the ground, to see Phil and get him out of there if he could. It was a snarl of red tape and not rendered any easier by the imminent storm. The base was being evacuated, and Phil had tumbled into the middle of that, presenting only his own questions and confusion, no doubt, and interfering with their schedules.

The modem ran through its sequence of clicks and whirs, then the sound—almost like a pay phone makes when the quarter drops home—rang out from the small speaker and after a quick, loud burst of static, the modem connected. Andrea didn't hesitate—the computer was as familiar to her as her own mind. She quickly activated the automatic data downloads from radar and the storm tracking software. While these were running, she opened her e-mail.

Five new messages blinked into her inbox, one at a time. The top one was from the Pentagon. She almost ignored it, and then opened it with an impatient click. The other names on the list of addressees were all men and women she knew, most of them working out of NOAA. The subject was simply, "The Storm."

Andrea scanned the message ruefully. They were a slow-moving lot, but it had taken only a day for the government to get around to asking her whether there was anything she thought they could do about Hurricane Andrea. They didn't call it that, of course. They called it simply "The Storm," not bothering with the niceties that would give it a human name to splash across the banner headlines of newspapers around the world. This was too close, and too powerful. They didn't want to name it; they wanted a way to stop it.

Andrea hit the "reply to all" button and left a short, concise message to them all.

To all concerned. We have been waiting for a chance like this. My people are already underway. Details can be verified through Keith Scharf at my complex in North

Carolina. Simulations indicate that what I'm about to at-tempt may work. If not, I hope you all have long lives, and that you have sense enough to get out of the way of this storm. I call her Hurricane Andrea, and she's a monster.

Andrea signed the note and hit send. Then she quickly ran through the rest of her messages. Three were unimportant, but the last one was from Keith, and she opened it breathlessly.

"Phil has landed," it said. "Gone to Norfolk to try and bust him out. If not, will locate him after the storm. No worries at this end—go get that thing and make it go away."

Andrea stared at the screen, and it blurred as tears filled her eyes and rolled down her cheeks. She closed her eyes for a moment, and when she did, she saw his face, rugged and handsome, staring at her through his bright blue eyes. She wanted to reach out to that image, take his hands and step to the side.

Quickly, she hit reply and typed simply, "Tell him that I love him. I will be home soon—Andrea."

She hit send, but at that same moment the boat lifted and dropped from a particularly high swell. The dip of the antenna must have caused the already shaky signal to break. The modem light died. She had no idea whether or not her reply had gotten through.

Andrea pressed the connect button again, but though the computer tried several times, a solid connection could not be made. Andrea closed the program and brought up the map quickly. She worked as fast as her fingers would fly, her lips pressed very tightly together, fighting the urge to slam the lid of the laptop so hard that the thin, powerful computer was smashed.

The work calmed her, and she printed out her results carefully. This done, she tried to connect a final time. There was no answering tone from the far end at all, and she closed the laptop with a long, heavy sigh. She took the printout from the computer, stepped to the chart table, clipped the paper in place and removed the previous update. She crumpled the old sheet and tossed it in the garbage can tied to the bulkhead. There was no sense keeping it; all of the files she was receiving were archived and analyzed back in the compound.

"This might be the last update for a while, Seth," she said. "We'll be on our own unless we can connect again."

The young sailor nodded. "That's fine, ma'am," he replied. "We pretty much navigate by our own radar, and we have our course. All those maps do is remind us of that storm, and I'm as happy not knowing just how close we're going to cut this, for myself."

Andrea smiled. She hadn't considered that. When she'd had all of this equipment lugged on board and set up, it had been more out of habit than out of thought. Seth was right, of course. Her charts could show them the position and speed of the storm, the position and speed of the other boats, and the other barges, but it wouldn't matter much as far as navigating this particular boat was concerned. That was in Captain Greenwood's hands, along with Seth and the rest of the crew.

"Have we heard from the cutters yet?" she asked.

The two larger, faster craft should have come out of port about a half a day behind them, but as of the last time Andrea had checked, there was no report of them. She scanned the printout she'd clipped to the table. There was one blip behind them that looked like it might be one of the two ships, but the other was nowhere to be seen. Frowning, she stepped over to the computer, sat down, and brought up an enhanced view of the data she'd downloaded.

The same boat showed up, but there was no sign of a second.

"Nothing so far," Seth answered. "If we had satcom, we'd have picked them up right away. We won't get them on the line-of-sight until they get within range. They were pretty far behind, and even as fast as those boats are, they'll take some time to get in close enough."

"I only see one of them on the printout," she said, talking as much to herself as to Seth. She was trying to figure out what might cause a glitch that would prevent one or another of the boats from showing on the radar. The barges and their tugs, even the one slipping around from the far side of Bermuda, were all accounted for, but where there should have been two cutters, there was only one.

One of the ships could carry all of the crews, if it was necessary, but she wasn't at all sure there would be time for them to come alongside the barges, one by one, and get the people out. Not with only one ship doing the work.

"Keep trying to reach them," she told Seth. "Call once every fifteen minutes until you make contact. I'm going to go discuss the situation with Captain Greenwood."

Seth nodded, and Andrea grabbed Phil's coat, wrapped it back around her slender frame, and stepped back onto the tugboat's deck. She shivered, not just from the wind, but at the thoughts now whirling through her mind.

If they didn't have all of the cutters, they weren't all going to get off of those barges in time. The worst of it was, with communications out at this point, there was no way to know for sure if her fears were ungrounded, or to try and make changes in their plan that would solve the problem before it happened.

The thought of anyone stuck on one of her barges with the hurricane bearing down on them was not one she wanted to dwell on—but what choice would she have? If she told them all before hand that she suspected some of them would be stranded, what would they do? Mutiny? Would they head off to sea around the far side of Bermuda and let Hurricane Andrea devastate their homes, and in most cases, their families? She didn't think so. She thought they would stick with her no matter what, but she didn't know. One more thing, she thought, that she just didn't know.

She saw Captain Greenwood assisting two seamen with one of the tow cables, and she turned away, moving back to her spot along the railing and staring off toward the distant storm. It didn't matter yet. She could talk to the captain about it later, and probably she'd find out, after worrying herself sick over it, that both of the cutters were right on course and schedule, and that her fears were ungrounded.

As she watched the nose of the tug press steadily through the waves, the weight on her shoulders doubled, and she closed her eyes, clinging to the rail for support. For the first time that she could remember, Andrea felt her sixty-nine years fully and completely. She was tired, and it was time to bring this all to an end. As her thoughts drifted, Phil stepped in to fill them. The tears were wiped heartlessly from her cheeks by the whipping chill of the wind.

Chapter Twenty-One

As it turned out, Phil didn't get a lot of time to tour the new facility, or to rest. Once the odd silence his entrance ushered into the room dissipated, and the first tentative questions were asked, they were all sucked back into the moment. The screen, bigger and more colorful than anything he'd ever seen, reminded Phil enough of a radarscope for him to get the gist of what he was seeing, though it was hard to shake the sensation of walking onto the set of some weird science-fiction movie.

The storm was displayed as a whirling white mass, the eye a focused pool of black in the center. It was enormous. Bermuda was clearly marked on the map, and the storm would have stretched out and blotted it out with just a single corner of the covering, whirling clouds, that it might not have existed at all.

There were a number of colored blips on the screen, also very small. Some converged on the path of the storm. One circled around from the far side of Bermuda, and one other followed behind the first two.

Keith grabbed Phil's arm and pointed. "The four markers in front, and the one coming from Bermuda, are the tugs with the barges I told you about. They will converge along that light green line." He pointed to the projected placement for the barges.

Then Keith frowned. Releasing Phil, he stepped to the

screen and pointed at the single marker trailing behind the barges.

"Where is the other cutter?" he asked.

A young man stepped forward and handed him a memo. He read it quickly, his face growing ashen, and he suddenly glanced back up at the screen. "Damn."

Phil stepped forward and Keith handed him the note. The text of it read simply, "Engine trouble in Cutter # 2. Crews working around the clock. If repairs are complete in eight hours, we can make target. If not, will be moving the boat out of the storm's path."

The top of the memo, a format Phil didn't recognize, had a date and time. He checked his watch. It was stopped dead, and he glanced around. Keith caught the motion and showed him his own watch. The memo had been received four hours earlier.

"Have we got an update on their status?" Keith asked the young man who'd handed him the note.

"The last time we heard, they were on schedule, but barely," was the reply. "There's more."

Keith took the second printout and read it carefully. This time he handed it to Phil more slowly.

Phil took it and read Andrea's note.

"We've lost communication with the barges," the young man continued. "This was the last thing that came over the computer. It was addressed to you, sir," he nodded at Keith, "but considering the situation . . ."

Keith gestured for him to go on, though he was still reading. "We're hoping the first cutter can get through to them via radio when it gets closer. It's equipped with more powerful transmitters, and if they can relay, we might re-establish comms. It's also possible that the station in Bermuda will get through, but everything from that area is spotty. The storm is causing some of the strangest interference we've ever seen."

Phil glanced up at this, and then down at his stopped watch. "I believe that," he said. "I'd say calling what's out there 'interference' is a bit of an understatement."

Everyone grew silent again, waiting to see if he'd say more, or if they'd offended him. Phil stared at them, and then waved his arms. "Well?" he said. "What other options do we have? Surely that broken down cutter isn't the only answer?"

The tension snapped like a twig and everyone moved at once. Keith led Phil to Andrea's seat, a comfortable leather office chair. "We have another boat on Bermuda," he said. "It's smaller, and not quite as fast. I don't know if it's ready to go, but I'll find out."

Phil nodded. He was staring at the smaller computer screen—he assumed that was what it was—on the desk in front of him, but he didn't really see the display. He was tired, but Andrea's message—those simple words, in all the madness he'd flown back into—had given him new strength. He knew he was completely out of the loop here. Everything they'd been doing, all the programs that had been underway when he'd taken off on that last mission, were as old as he felt, and about as useless. Still, there had to be something he could do, some way he could help. He knew he couldn't just sit in this room and watch the others work; that would drive him crazy.

"Is there any way to get to Bermuda by air?" he asked.

"We could probably get to the island," Keith said, shaking his head slowly, "but I don't think they'd let us land. Not now. If the storm breaks, or continues on course toward the U.S. coastline, maybe then, but by then this is going to be a done deal. The best thing we can do is to keep contact with them and make sure that we take all precautions so that, if and when they get back, this place is still here to greet them."

"Sir?" A long-haired woman with thick glasses turned from her console.

Keith paused and turned to her. "What is it, Susie?"

"We've raised the first cutter, sir. They are on course and on schedule—a little ahead of schedule, actually. They have no communications with the barges, but should be within range soon."

"Keep on that," Keith replied. "And see if you can raise Bermuda. We need to get the older boat underway, just in case."

"What if you don't have the two cutters when the barges are in place?" Phil asked.

"The plan would be aborted, if it was a normal storm," Keith said, "and if Andrea was here, running the show, and not there." He pointed vaguely at the center of the screen.

"And now?" Phil gripped the armrests of the chair tightly.

"I don't know. The smart thing for them to do, if they don't know they have a way out of there, would be to release the barges and get those tugs moving as quickly as possible. They could probably outrun the storm around that side and be out of harm's way."

"But you don't think that's what she'll do," Phil added.

"Do you?" Keith asked in return. "I don't know. If it was her own life on the line, and no other, I have no doubt she'd do what she could to stop this storm or die in the attempt. With so many others along, I wouldn't want to bet on it.

"You know she feels responsible for this. Hell, for all I know we *are* responsible for it. It was a big storm when you flew out to meet it, Phil, but it has grown way beyond that, and the probability is that the slick of oil I laid down in its path all those years ago was the cause. We've had a lot of chances to run the simulations since then. We've checked it every which way you can imagine, throwing in different weather conditions, wind speed, temperatures, varying the amount of oil, the location of the slick—even the seeding." He glanced up at that.

"We never knew whether you dropped that load, or whether the timing was so screwed up that it didn't matter. The others all claimed to have dropped their pellets at the same time, but they couldn't be certain of it because time was—odd."

"You can say that again," Phil muttered.

Keith went on as if he hadn't heard. "The only thing we are certain of is that the lead pilot of the cargo planes signaled for the release of the oil too soon. We know this now, not from asking them, or from any data gathered at the time, but from the simulations themselves. The storm hit the oil slick well ahead of the time your men began to drop the silver iodide, and the temperature difference to the south and west was all it took."

"We've got Bermuda on line," the woman named Susie called out from her radio console. "It's Gabrielle."

Gabrielle held the microphone close to her chest and hunched over it. The storm hadn't reached Bermuda, but the outlying wind, rain, and swell was making itself known. It wasn't as bad now that they'd reached the far side of the island, but it wasn't what you'd call a good day for sailing.

"The tug and the barges are ready to get underway," she said, almost screaming into the microphone. "The weather's pretty bad, but once they are clear of the reef we can ride it out. We'll be moving more quickly than the storm, and at an angle, trying to get well ahead of it and rendezvous with the others down south and west."

"What about the cruiser?" Keith asked.

She wasn't certain she'd heard him, but she answered anyway. "We aren't taking the cruiser, Keith. We have barely enough staff here to man the barges. It's been hard to get anyone off the island and we have to have every one of them to make this happen. If we tow the barges into place without enough trained personnel to operate the pumps, we're wasting our time and risking lives for nothing."

"We only have one cutter," Keith told her. "If you go out there, we can't guarantee everyone will get out alive. The last cutter may make it, but they are making emergency repairs. We can't guarantee they will make it, and if they don't, there won't be time to get everyone out."

Gabrielle pulled back and stared at the microphone in her hand in disbelief. "So," she said at last. "If we go out, but can't take the cruiser, we're just going to our deaths?"

There was no answer and she cursed, though not loudly enough to be heard over the radio.

"Can you find another crew?" Keith asked at last. "Isn't there someone there who could man that cruiser and follow, someone you trust?"

Gabrielle was about to launch into one of longest and most colorful strings of curses of her adult life, but she never gave it breath. Just at that moment, a battered old truck rolled up to the pier. She didn't know for sure who, or how many were on that truck, but she'd seen it before. Then, when the old man stepped out from behind the wheel, pulled a battered cap down over his eyes and hunched against the wind, she started to laugh.

"I might have something," she said into the microphone. "No promises, but I just might have an answer here."

"God knows we could use some good news," Keith replied. "They're out there, Gabrielle, and we can't reach them on the radio. Andrea doesn't even know there's a problem."

Her heart nearly stopped in her chest, but Gabrielle's chin stiffened with resolve. "I'll do what I can," she replied. Then she put the microphone in its clip, exited the cabin of the tug, and worked her way carefully across the swaying bow to the shore.

She met the old man halfway across the dirt parking lot. It was the same fisherman she'd taken out to the fish farm. She glanced over his shoulder and saw that his old truck was filled with others, their faces planted against the rain-washed glass, staring at her.

"I hear," the man started in without hesitation, "that you go to fight the storm. I hear this, but I do not believe it. I also did not believe that you could bring fish from dead water, so now I wonder."

Gabrielle didn't answer, sensing that he wasn't finished.

The old man turned and stared out into the choppy surf. "I have come to help. When you said you could bring the fish, we laughed at you. We told you we knew all there was to know about our home, and our fish, but you have brought things we have never seen, and we were wrong.

"Today they told me you would fight the storm, and I laughed. I told them that you could not fight a storm from a ship, and that you would all die. Do you know what they told me?" he asked with a twinkle in his eye.

Gabrielle shook her head.

"They tell me that if you can bring fish to dead water, maybe you can stop the storm—and that it would be something to see." He turned back to face her and smiled. "I've lived a long time, and I think I would like to see you fight this storm."

Gabrielle smiled. She turned and pointed at the boat she affectionately called "The Cruiser." It was much newer and more powerful than the boats the fishermen took out every day, but there was nowhere else to turn.

"Do you think you can pilot that boat?" she asked him.

The old man stared at the cruiser for no longer than a second, then he nodded. "Of course," he said. "It is a boat, and I am a captain." He shrugged as if her question and its answer were academic.

"Then you can help, and I welcome you," she told him. "We are going to stop that storm, if we can, and I think that we can." She pointed at the barges, anchored out a few hundred yards, and the ocean-going tug being prepared for sea at the end of the pier. "We have to get those barges into place, and once we do, we will need our people brought to safety. The boat that was going to do this for us may not make it—but if you and your men . . ."

He held up a hand. "We can do this," he said.

Gabrielle nodded. "I'll send one of my people with you," she said. "They are familiar with the controls and can go over them with you while you get underway."

"Good hunting," he said to her, his smile widening. "Perhaps we will meet in front of the storm and see whether growing fish is the limit of your magic."

"It's not mag . . ." she stopped herself. That conversation would have to wait until there was a *lot* more time. For now, if the man thought she had magic to offer, that was fine. All she needed from him was the possibility that she'd see another day when this one was done. Beyond that, there was plenty of time to teach the science of fish farming, and maybe for her to go out on their boats and learn how to man the nets. Who knew?

She hurried off to the tug to reassign a person to the

cruiser, and the fisherman called his men from the truck. They were already boarding the cruiser when Gabrielle reached the tug's deck.

On the cutter *Daybreak*—four hours behind her sister ship *Moontide*—the order was given to turn over the engines. Repairs were complete, but all hands waited, breath held and eyes closed in silent prayer, for the roar of the diesel engines. A sputter wouldn't do. They were heading into the most dangerous cruise of their lives, and anything less than fully operational was not going to be enough.

The engines coughed only once, then caught with a thrumming roar. Moments later, the decks rang with the cheers of the crew, and the captain, George Clayton, stood on the bridge, staring out over the darkened waves. He wasn't sure, even at that moment, whether he was glad to hear the engines, or terrified, but he let none of this show. He couldn't afford to pass any doubt or weakness on to his crew—not now.

"Get us moving," he growled, and the merriment on the bridge slowed and became a deep silence. The cutter accelerated smoothly, and Clayton fingered the small St. Christopher's medal dangling by a chain from his throat. He was no more superstitious than the next man, but these were extraordinary circumstances, and he was taking no chances.

"Give me as much speed as you can," he told his helmsman, "but be careful. We aren't so far behind we can't catch up, but it won't help anyone if we beat ourselves to hell on the waves."

The young seaman nodded. If nothing changed, and the engines held, they would come even with the first cutter late the next day. None of them wanted to think about what would happen if there were more problems, but they all understood the situation. The barges were well ahead of the first cutter, and there had been no communication since just after *Moontide* pulled away from the pier. If they didn't make it to the rendezvous point at the scheduled time, then people were likely to be stranded in the path of the most powerful hurricane in history. None of them wanted that on their conscience.

The moon shone down clear and bright. Only light cloud cover blurred their view of the stars. The waves were light, and it was difficult to believe the storm waited not so many hours distant.

"Get Scharf on the radio," Clayton said, turning from the window and heading for his cabin. "Tell him we're on our way."

As Captain Clayton stepped off the bridge, the cutter plowed through the glittering, moonlight glazed waves, rushing against the clock.

Chapter Twenty-Two

Andrea tried several times to sleep, but she could not. It wasn't the waves, though the wind had picked up considerably. She knew she should be resting. She wasn't as young as she'd been, and despite her health and the fact that she felt—in her mind—no older than she'd been the day she'd watched Phil take off thirty years in the past, her body knew better. She was going to have to draw on reserves she might not even have before this was done, but sleep eluded her, and she tossed and turned on the hard bunk, fighting her restless mind for release.

Everything had taken on the unreal, slow motion aspect of a dream. She'd felt similar sensations in the green-gold calm before a thunderstorm, or on occasions when she'd known some important confrontation or meeting would take place. The energy was building up inside her, ready to release on a hair trigger, but it was impossible to keep it from leaking through to her conscious mind and into the moment.

They had not heard from the cutters, or from Keith, since she'd sent her last e-mail. They weren't in position yet, but they must be close enough to the storm to pick up some sort of odd interference. There was no way to know what exactly was preventing them from getting through, but they were able to communicate with the other boat, and with the barges, so there was nothing wrong with the equipment.

She lay awake, thinking about the placement of the barges. She forced herself not to think about the cutters following behind. She hated being out of touch. In her world, back at the compound, she could reach literally worldwide for anything she needed. The Internet had become second nature to her, and the thought that the one person in all her life she most wished she could just talk to was sitting back in that complex, waiting for her and that she couldn't reach him would have driven her quickly mad if it had not been for the storm.

She couldn't run a full simulation from the laptop without access to her network, so she couldn't even tell what was likely to happen when they got their pumps into place. She'd spent most of the day calculating the placement, taking into consideration, as much as possible, the smaller capacity she was working with. It was infuriating, after so many months of research with the pumps, to be thrown into this so quickly that she had no time to use the full set of tools at her disposal. With the computers back at the compound she could have gone into this with more confidence—though if the simulations had not been as good as she hoped, she knew she'd have gone through with it anyway—but maybe it was better not to know. They were, after all, only simulations, and putting too much faith in simulations and calculations was what had brought them to this point in the first place. There was no way to plan for the "joker" in the deck—the random factors of nature, the universe, and fate.

The tug's engines chugged rhythmically, and though she couldn't sleep, the sound was soothing, almost hypnotic. She drifted, her mind not really anchored to any one thought or image. She remembered Phil as she'd last seen him. She thought of the hangar, and wondered if he'd seen it and known why she had left it the way she had. She thought of Keith, and the computers, and wondered if he had done what she hadn't had the time to do. She wondered if he'd run the simulations and if he knew—better than she did—what they faced.

The waves pounding against the hull of the big tugboat were rougher than they had been when she'd first laid down. The boat rolled up and then back down, sliding over the water. Every now and then she glanced over at the digital clock on her small desk. She'd not brought any clocks with dials, and she had insisted that all hands be equipped with digital chronometers. She didn't know if it would matter, but in the years since Phil's disappearance, she'd become somewhat of an expert on disappearances in "The Devil's Triangle," and she'd not read any reports of digital devices being affected in the way analog watches and timepieces seemed to be. They didn't need any further confusion, and if they were going to disappear for the next thirty years, she would wait to find out the hard way. If the interference with the radio sets was a symptom of what Phil had experienced, she didn't want to know until the U.S. Navy of 2036 was pulling her from the battered shell of the tugboat.

Finally she gave up, rolled off the cot, slipped on her boots and Phil's peacoat and headed for the bridge. She found Captain Greenwood there ahead of her, and without a word, he handed her a hot cup of black coffee. The night was dark. There was still light from the almost full moon, but clouds scudded across the sky, and the wind was much stronger than it had been when she'd first gone below.

"We'll be in position to release the first barge by eight o'clock this morning," he told her quietly. "We still haven't heard anything from the cutters."

He let the silence hang, as if expecting her to fill it, but Andrea merely nodded, sipping her coffee.

Captain Greenwood turned to stare out over the choppy sea. "We should have them all in place by no later than one o'clock in the afternoon."

"How far out is the storm?" Andrea asked.

He turned back to her. "It hasn't changed course or speed. The projections you gave me match precisely what we're getting off the radar. If we get in position on schedule, the boats can get out ahead of the storm."

Andrea nodded again, thinking. "But if the cutters don't show up soon, the crews will be stranded."

"Exactly," he replied. "I'm not sure what to do, to be frank. We have a commitment to keep these people safe, but . . ."

"But the storm is going to kill thousands before it's done," she continued for him, "and if we can stop it . . ."

Captain Greenwood nodded. "I don't like being the one to leave," he said at last. "I wish I could take the place of someone on the barge and meet the storm myself. Then I would know I'm doing the right thing, but I wouldn't be making that decision for anyone else."

"We'll gather the crews at sunrise," Andrea said, deciding on the spot. "If there are those who don't want to go through with this, we'll transfer them to the tug. Whoever is willing to remain will transfer to the barges and get the pumps running. There *is* shelter on the barges, and in the last test most of them rode out the storm, so it isn't a suicide mission, though with this storm it might be close . . ."

Captain Greenwood nodded slowly. "If there are not enough to stay," he said at last, "I'll put the first mate in charge and take one of their places. I don't know if we can really do what you say we can, but . . ."

He waved his hand in the direction of his radarscope. "I've never seen anything like that. I have family back on the coast, and if I can keep that thing from crashing down on their heads . . ."

Andrea smiled. "Let's just hope the cutters show up in the next few hours, and it isn't an issue. I think most of those who are out here with me will stick through to the end, cutter or no cutter. We've worked together for a long time, and sometimes you just have to know if you were right. That probably doesn't make any sense," she mused, "but it's true. I've been fighting this storm in one way or another for three decades. I've seen that swirl on my computer thousands of times, gone to bed with it running into the coast as I slept and seen it stopped cold any number of times—and none. It's become very personal."

Greenwood nodded.

There was a burst of static from the radio, and both turned toward the cabin. A voice called out, breaking up every few syllables, but loud enough to be made out over the dull throb of the engines.

"What was that?" Captain Greenwood called to the seaman on watch. "Did you catch that?"

"Not sure, sir," the young man answered. "I couldn't make it all out, but I think . . . sir, do you know a ship called the USS *Cyclops*?"

Greenwood didn't answer. He stared at the cabin in silence.

Andrea studied his face, but she couldn't read his expression. "What is it?"

The captain shook his head. "Static," he said. "It was only static."

The message wasn't repeated. Andrea thought about asking what was wrong, but he turned away before she had a chance. She thought he was going to ignore her, but at last he spoke.

"The USS *Cyclops* pulled out of Rio de Janeiro in 1918, stopped in Barbados, and entered the Devil's Triangle," he said, watching the waves as if he expected something to sail out of the shadowy mist at any moment. "It disappeared with more than three hundred crew members and was never seen again. No trace of wreckage, no storms to speak of—she just vanished."

Andrea stared out at the sea, following Captain Greenwood's gaze.

"Wouldn't the radio be on a much lower frequency?" she asked, her heart suddenly pounding, though there was nothing to see, or to hear.

"If those men can still broadcast out here," the captain said, "anything is possible."

They fell silent again and watched together as the last hazy shroud of night slowly leaked from the sky and the sun tinted the skyline bright red. Andrea closed her eyes, and couldn't suppress a shudder. The captain, if he noticed the red sky at all, showed no sign of it. He was absorbed in his own thoughts.

When the radio crackled a second time, they both jumped. The young seaman on watch had grabbed the headset before either of them could react. The speaker crackled again, and then they heard a voice clearly.

"Stormfury One, this is *Moontide*, over."

Andrea turned to Captain Greenwood, and they almost collided in their efforts to reach the radio set. The young sailor, Seth, who'd been on the helm the night before, was the operator. He pulled off the headset quickly and handed it to Greenwood. Andrea stood by anxiously as the captain took the microphone.

"This is Stormfury One, calling *Moontide*. Read you five by five. Good to hear your voice."

There was a momentary silence, then a new voice washed out through the speaker, older and with authority. Andrea assumed the captain at the other end had taken over the radio set as well.

"Is that you, Jay?" there was no attempt at protocol this time. The voice was steady, but tense.

"Yeah, is that you, Al?"

"Affirmative," came the immediate reply. "Listen, Jay, we may have a situation."

Captain Greenwood said nothing, and the *Moontide*'s captain continued. "We left the second cutter just off the coast," he continued. "They were having engine trouble. We last heard from them about three hours ago. They had completed repairs and were on their way—but we lost them. I can't contact them on the radio, and I can't reach base."

"So you don't know for sure they're still behind you," Captain Greenwood finished.

"Exactly. I assume that they are, and that the same interference that cut us off from you is now preventing us from communicating with them as well, but they could have had more trouble and veered off course to avoid the storm. There's no way that I can see to find out without turning around and going back far enough to pick up their signal. If we do that we might not be on time to get you guys out of there."

"Come on ahead," Captain Greenwood said without hesitation. "We'll tell the crews what the deal is, and we'll put those most concerned on the last two barges. You can pick those two crews up, and the second barge will have to get the last two. If it doesn't show up . . ."

"Are you sure, Jay?" the voice at the other end seemed anything but sure.

"I'm sure," Captain Greenwood replied. "We lost radio

communications a long time ago, and there's no reason to assume that isn't the case now. We'll hear from the other cutter in time."

"Roger. And Jay?"

Greenwood didn't answer.

"Good luck."

"You too," the captain replied. "You too, Al. Let's go kick that storm's butt, what do you say?"

"You got it. *Moontide*, over, and out."

The radio fell silent again, and Jay turned to Andrea. "Well, it seems the odds have shifted slightly in our favor. Let's get everyone out on deck and tell them what's going on. Then we'll contact the crews on the barges. I want to give everyone a chance to think this through. It won't do you or anyone else any good to have someone panic out there."

Andrea nodded. The sun was rising now, but the daylight was as ominous as the twilight had been the night before. The storm's presence was heavy in the air, and she felt her nerves tingle with some indefinable energy. She thought the crew felt it too. Every movement was a little too crisp, and more than once she caught others staring off at the horizon. The closer they got to the drop zones for the barges, the more real their situation, and the inherent danger associated with it, became.

As it turned out, only two members of the barge crews had to be transferred, and they were able to handle this easily enough with a sling that was sometimes used during underway replenishment details. They rigged what was known as a hi-line and using pulleys and ropes they were able to transfer goods, or personnel, from one boat to the other. Most of the personnel had been handpicked by Andrea long before, and they knew the risks. It was difficult to know if the actual seriousness of those risks had sunk in, but they weren't backing down. Once everyone was in place for his or her final assignment, they moved into position, and the first barge was detached from the second tug. Immediately the crew began dropping the anchors at each end, and on each side.

Once the barge was locked as firmly in position as possible, they set to work priming and activating the pumps. Andrea saw them scurry about the deck of the barge, growing smaller and smaller in her sight as the tug paralleled them and moved on toward the next drop. They would be long out of sight of the first barge when they placed the second, even further than she would have liked, but they had to make do with what they had.

Andrea and Captain Greenwood stood at the bow of their tug. They were making much faster time than the second tug. Their own first drop wouldn't be until after the first three barges were in place, and they had to move as quickly as they could if they wanted to allow for enough time. If it hadn't been necessary to meet with all the personnel at once, they would have veered off early in the morning, reached their positions, and been gone. Now they had to make up the time, and they were running across the swells, which were growing taller and rougher. Time had grown critical, and there was still no word from the second cutter.

Around ten A.M. they reached their first drop. Captain Greenwood was everywhere at once, calling out orders to the hands on the barges and overseeing the release of the lines. Andrea stayed out of his way, but she watched anxiously as the seas tugged at the barge, making it dance like a cork. She was afraid the lines would snap before they were able to get it in place and drop the anchors, but soon four solid lines were grappling the bottom, and she watched the crews fan out around the pumps as the tug's engines revved and they moved on down the line. They had three more to release before the final barge, and that was the one Andrea would board.

As they moved north, the seas calmed somewhat, but it didn't take long for the swells to rise again. She hoped they had not miscalculated how far ahead of the storm they would have to start the pumps, or how close they could *be* to the storm and still safely pick up the personnel with the cutters. There were so many factors that you could talk about and think about, but never really foresee. So many ways this could go horribly wrong.

If they had had a perfect setup, she would have been much further ahead of the approaching storm, and the pumps would have been in place and operational hours earlier. The cooling action was intense, and would not take very long, but they were spreading the pumps so thinly that there would be shifts in the temperature across the face of the storm. At the center of the gap between any two barges, the temperature would be warmer. What if the storm just burst through the gaps, swallowed the barges and pumps and blasted on its way?

She shook her head and concentrated on watching as the lines for the second to last barge were released. The waves were still heavy, but did not seem any worse than they had when the first barge had been released. She saw her people scramble over the flat, bobbing decks like mice. Each time the barge was lifted on one of the long, flowing swells, it dropped on the far side, shuddering as it fell. When this happened Andrea knew the men and women on that deck felt as if they'd tripled their weight as gravity dragged at them unmercifully.

She smiled ruefully and flexed her knees, wondering how her sixty-nine-year-old legs were going to take that kind of stress. She was in good condition. She'd worked out every day of her adult life, and had competed in two marathons over the past ten years, just so she could add that to her list of accomplishments, but this was not going to be easy. A world where people ran for pleasure and fitness seemed a million miles away from where she stood at that moment.

They made much faster time with only the one barge attached, and before she knew it they were in place. She knew that there were five more barges down the line—or there would be if Gabrielle had come through. She stared out over the ocean in every direction, but there was nothing but the rolling expanse of waves. The sensation of entering another world was so sharp that she wondered, just for an instant, if they'd already disappeared into that other place, where Philip had been for so long. That place where nothing worked right, and watches spun backward.

Seth was at the helm again, and he glanced over at her with a smile. She smiled back, her own expression more tentative. Then the speaker crackled. She rushed into the bridge, closing the door against the sound beyond and waited. No one was manning the radio at that moment. The speaker crackled again, and a voice came across, faintly. She stepped close, leaning down to listen, but couldn't make out all the words. She heard the words *Daybreak—Moontide*—and 'over,' but that was all.

She grabbed the headset and slipped it on, keying the microphone quickly. "*Moontide*, this is Stormfury One, over." There was no response. She repeated herself several times. Once there was a faint break in the static, as if someone had keyed a microphone far away, but no message followed.

She removed the headset and turned to Seth.

"They said *Daybreak*," he confirmed, nodding as if she'd asked a question. "That's the other cutter."

Andrea took a deep breath and nodded. She wanted to say something, to thank him for . . . what? Confirming her own senses? She couldn't quite get the words out, but she did manage a slightly better smile. Then she turned, exited the cabin, and readied herself to transfer to the last barge. It was time to get to work, and if that last message had been nothing more than a tease from God, at least she'd do what she could.

On deck, Captain Greenwood had rigged the hi-line to the barge, and the sling was in place. The rest of the barge's crew was already in place, and they were standing by to drop the anchors, once the lines from the tugboat were released.

Andrea slipped into the harness and tugged at the lines nervously. It had not seemed a big deal when she'd watched the others doing this earlier, but now, with the seas rolling beneath her and the sensation of the lines growing taut, then slack between the barge and the tug, it was an entirely new proposition.

Captain Greenwood laid a hand on her shoulder. "Are you sure you want to go through with this? They have enough people over there to get the job done."

Shaking her head, Andrea tightened the last strap. "I have to go. I have to see this through. And if I were to leave with you, and something went wrong . . ."

The captain nodded. "I wish I was going with you, but it seems as if you'll have enough people without me, and I might just be in the way."

She smiled at him. "You get your boat and your people out of here," she said, "and thank you for everything, Captain."

He nodded, but didn't speak, and she thought she caught an odd glitter at the corner of his eye, just before he turned and gave the order to lower her.

After that, she could think of nothing but the wind, the roaring of the water below her, though she could not for the life of her remember it being so loud moments before, and the swaying of the ropes. Just for a moment, as one swell passed, the rope dipped, and she shot down toward the surface, but the crew of the barge worked the lines quickly and with her eyes closed and her hands gripping the rope harness tightly, she shot across the gap as quickly as they could draw her.

Then she was loose, standing on wobbly knees as they supported her long enough to get the harness free and get her to a seat. The lines were cast off quickly, and she felt the deep, vibrating grate of chains sliding through chocks as the anchors were dropped, first on both ends, then in the center.

Captain Greenwood stood on the fantail of the tug as it pulled away, growing to a tiny speck on the horizon. Andrea shook her head and rose unsteadily. Then, as her balance returned, she turned to the others. "Let's do this!" she called over the sound of the water splashing against the sides of the barge. "We don't have much time!"

They moved without further instruction, one group to each pump. As she worked, Andrea scanned the skyline, but there was no sign of the cutters. Above them, and to the south, the sky had started to darken with the first hints of rain.

Chapter Twenty-Three

Phil heard the helicopter first. It roared in over the compound, circled once, and dropped without ceremony in the center of the large parking lot below. They had cleared the area for just such a landing, but there were no flights due in. Keith and Phil hurried from the control room toward the main doors of the building. As they stepped out of the building, they saw several men in uniform and one man in a dark suit debark a large U.S. Navy chopper, ducking as they passed through the wash from the rotor blades.

The three approached and without preliminary, the man in the suit, tall with dark hair going to gray, stepped forward. He ignored Keith and stared at Phil in what might have been shock. The briefcase dropped from his hand, and he glanced down at it, just for a second, before snapping his head back up to stare again.

"Phil?" he asked. It wasn't really a question, and sounded even less like one when he repeated it. "Phil Wicks?"

Phil returned the gaze for a moment, and then broke into a grin. "Matt Schmidt. My God. And in a suit, no less. Shouldn't you be out flying something?"

Matt's shock broke and he returned Phil's grin. "They told me, and I didn't believe it," he said. He gripped Phil's hand tightly, then drew him closer and gave him a quick hug. "Unbelievable," he added for emphasis.

Keith, who had been standing quietly by, tugged on Phil's

arm, bringing him back to the moment.

"What's up, Matt?" he asked quickly. "We have kind of a situation here . . ."

"You always were one for understatement," Matt laughed. "That's why I'm here. And no, I don't fly anymore—eyes aren't quite what they used to be. I took a position with the State Department when I retired. After your hasty exit from the clinic up in Norfolk, they ran some checks on you. When they found the files and figured out what you were up to when you disappeared, it didn't take them long to make the connection to that storm out there."

He pointed in the direction of the ocean. "It also didn't take them long to put you together with my name and to call me. We have to talk, Phil."

"Not a lot of time for talk just now," Keith cut in. "We have to get inside and monitor the operation. Lives are at stake."

"Matt was with me on Operation Stormfury," Phil said, turning to Keith. "He might be of some help."

"Let's get inside, and we can find out what these gentlemen want from us while we check on Andrea and the boats."

"Ah," Matt said, "then it *was* her. We got reports from the USCG that they tried to warn off a couple of ocean-going tugs, loaded to the gills with barges and heading directly into the path of the storm. Somehow, all of the details only pointed in one direction."

"You know Andrea," Phil said bleakly.

Matt put a hand on Phil's shoulder. "I know you're worried, Phil, but the government needs to know what's going on, too. I have a lot of resources at my command, and I'll tell you—if they can stop that storm, divert it, or do anything useful to it at all—I'm here to help."

"Just like the good old days," Phil said.

The two uniformed officers stepped forward then, and offered their hands. Phil and Keith each took one, then swapped.

"Captain Jason Barnes," the first one said. "I'm with NOAA."

"Lieutenant Mike Penn," the second officer said, in turn. "I'm a pilot out of Oceana Naval Air Station. They sent me down to cover all the bases. I have experience flying over hurricanes." He smiled at Phil. "Apparently we have something in common, sir."

They turned as a group and entered the main building. Keith led them through the clean room and into the control center. As they glanced around, taking in the sophisticated equipment and the confused expressions of the operators, Matt laughed.

"Man," he said, turning to Phil once again, "this is as good as anything we have at the Pentagon. Sure is a long way from the old days."

"I was thinking the same thing," Phil replied. "This is all new to me, too."

Matt nodded soberly. "Forgot, just for a minute there, why I was here. You were gone a long time, Phil. I'd like to hear about it, when we get a minute. Questions are being asked about where you've been, how your plane could have flown in the condition it's in, and a few other things."

"There was nothing wrong with my plane." Phil frowned. "I know the landing was rough, but under the circumstances . . ."

"That's what the ground crew said," Matt nodded, "but . . . well, here."

He opened his briefcase on one of the tables and pulled out a small stack of Polaroid photographs. He handed them to Phil without a word. Keith drifted past them to the main screen and was talking quietly to the operators.

Phil stared at the first photo and frowned. "This must be a mistake," he said at last, flipping past it through the stack.

"I'm afraid not, partner," Matt said. "I took these myself, just before we took off. We were one of the last aircraft to evacuate. They left your plane right where it was towed after the landing."

The photographs showed the decrepit, desiccated hull of an airplane. The sides hung in rusted shreds. The tires were nothing but piles of windswept dust. It looked as if it had been parked and ignored for—well, for thirty years. No way had it flown only a few short hours before. No way had he been in it.

Keith stepped up, and Phil handed the photos to him, but before a word could be spoken, Susie called out from her console.

"We just heard from *Daybreak*," she said excitedly. "Their engines are on line and they are en route. They should have time to catch up, if nothing else goes wrong. They have no comms with *Moontide* or the barges, though, and we've lost contact with the boats out of Bermuda, as well. Interference is heavy out there."

"We had the same problem," Captain Barnes said, stepping closer to the screen. "We have good radar images, like these," he pointed at the swirling white mass on the screen, "but we can't seem to raise anyone close to the storm on radio. It's like everything within four hundred miles of the thing has been cut off from the rest of the world."

Matt turned to Keith. "What's going on out there? What is Andrea up to—and more importantly, how can I help?"

"It will take a while to explain what she's trying to do," Keith replied, moving to one of the consoles, "and at this point, I'm not sure what might help. I may be able to give us a better idea whether she can pull it off or not if I can get a simulation running. We've run the simulation with all of our equipment operational, but unfortunately, that isn't the case here."

"You run the simulation," Phil said, turning to Matt suddenly. "Can you get me to Bermuda? I'm told we can reach the island from the far side, away from the storm. It will take a while to explain why, but I know the hurricane is going to miss the island. It's already been as close as it's going to get, so conditions shouldn't get any worse."

Matt thought for a second, and then nodded. "Give me a phone and about ten minutes to arrange it. I'll get us something out of Norfolk, if there are still any aircraft that haven't been evacuated. We can be there in twenty minutes, transfer, and be airborne."

He turned to Lieutenant Penn. "You willing to take us?"

Penn grinned in return. "Always ready to fly, sir. That's why I'm here."

Matt stepped away to a desk, and a phone that Keith pointed out.

Phil only nodded. He was already seeing Andrea's face, trying to etch the lines onto it that the years would have brought her, and wondering what it would be like to hold her now—whether she'd remember him, still love him, or just stare at him in shock, or horror. He certainly wasn't the man he had been when they'd last seen one another.

"It's set," Matt said, replacing the phone on its hook. "Let's roll."

Keith gripped Phil by the shoulder. "Are you sure? Are you up to it?"

Phil shrugged. "Only one way to find out. I can rest on the flight. I know you have a lot to do here, Keith, and I'm mostly just in the way. I'm so far out of the loop I don't even recognize it. Over there, though," he waved in the general direction of the storm, and Bermuda, "over there I may be able to find those boats, or even a way out there myself. I don't know what I might find, but at least I'll be doing *something*."

Keith nodded. "Good luck, then." He turned to his radio operator. "Susie, give Mr. Schmidt our frequencies. Once they're in the air, we can stay in contact as long as the storm allows it. Maybe they'll be able to spot the barges from the air and relay information."

Susie jotted a couple of numbers onto a pad and ripped the sheet off, handing it over.

"We'll check in as soon as we're airborne," Matt promised.

"I'm going to stay here, if you have no objections," said Captain Barnes. "This is fascinating, and I have a lot of questions. If this is the heart of the operation, I'd like to be here to observe."

Matt nodded. "That's fine."

Then Phil, Matt, and Lieutenant Penn turned and headed for the door, and the chopper waiting in the lot outside.

"Are you sure they'll give us a plane?" Phil asked as they hurried past the computer bays. "They didn't seem too happy with me when I touched down."

"They'll give it to us," Matt replied, shouting now as they exited the building and neared the helicopter, which sat with its blades still spinning. "As long as they believe there's a chance that Andrea can pull off a miracle, they'll support it. I can't say what they're going to do when it's all over, but for now, we've got as close to a free shot as the government ever gives."

He stopped for a second, so that Lieutenant Penn would

pull ahead a few steps, then said more quietly, "It'll be good flying with you again, Captain."

They hurried after Penn and stepped up into the helicopter. Moments later they were strapped in and soaring over the Dismal Swamp through hazy cloud cover, banking off into darkness.

Gabrielle cursed under her breath as the last of their barges swayed and tossed in the waves. The sky was gray and overcast. There was no rain yet, but she felt it in the air, heavy with potential threat. The other four barges were in place, and she'd seen the cruiser pass earlier, heading out to bring in the first crew. It was too tight. They should already have been in place and gone, but the roughening seas and the abbreviated crews had held them back. Now they had to get this final barge anchored and running.

At the helm, a grizzled old native seaman clung tightly, his face ashen. He was a very good sailor, as were the other five who would aid him in getting the tug out of harm's way. He'd been sailing and fishing around the island all his life, and he could read the signs. He felt the storm, just as she did, but where Gabrielle's fear was tainted with frustration, his was pure and absolute. He had seen hurricanes tear across the island too many times not to fear them, and he had been sailing long enough to know the foolishness of being at sea when they hit. Only his loyalty and the vague hope of "magic" kept him from veering away from the bouncing barge and making for the open sea.

The last of the crew, with the exception of Gabrielle, was lowered down the hi-line and hit the deck of the barge with a thump as a new swell raised it suddenly to meet her. There was a wild moment when it seemed she would be yanked back over the side, but strong arms grabbed her from both sides, and the harness swung free. They pulled it back to the tug, and the two seamen who were handling the lines turned almost frantically to Gabrielle.

She took a last glance at the darkening sky, gulped in a calming breath of air, and nodded. The two men helped her quickly into the harness, and over the side. Before she knew what had happened, she was stumbling on the deck of the barge, and the harness was torn free. As soon as she was down, the lines were released, and the tug throttled up, pulling a safe distance away so that the two vessels wouldn't collide.

Gabrielle waved them off, and with a deep-throated rumble, the tugboat turned away from the barge, and from the path of the storm, and headed straight out past the island toward the open sea. As long as the storm moved parallel away from the island and didn't turn straight into them too quickly, they had time.

Gabrielle turned to stare in the other direction, where the cutters should be coming from, but she could see nothing—not even the next barge. They were alone, and the waves rolled in huge sloping bulges beneath the barge, tugging at the anchor lines. They held.

With a few sharp commands she got them all moving, and the work of the moment took her mind off her growing terror. The pumps had to be started, and they had to be running long enough in advance of the front storm wall to make a difference in the overall temperature. She knew this could happen fairly quickly, but there was no way to gauge how much time they might have. She could call on the radio in the control shack when they were done, but for the moment they had to work, and the pitching, bucking deck fought them every step of the way.

It was almost half an hour before the first two pumps were

operational. The third was quicker. They had their rhythm down by that point, and when it came time to start the two pumps on the far side of the barge, she broke them up into two groups. One hour and ten minutes after the tugboat veered away from the barge, all five pumps were pounding compressed air beneath the surface, forcing the cooler water up from below and sending rhythmic pulses through the barge, like giant heartbeats, slightly out of sync with one another. It was jarring, but bearable.

They gathered in the small shack around the radio and Gabrielle powered it up and began to call out. There was no response, and they could see nothing in any direction. The cloud cover had lowered over the surface of the water, and visibility was low. One of the others flipped a large circuit breaker, and huge strobing beacons flashed on poles at either end of the barge. It was impossible to tell how far they could be seen through the murky shadows. Gabrielle continued her message, reporting they were ready for pickup, but the radio spit back only silence—and the waves continued to grow taller and wider.

On the cutter *Daybreak* the radio operator turned to his captain. "We've lost contact with the base," he said. "Shall I continue to try them?"

"There's no point in that," Captain Clayton replied, shaking his head with a frown. "We've lost comms with every ship that's headed into this mess. We almost had the *Moontide* earlier, keep trying them, and keep trying for the barges. We're in this for keeps, now—the only way to go is ahead, and we have to assume that we'll find them where they're supposed to be and get them out of there. We have time to get out, either way."

The radioman nodded. He flipped the frequency dial to

the circuit they had established between cutters, and began to call out to the other ship at regular intervals, each time waiting patiently for a response. The sky had grown hazy, and the endless static was almost maddening, but he kept at it. They were four hours out, and the closer they came to the target zone, and the place where the other cutter, and the barges, were supposed to be located, the more likely it was he'd raise somebody. At this point, if he'd raised a Nazi U-boat, he'd have been happy, but he kept this thought to himself. The cutter sliced easily through the waves, making good speed.

Clayton, who normally would have turned over the bridge to his mate and rested at this point, stood with his hands clasped behind his back, staring out across the water ahead. The red sky at sunrise was still fresh in his mind, and he hoped he wasn't making a fatal error. It might be that the storm had screwed up reception, and that everything was fine. It might also be that something else had gone wrong, or, if the stories he'd heard about Captain Wicks' last flight were true, it might be that no one was out there at all—that they were simply gone, and he was leading his own crew right in after them. He thought about his wife, and his son Bobby. He wondered what it would be like to return to them after thirty years, a very old man, and his skin grew clammy at the thought. He kept the thoughts to himself, and the miles skimmed away beneath the hull.

He thought about the *Moontide*'s captain, and he whispered to him across the waves. "Where are you, Al, you old son of a bitch? Where the hell are you?"

Only the waves, and the wind, answered.

The cutter *Moontide* pulled away from the third barge with the crew safely aboard and turned toward the fourth. Things were going smoothly, but that wouldn't help the crews on the second set of barges. Visibility was growing worse, and the rolling seas were making it difficult to get in close enough to take the crews aboard safely. Already there had been close calls, and they had at least three more barges to go.

The radio crackled, but no one paid much attention. The static pops and cracks had been grinding out of the speaker for hours, but they hadn't heard another radio operator's voice since they'd heard the half-message from *Daybreak* and gotten the garbled news that the second cutter had made repairs and was on its way. With the seas as heavy as they were, it was almost too late. It was something they hadn't accounted for—the surge reaching them so far ahead of the storm wall. Even a Category Five should have given them enough time to get in and out with the crews. This one, though? It was simply too large and too powerful to predict.

The radio crackled again, and Captain Al Menard turned with a scowl on his face. He strode briskly to the set, thinking he'd turn up the squelch and stop the infernal squawking sounds, but he stopped about a foot short and listened intently. At first what he heard seemed to be the ghost of a voice, not really in phase with the signal. He couldn't make out any words clearly, but there *was* something there. He hurried the last few steps and grabbed the headset.

"*Daybreak*, this is *Moontide*; do you copy, over?"

There was another scratchy burst of static, and then, weak, but discernible, came the response. "*Moontide*, this is *Daybreak*. Have you weak, but readable. Are you in position, over?"

"*Daybreak*, this is *Moontide*. Affirmative. We have completed pickup number three. I repeat: we have picked up three."

When he got a response, he quickly gave the operator on

the *Daybreak* the coordinates of the sixth barge. "Get there as quickly as you can," he said, before signing off. "The seas are rough out here, as you may have noticed. It may take you longer than planned to get them out, and we don't know where the Bermuda barges have anchored. We have no comms at this time."

"Roger, *Moontide*, this is *Daybreak*, out." There was a silence, then the speaker crackled again, and the voice returned. "And might I add," the operator on the *Daybreak* said, "it's damn good to hear your voice."

Captain Menard almost laughed. "Let's take 'em home. *Moontide* out."

Chapter Twenty-Four

Andrea stood on the deck of the barge and watched the nose of the cutter plow through the surf toward them. The sky was very dark, and the wind had picked up to the point that, between the gusts and the choppy, rolling seas, it was difficult to remain on her feet. She was tired. She had never been so tired. Making her way up and down the length of the barge, fighting the shuddering gravitational pull each time they rolled down the side of a new wave as her weight seemed to multiply, then recede, had put a strain on her joints that would ache for weeks. It didn't matter. The pumps were operational, the anchors, for the moment, were holding, and now their salvation was in sight. She had never been happier to see anything in her life.

The *Daybreak* was making slow headway, but she knew this was mostly due to running across the seas, trying to get into position. They would be alongside, or as close as they dared to come, in moments. She called her crew close in about her and clung tightly to a pipe just outside the barge's control cabin.

As the *Daybreak* pulled alongside, she heard the sliding roll of the cutter's anchor snaking down through the depths, and a man standing on deck, Captain Clayton, she believed his name was, called out to them to stand by through a battery-powered bullhorn. They were soaked and shivering. The wind was heavy with moisture, and the clouds grew lower and denser with each passing moment.

There was the POP of a line gun, and a balled-up and weighted knot of rope soared over from the cutter to land on the deck. Her people gathered it in, working quickly to haul the heavier lines across. Within moments they had rigged the lines, and though they creaked with the strain, they held.

Andrea pushed the others forward, youngest first, and one by one they were hauled up the line, the harness swaying in the wind and threatening to slam them into the hull of the cutter. Each time the men on deck managed to avoid disaster, swinging the sling up and over the railing and hurriedly passing the sling back down. It seemed to take forever, but Andrea knew they couldn't have been at it more than fifteen minutes when it came time for her to be placed in the sling. One young man remained behind, and she protested, but he pushed her firmly into the harness.

"I'll be fine," he told her with a fierce grin. "I can strap myself in more quickly than I can show you how to do it. Get up there, ma'am."

She nodded, and in moments she was swinging crazily out over the waves. She closed her eyes and prayed then. She prayed for herself, and for Phil. She prayed for the crews of the other barges, and for the storm to pass. Before she could get to Keith, the compound, or Gabrielle, she felt a sudden lurch and was hoisted up and over the cutter's rail.

She stood, shaking, with one of her assistants helping support her weight as they watched the sling take its last journey down. The young man was as good as his word. He was into the sling and back up onto the cutter's deck in what seemed less than a minute. Without hesitation, the rigging was released from the cutter, tossed over the side, and left to dangle from the side of the barge. With a roar they came about, swung away from the barge and into the seas, and angled off toward the open ocean.

The crew helped Andrea into the bridge and sat her down in a padded chair. She brushed them off, though she still felt too shaky to stand on her own. "Have we heard from the others? Has anyone heard from Gabrielle?"

"There's another boat," the captain assured her. "I didn't recognize the pilot's name, and I couldn't make out much of what he said through the static. In any case, we're out of time. I'm setting a course away from the storm. I sure hope those damned things," he poked a thumb back over his shoulder toward the barge and its five pumps, "can make a difference. We're going to be lucky to get out of here with our skins."

Andrea slumped back on the seat, drained. She needed to know that the others would be getting out as well, but there was nothing she could do. Everything she had to throw at the storm was already in place. She knew she should feel a sense of exhilaration or accomplishment, but all she felt was exhausted and worried, frightened for her friends and her colleagues. She wanted to talk to Phil, and Keith, and she wanted her computer. None of it was possible, so she drew her legs up with her knees against her chest, circled her legs with her arms, and rocked slowly, face pressed into the damp denim of her jeans.

The *Daybreak* sliced powerfully through the waves, knifing away from the barge and into the dim, lightless void.

Gabrielle could barely see the flashing lights at either end of her barge. The wind howled around them, and she was so cold her teeth chattered wildly, and her jaws ached from trying to prevent it. They huddled together in the control cabin, taking turns standing and watching. She had repeated that the boat would come for them, and that everything would be fine until the words were a mantra, chanted into the face of the coming storm and swallowed up unheard. No one believed her, she knew, but she kept repeating it anyway. There was nothing else to do but to give in to despair, and if she did that, she knew, she might as well dive over the side now and let the waves dash her against the side of the barge until she was senseless.

They had been finished with the pumps for an hour and a half. They should have been picked up by now, should have been on their way out around the island to safety. Instead, the winds ground at the walls of their small cabin with a fury that threatened to rip it from the frame of the barge, and the waves rolled up and back like the sinewy curves of some giant serpent. They were alone. Gabrielle had never felt so alone. Even with Jason at her side, her arms around him and clinging, she felt the darkness pressing in, separating her from him, from the others, and from the world.

She thought about praying. It had been a long time since her last confession, but she knew the words well enough. The rituals of childhood, particularly a childhood riddled with Mass, penitence, and communion, were hard to shake. She actually had the first "Our Father" on the tip of her tongue when an image burst into her mind. It was an image of God the Father in all his white-haired, bearded holiness listening to her prayer and then shrugging. Like, what did she expect him to do? "You don't have sense enough to get in out of the rain" hardly covered it this time, did it? She snorted and almost burst into hysterical laughter, but bit it back. There would be no coming back from hysteria, either.

It was Sandra's turn to watch. She was a large, blonde girl—a former Olympic swimmer with strong shoulders and fierce green eyes. It took a moment for Gabrielle to drag herself out of her self-absorbed misery to understand the girl was shaking her and saying something.

"Wha . . ."

"The boat!" Sandra screamed. "The boat is out there."

Gabrielle leaped to her feet with Jason right behind her. The others crowded around the windows and rubbed the fogged glass, trying to see. Sandra was right. The cruiser was out there, rolling in slowly, turned parallel with the barge. The throb of the engines was buried in the pounding of the surf and the pumps, but the sleek lines of the boat were clearly visible, and there were men clinging to its railings, waving their arms.

Gabrielle tried the radio. At first she got nothing, then, remembering it wasn't one of the cutters, she flipped the frequency dial frantically. A moment later she heard the scratchy static-laced voice of the old captain. "Stand by for lines," he said, and she nearly collapsed with relief.

It was far from over, though. The seas were much too rough for a standard transfer. They got the lines across fine, but when they had been tied off on the barge, they threatened to snap almost immediately. The backlash of such an action would cut a man in half as cleanly as a giant cleaver, and they all knew it. The lines were cast off again hurriedly.

Gabrielle thought frantically, and then made up her mind. The barge was equipped with several standard U.S. Navy lifeboats. She returned to the radio. She quickly relayed her idea to the cruiser, and after only a moment's hesitation, got the green flag. The crews from the first four barges were already aboard. There were plenty of experienced hands on the ship—but their combined skill couldn't change the seas that threatened to capsize them. Something had to be done, and quickly.

Working together, they unfastened one of the lifeboats.

They were stored in huge orange canisters designed to open at a certain depth from the pressure of the water. They could also be opened manually and that is what Gabrielle ordered. The boat hissed to life, and her crew scrambled around it, fighting not to be drawn or washed overboard, but fighting at the same time to secure the boat before the wind could yank it away from them. When it was fully inflated, Gabrielle climbed inside and tied off the raft to the barge to hold it in place.

The rest of the crew scrambled aboard, and one by one they fastened themselves to the boat using short lines, ropes, and whatever was available. When all of the crew except for Jason was in place, they signaled the cruiser, and another line was shot across. Jason lunged, grabbed it, tripped on the deck and sprawled headlong. He clutched tightly to the line as the barge tilted, and scrambled crab-like, barely managing to cling to a stanchion and wrap his body around it before he was swept overboard.

As the barge rose again, tilting the other way, he launched himself into the raft and helped Gabrielle tie the line off at the front of the small craft. Then, releasing the lines that held them in place, she waved frantically at the cruiser.

The raft scraped alarmingly on the deck and lurched forward. The rubber craft bunched, dipped as the line was pulled taut, and then slid off the side of the barge and down about fifteen feet to the surface of the water. The crash knocked all the wind from Gabrielle's slight frame, and she gasped. Water rolled over the edges of the raft, and it plunged forward, held by the line and drawn slowly through the waves toward the side of the cruiser. Men scrambled on the deck and wrapped the line that joined them several times around a post on deck to keep tension. The waves rolled up, then down again and the line thrummed with tension. Gabrielle ducked her head—gasped as she took in a mouthful of seawater. She clung to the boat with all her strength, and slowly—very slowly—they were dragged closer.

It seemed to take hours. Water pounded them, and each time the seas beneath them rolled, the line threatened to snap, but it held. It held, and at last they felt the heavy bump of the cruiser's hull on the front of their raft. Ladders dropped over the sides, and more lines, and the crew scrambled up like rats until they were grabbed and hauled on deck by those waiting above. Finally, only Gabrielle remained. She was tired, too tired to rise, and certainly too tired to unbind the lines that held her to the rubber boat. She waved feebly to those above, but she was unable to cry out—and they would not have heard her in any case.

The lifeboat slammed into the side of the cruiser, and all the breath left her body. The world spun, and she took in another mouthful of the salty water, choking weakly.

Then—very suddenly—strong arms wrapped around her. She felt the lines that bound her to the lifeboat cut free, and she was lifted like a child. Next came a whirling, dizzying climb. She could only flail her arms and legs weakly, and in moments she felt more hands, lifting her over the rails and onto the deck.

She stared up and saw a toothy grin returning her gaze. The old fisherman smiled at her. "If you drown, who will bring the fish?"

She tried to laugh, but the seawater choked it, and she slipped into darkness, visions of nets filled with flopping fish filling her mind.

The cruiser shot out into the waves and fled for safety. The wind picked up another notch as Hurricane Andrea screamed her fury and drove toward the thin, but strengthening wall of cold water in her path.

The small boat bounced and shuddered as it rode up one swell and down the next, but the captain piloted it expertly, angling to the north toward open water and safety. The radio was silent. Even the empty squawks of static had died away. Everyone huddled below deck except for Jason and the old fisherman, who manned the helm and tried to watch the water ahead through the rain-washed windshields. Their lights were feeble in the murky darkness, and gusts of wind tore around and through the seams of doors and under cracks, whistling and screeching.

Behind them, the pumps thrummed and pounded at the water, their voices small and lost in the face of the coming storm.

Chapter Twenty-Five

As they soared over the storm, keeping well above the ten thousand foot level, Phil felt a dizzying sense of déjà vu. The sensation was heightened by the fact that Matt was there, driving the images of his first storm experience, and his last, into sharper perspective. This was, of course, much different than either of his other experiences. They were in a DC-8—the aircraft that Lieutenant Penn had explained to him was one of the current standards for hurricane research. Phil had always been a propeller-driven pilot; the jet was a new experience, and despite his weariness and the disorientation the last day had brought to him, he got little rest on the flight.

They took off out of Oceana Naval Air station and in only about an hour they closed on the near edge of the storm. They had a brief glimpse of the lights on Bermuda as they flashed overhead. Lieutenant Penn tried the radio frequencies for the barges, and for the cutters, but they got no response. It was just not possible to cut through the odd interference the storm was causing. Either that, or there was no one at the other end to answer. None of them wanted to think about that.

"We're over the line where the barges were expected to anchor," Penn called back to his two passengers. "We're up pretty high, and the storm has dropped visibility to nothing, but I'll make a run over in case we can spot their lights."

Matt nodded. He stared intently out his own window and

down on the rolling clouds below. They were high enough that the moon was clearly visible above them, but all they could see below was an endless, twisting mass of clouds.

"You remember that day, Phil?" Matt asked at last, turning away from the spectacle long enough to meet his old captain's gaze.

Phil nodded. "You know I do. Like it was yesterday. I still wake up—or I did thirty years ago—screaming, thinking that spout is driving at me to drag me down. You don't shake a memory like that."

Matt nodded, as if it was the response he'd expected, and turned back to the window again.

"Can we still reach Keith?" Phil asked.

Lieutenant Penn flipped a couple of switches, and spoke into his microphone. A second later he turned and gave Phil a thumbs-up. It was difficult to speak over the roaring of the engines, and since all three men were pilots, they dropped easily into the silent hand communications. The lines were still open.

"Ask him if there's anything we should be able to see from here, or any sign we should watch for to know that it's working," Phil shouted, raising his voice to be heard. "I don't want to just fly around up here—we should be doing some good."

Penn nodded, and Phil turned to his window, opposite the one that Matt was staring out of. There was nothing below but endless dark clouds, stretching so far to either side that the thought of Andrea, her barges, and a bunch of compressed air pumps actually doing battle with the thing had the bitter taste of futility in his mouth.

How many years of his life—of her life—had been thrown at the walls of these storms, only to be slapped back into their faces with disdain? Andrea had lived with her father's death for more than sixty years, but did that stack up to having thirty stolen out from under you? He gritted his teeth against the thoughts that threatened to spill in and jumble his mind. He focused on the clouds below and willed his mind, and his suddenly failing eyesight, to pierce the gloom.

Once he thought he might have seen a glimmer, a flashing light, strobing in the darkness, but it was gone so quickly that he convinced himself it had only been a will-o-the-wisp, moisture in the storm reflecting back some light from the DC-8 itself, or a glimmer of moonlight.

Lieutenant Penn turned back to them.

"I'm going to bank back and run along the storm wall again," he shouted. "Scharf says that if we are going to see any change in this storm, that's where it will show up first. He also said to watch the eye."

Phil nodded. If he were thinking straighter, he'd have known this.

Matt glanced at his watch. It was working fine, and he tapped it. Phil raised an eyebrow, and Matt yelled, "The storm wall should reach the point where the barges are supposed to have created their wall of cold water in about ten minutes."

Phil nodded again.

"Where are you, Andrea?" he whispered. He turned back to the window and watched the endless roll of the clouds with growing frustration.

Along a line hundreds of miles long, eighteen barges rolled and tossed, pounded by the relentless front edge of the storm. The assault was brutal, but the anchor chains were strong and somewhat more flexible in their strength than was standard, another innovation by one of Andrea's people. Somehow, they held, though the aft anchor on one barge snapped loose near the end. The pumps functioned beautifully. Each was self-contained and held enough fuel to keep it operational well beyond the time period allotted. Either they would cool the water and break up the storm, or they would be picked up, shattered, and blown away in the monstrous grip of the wind, but they would not run out of fuel.

Around each barge, and stretching in all directions, the temperature of the water slowly dropped. The process was simple. Compressed air punched down into the water. The water that was driven downward displaced large amounts of very cold water from below and forced it up to the surface. Each barge was miles from the next, but the pumps were large. The cooling effect spread, and the further the water was cooled, the more this sped and aided the process of further cooling.

By the time the storm front arrived, the water temperature was a ragged, varied line directly in its path. The average temperature had dropped nearly twenty degrees, but there were pockets of warmer water along that length, and the water to the west was warmer still. There was no way this could have been seen from the air, and the simulation that Andrea had run had created the line with much greater symmetry. Like a broken, haphazardly gathered horde, the pumps held their ground and Hurricane Andrea, all disrespectful, fell on them in a fury.

At first it seemed that the storm wouldn't even slow. It rolled up against the wall of cold water and the barges were swallowed. Waterspouts erupted along that strip and ripped up into the air, twisting like trapped serpents, held to the ocean by having their tails nailed in place, and furiously fighting to be free.

Then, as if someone had grabbed the winds and gripped them, giving them a good shake, the eye began to grow ragged. The storm shifted, listed to the south, and to the west, but instead of roaring off unchecked, it rolled more slowly, as if unraveling.

Phil saw it first. They banked in toward the center of the storm and skirted away from the band of waterspouts, though the DC-8 was safely above the altitude these reached. They turned toward the eye, and as they did so, Phil watched the side of it stretch. It elongated, leaving behind the near perfect circular shape, and breaks appeared. The winds washed in, quickly filling those gaps and driving into the symmetry of the storm's heart.

"I'll be damned," he breathed. Matt didn't hear him, he'd spoken too softly, but Matt saw it at almost the same time.

The two turned, met one another's gaze, and shook their heads in amazement.

Lieutenant Penn had also spotted the shift in the storm, and he brought them about in a long, sweeping arc. By the time they roared back over the center of the hurricane, the eye was little more than a misshapen blotch on the roiling clouds below.

They continued on back toward the storm wall. The clouds were shifting away from Bermuda. The entire mass of the storm, ponderous and slow now, turned like an injured beast. It rolled along the wall of cooler water, breaking it up as it went, but being eaten at the same time. As more of the storm reached that point, the effect of the temperature shift rippled back through.

They shot past the storm and Lieutenant Penn turned to them. "I just heard from Mr. Scharf," he reported. "He says we should watch it. He ran a simulation with the reduced number of barges. The storm's eye reformed."

Phil frowned. He glanced over his shoulder, out the window and back toward the hurricane, which seemed to be breaking up beyond recovery. He shook his head, but even as he did so, he felt the DC-8 slip into another long, arcing curve.

As they crossed the storm again, it was difficult to tell what was happening. There was not a very clear center, but the breadth of the thing was huge. It undulated to the southwest. When they curled around yet again and passed over it, however, it was clear. The eye *was* reforming. It had opened back into a vaguely circular shape, much smaller and tighter than before, but still there. The storm whirled and writhed about it as the entire mass shifted direction.

"Damn it," Matt said, smacking his hand into his knee.

Phil just stared down at the storm. He watched it as it whirled and roared its fury, and then, looking up at Matt, he smiled. The other man stared at him as if he'd lost his mind, but Phil held up a hand before his old friend could speak. "Look at it closely."

Matt did, but nothing clicked. He glanced back at Phil and shrugged, as if to say *what,* and Phil's smile only widened.

"Look how small it is," he said at last. "Matt, she didn't stop it, but look at that storm. It's no Category Five, or even a four. I'd be surprised if it holds at a two. Even if this hits ground, this is a success. We didn't have to stop it, just cripple it."

Matt stared at him, still frowning. Then, as the implications of what he'd just heard sank in, he sat back and looked a little dazed. The storm they had first flown over had exceeded any Category Five in history. The winds had been well over two hundred miles per hour, and the devastation predicted had been so catastrophic that most of the southern east coast had been evacuated to hundreds of miles inland.

Yes, there was still a storm, but no stronger than your average tropical depression. Powerful? Yes. Dangerous? Of course it was dangerous, all storms were, but this was manageable. Natural. Finally, shaking his head again, Matt started to laugh.

Lieutenant Penn stared back at them both as if they'd lost their minds, but they were too far gone to explain. It would have to wait.

At last, catching his breath, Matt managed to call out to the pilot. "See if you can get us clearance for Bermuda," he gasped. "Get this thing on the ground. Oh—and tell Mr. Scharf he has a Category One hurricane breathing down his neck—he should close the windows."

The sun rose and the skies were washed in yellow, gold, and light lavender. There was no red in sight. Andrea lay curled in a coil of rope on the deck of the *Daybreak*, blinking her eyes and feeling as if her body was so stiff it might never move again. They slid smoothly through the water, and with an effort she managed to sit up and look over the side.

Another boat ran alongside, just a bit behind them, and beyond that was a third, smaller and sleeker craft. It took her a moment to realize the dark-haired woman waving to her from the deck of that boat was Gabrielle, and that it must be the "cruiser" she'd heard about.

Men and women lined the rails of all three boats, and all of them stood with their faces uplifted to the morning sun. All of them smiled. Andrea groaned and rolled out of the mooring line she'd slept in. She stayed on her hands and knees for a moment, getting her bearings, and then, very slowly, she got to her feet and turned toward the rail once more.

She returned Gabrielle's wave, smiled feebly at those waving to her from the next boat, and turned toward the cabin. She needed coffee. She remembered vaguely that everyone was accounted for. They had gotten in, and the barges had been placed. The pumps had been lit. What happened after that was beyond their control now, but she needed to know.

And she needed to know about Phil.

As she entered, Captain Clayton smiled at her. She returned the smile bleakly, and he pointed her toward a large stainless steel coffee urn. Beside it was a stack of foam cups, and she took one gratefully, filling it with steaming black coffee.

Then she turned to the Captain. "Have we heard anything about the storm?"

He nodded, but at first he didn't speak. Andrea saw he was trying to form his response carefully, and her heart sank. If the news were good, would he hesitate?

"The storm broke up when it hit the barges," he said at last. "The bulk of the wind and rain kicked to the southwest, just like you thought it might. Then it reformed."

The words hung in the air, and she stared at him, uncomprehending.

"The eye of the storm reformed," he repeated. "They are *all* calling it Hurricane Andrea now—it's a Category One storm, hovering off the coast of North Carolina."

Andrea couldn't process it.

"Category One," she repeated numbly. "But."

Captain Clayton's smile returned, full force. "You did it," he said. "The storm may not even make landfall, but even if it does, it won't be much more than a tropical storm. You stopped it."

She nearly dropped the coffee cup, and when her weak, trembling hands continued to refuse her order to grip more tightly, Andrea set it on the edge of the chart table and fell back against the bulkhead, shaking like a leaf. She hadn't realized until that moment just how worried she had been—how sure it would be just another failure.

"You . . . you're sure?" she asked.

He nodded. "I've been on the radio with Mr. Scharf. We've been ordered into Bermuda."

Andrea nodded numbly. "How long will it take us, do you think?"

"I figure we should be tied up no later than two o'clock this afternoon, if there isn't a lot of damage to the piers. The winds hit the island pretty hard, and there was some flooding before the storm shifted toward the coast. No later than five."

She nodded, barely hearing his answer as her mind raced back over all that had just happened, and at the same time tried to process what might come next.

"If you don't mind my saying so," the captain interrupted her thoughts, "you don't look very well, ma'am. There's a cot in my cabin, just through there," he pointed toward the single door exiting the bridge. "Maybe you should lie down for a while. We still have quite a while before we catch sight of land."

Andrea nearly turned back toward the decks outside and declined, but as she pushed away from the bulkhead, her legs threatened to give way beneath her. He was right, she was in no condition to walk, let alone wander around the cutter's deck. At a nod from his captain, a young seaman escorted her through the door and down a short hall. He let her in the door, and she had no more seen the cot than she was on it, falling back with a heavy sigh. The moment her eyes closed, she slept. For the first time in years, no storms disturbed her dreams.

The cutter slipped in beside the pier without mishap. Andrea, feeling much more herself, stood at the rail and watched as men scurried about on the pier, tying off the mooring lines and lifting the bow into place. They would be ashore in moments, and she couldn't remember when the thought of solid ground beneath her feet had sounded better.

Everywhere she looked there was debris. Pieces of buildings, roofing, trees, and plants that had been broken, bent, or uprooted, lay sprawled across the end of the pier. They had cleared enough of it away to let the boats tie up. Gabrielle had taken the cruiser along the beach to its usual berth. She said they'd clear a path if they needed to, but their pier was well sheltered, and she thought they'd be okay. There was plenty of time to catch up with her, and her crew, later. For now, dry land and some food were in order—food better than the U.S. Navy MRE she'd been fed on the cutter. They'd been purchased from surplus government stock, and had about as much taste as reconstituted dirt—though they had dulled the hunger.

As she waited she saw a flash of color on the road. At first she couldn't make it out, but then she saw that it was a red Jeep. The vehicle was picking its way in and around fallen trees, and she saw it roll up and over at least one.

She didn't know why the sight of that Jeep started her heart racing again, but it did. Maybe it was just the idea that the world was converging on them. First it would be whoever was in that Jeep, then Bermudan authorities, then the U.S. Government, and who knew what other agency, country, or interested party. She knew she'd be questioned until her head swam, and already it made her tired. She watched the Jeep's approach in silence.

Then she heard the captain's deep baritone calling "all ashore," and she turned from the rail. She had no luggage, so there was nothing to gather or carry. She stopped at the end of the bow, smiled at the captain, then stepped forward and gave him a quick hug.

"Thank you," she said simply.

Then she turned and walked down the short gangplank to the wooden pier. It was shaky, but solid enough and, after a few minutes, she managed to pick her way through the branches and leaves to the shore. As she did, the Jeep pulled to a stop about twenty yards away.

Andrea stopped and waited. No one got out—not at first. She could make out two figures inside, but no details.

Then, slowly, the passenger door opened, and a man climbed out. Andrea saw him—traced the lines of his face with her gaze—gasped—and fainted, falling to a heap in the damp sand.

Phil saw her the moment her foot hit the cutter's bow, and his heart nearly stopped. She looked enough like the young woman he remembered to send a thrill through him. He watched her, and his eyes filled slowly with the warm tears he'd been holding back.

Matt drove the Jeep carefully, not glancing even once at his old friend, giving him the privacy of the moment. They pulled to a halt, and Andrea stood, watching them—waiting.

Phil stepped out of the Jeep, and he saw her eyes widen. He saw her jaw drop into a small round 'o'—just for a second—and then he saw her fall.

Andrea had barely hit the sand when Phil was at her side, Matt right on his heels, the Jeep's engine still running. Phil slid one hand under her shoulders and lifted her slightly. He studied her face, reached out with his free hand to stroke a stray, light gray hair from her eye. She trembled, and a second later, she opened her eyes.

They stared at one another for a long moment, as if their

combined gazes could anchor them solidly in one place—one universe—one moment. Then she was in his arms, and he drew her tightly to his chest, breathing in the salty scent of her hair and feeling her slender form trembling against him. They stood that way for so long his back began to ache, and his legs trembled, and at last Matt cleared his throat, tugging them gently back into the world.

"You did it," Phil said. "You stopped it."

"We did it," she replied.

He nodded and smiled, then hugged her again. As she laid her head on his shoulder, they heard the wail of sirens in the distance, and knew that the authorities were on their way.

Phil disentangled himself from her arms reluctantly. She frowned, and then smiled tentatively, seeing that he was only reaching for something.

From his pocket, Phil pulled free two short lengths of rope, joined in the center. They were frayed, nearly rotted from age, but in the center, holding them tightly together, the knot still held. "A sailor's knot," he whispered.

Andrea took the rope in her hand, rubbed gently at the knot, and trembled. When she looked up tears streamed down her cheeks, and she fell back into his arms.

They turned back toward the line of official vehicles converging on them, together.

"So it begins," Andrea said wistfully, absently brushing her tears onto the collar of Phil's shirt.

"What next?" Phil asked. "After this, what do you do next? More storms?"

Andrea shook her head and bit her lip. She smiled at him, but didn't reply.

They turned and walked to the Jeep, where Matt stood waiting. Off the coast of North Carolina, Hurricane Andrea lost focus once again, twisting north and hooking back out to sea. A light storm surge lapped at the supports of some of the beach-side homes, and wind gusts rippled through the trees and off toward the Great Dismal Swamp, where they disappeared into the marsh and were lost forever.

The red Jeep did a quick U-turn and headed back down the road into the interior of the island.

Andrea, with her head on Phil's shoulder, finally broke the silence. "Phil," she said timidly.

He turned to her, his arms still wrapped tightly around her as if he thought one or both of them might dissolve into smoke. "Yes?"

"No more storms," she said simply.

He nodded gravely. "I was hoping you'd say that. I was really hoping you'd say that very thing. But . . . what will we do?"

She snuggled more tightly against his side and laughed softly before replying.

"How do you feel about fish farming?"

About the Author

David Niall Wilson is the author of twelve novels and over a hundred and fifty short stories. His books include *The Grails Covenant Trilogy*, *Deep Blue*, *The Temptation of Blood*, and *Ancient Eyes*. A retired US Navy Electronics Technician, he now resides in the historic William R. White home in Hertford, NC, butted up against the side of the Great Dismal Swamp. There he lives, loves, and writes with the love of his life, author Patricia Lee Macomber, their children, Billy & Stephanie, occasionally his boys, Zach and Zane, and a wildly varied number of animals. Wilson is a columnist for the Internet magazine www.chizine.com, a former President of the Horror Writer's Organization, and an Ordained Minister.